You don't *have* to read the Hiccup
But if you want to, this is the

WARNING

Any relationship to any historical fact WHATSOEVER is entirely coincidental.

YOU HAVE BEEN WARNED

Hiccup Horrendous
Haddock the Third and
his dragon TOOTHLESS

ABOUT HICCUP

Hiccup Horrendous Haddock the Third was
an awesome swordfighter, a dragon whisperer,
and the greatest Viking Hero who ever lived.
But Hiccup's memoirs look back to when
he was a very ordinary boy who found
it hard to be a Hero.

Innocence

Patience

Arrogance

Wodensfang

Toothless

HICCUP
(the
Hero of
this
story)

← Ziggerastica

Stormfly

STOICK the VAST

MUM

Fishlegs

Valhallarama

Camicazi

Bertha, Chief of the Bog-Burglar

Tantrum

← Gobber the Belch

HUMUNGOUSLY HOTSHOT

← Baggybum
the Beerbelly

The Hogfly

ALVIN
the
Treacherous

The witch Excellinor

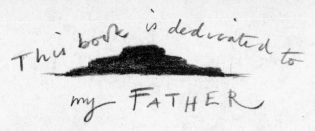
This book is dedicated to my FATHER

Text and illustrations copyright © 2015 by Cressida Cowell

Little, Brown and Company
Hachette Book Group
1290 Avenue of the Americas, New York, NY 10104
Visit us at lb-kids.com

Little, Brown and Company is a division of Hachette Book Group, Inc.
The Little, Brown name and logo are trademarks of Hachette Book Group, Inc.

The publisher is not responsible for websites (or their content) that are not owned by the publisher.

First U.S. Trade Paperback Edition: November 2016
First U.S. Hardcover Edition: November 2015
Originally published in Great Britain in 2015 by Hodder Children's Books

The Library of Congress has cataloged the U.S. hardcover edition as follows:
Names: Cowell, Cressida author, illustrator.
Title: How to fight a dragon's fury : the heroic misadventures of Hiccup the Viking / as told to Cressida Cowell.
Description: First U.S. Edition. | New York ; Boston : Little, Brown and Company, 2015. | Series: How to train your dragon ; book 12 | "Originally published in Great Britain in 2015 by Hodder Children's Books." | Summary: "The Doomsday of Yule has arrived, and the future of dragonkind lies in the hands of one boy with nothing to show, but everything to fight for. Hiccup's quest is clear…But can he end the rebellion? Can he prove himself to be king? Can he save the dragons? The stakes have never been higher, as the very fate of the Viking world hangs in the balance!"—Provided by publisher.
Identifiers: LCCN 2015024310| ISBN 9780316365154 (hardback) | ISBN 9780316299190 (ebook) | ISBN 9780316299206 (library edition ebook)
Subjects: | CYAC: Vikings—Fiction. | Dragons—Fiction. | Humorous stories. | BISAC: JUVENILE FICTION / Animals / Mythical. | JUVENILE FICTION / Fairy Tales & Folklore / General. | JUVENILE FICTION / Humorous Stories.
Classification: LCC PZ7.C83535 Hmf 2015 | DDC [Fic]—dc23
LC record available at http://lccn.loc.gov/2015024310

Paperback ISBN 978-0-316-36516-1

10 9 8 7 6 5 4 3 2

LSC-C

Printed in the United States of America

How to Fight a Dragon's Fury

by Cressida Cowell

LITTLE, BROWN AND COMPANY
New York   Boston

THE OPEN OCEAN

← sky burial place
MOUNT MURDEROUS

(Home of the Mighty Monster:
Seadragonus Giganticus,
the Doomfang, the Darkbreather)

THE MURDEROUS MOUNTAIN

Hero's End

WRECKER'S BAY

Reef Warrior

THE REEF

To America
(if there
is such
a place)

The Summer Curre...

TOMORROW

THE FROZEN ISLE
OF NOWHERE

NOTHING

ICE GORGES

ISLANDS
OF
ICE

GRIMBEARD'S
DESPAIR

The Winter Wind

VISITHUG
TERRITORY

THE BARBARIC ARCHIPELAGO

BASHEM

Isle of
the Skullions

PUFFIN ISLES

SILENCE

The Sullen Sea

VILLAINY

THE WRATH OF THOR

Bog-Burglar Islands

HYSTERIA

VA-LOUT
SLAND

THE DUNGEONS
OF THE
DANGER-BRUTES

(beware
Slitherfang)
THE
SWALLOWING
SANDS

SWALLOW

~ CONTENTS ~

THE STORY SO FAR

"There were dragons when I was a boy."

Those were the first words of the beginning of this story.

Once there was a boy named Hiccup Horrendous Haddock the Third, who lived on the little Isle of Berk with a hunting dragon called Toothless and a riding dragon called the Windwalker, wild and happy, in a world full of dragons.

Hiccup was the son of Chief Stoick the Vast and was the most unlikely Viking Hero you could possibly imagine: a skinny string bean of a boy who was nonetheless an awesome swordfighter, and a dragon whisperer, one of the few people who have been able to speak Dragonese, the language dragons speak in to one another.

One dreadful day, Hiccup accidentally released a great Sea-Dragon called the dragon Furious, who had been chained in the terrible forest prison of Berserk for over a hundred years. The dragon Furious began a dragon rebellion that aimed to kill the entire human race, and the humans and the dragons are now fighting each other to extinction.

The dragons have set fire to the little Hooligan village where Hiccup grew up, and the humans have been driven out of their houses and are now gathered on the island of Tomorrow, waiting for the final battle.

There is only one thing that can save the humans now. A new King of the Wilderwest must be crowned on the island of Tomorrow. Once the King is crowned, he will be told the secret of the Dragon Jewel, and this secret has the power to destroy all dragons forever. But a King can only be crowned if he has gathered together the King's Lost Things, ten objects that have been scattered across the Archipelago and lost for a century.

Over the course of eleven exciting and long adventures, slowly and painfully, Hiccup Horrendous Haddock the Third has gathered the ten Lost Things together, with the help of his best friends Fishlegs and Camicazi, an ancient old Sea-Dragon called the Wodensfang, and a beautiful three-headed riding dragon called the Deadly Shadow, who can camouflage himself so effectively you think he is invisible.

But the wicked Alvin the Treacherous (the clue is in the name, really) has stolen all of the Lost Things from Hiccup. Alvin is on the island of Tomorrow right now, and he is about to be crowned King. If Alvin is made King, he will use the power of the Dragon Jewel to make dragons extinct forever.

Everybody believes that Hiccup is dead, shot through the heart by Alvin the Treacherous's Warriors, but in fact Hiccup survived and is lying unconscious on the little beach of Hero's End, an island a little way from Tomorrow.

But Hiccup has no riding dragon, no boat, and no Lost Things. And only the one with the King's Lost Things can land on Tomorrow and live. If Hiccup sets one foot on its beach, the dragon Guardians of Tomorrow will rise from beneath the sand and carry Hiccup up into airy oblivion…

This is a dreadful predicament indeed.

Today is the Doomsday of Yule, the day of the final battle between dragons and humans.

There is only one day left now for Hiccup to become the King of the Wilderwest, and to save the dragons.

One day more…

CAN HICCUP SAVE THE DRAGONS?

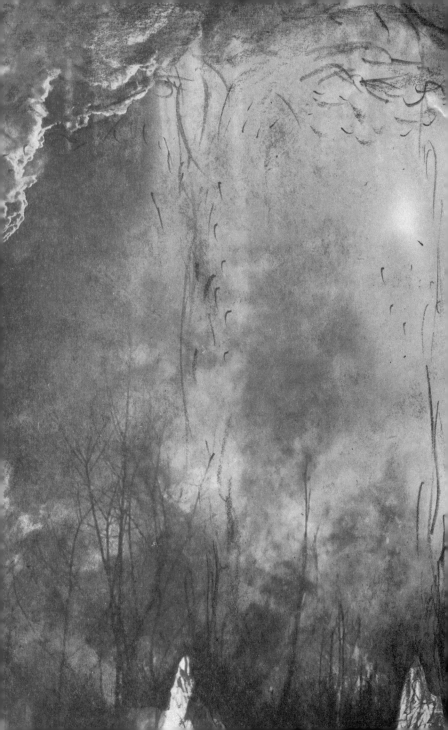

THE WORLD NEEDS A HERO

It was the darkest hour that humanity had ever faced, and a terrible doom had come upon the Archipelago.

Once, not so very long ago, these little green islands had been bustling and full of life, with a cozy little village nestled on every hilltop. Now, those same villages were blasted all to smithereens, and even the scorched hills themselves had great bites torn out of them, mountainsides upended, rivers rerouted, trees turned upside down with the sap weeping out of them, and great gouges in the face of the earth caused by the raking of angry dragons.

The smoke of the burning villages and the flaming of the forests had combined with the early-morning mist to create an eerie fog, out of which the dragon Furious and the numberless forces of his dragon army gathered in Wrecker's Bay loomed spookily like ghosts. The majority were still sleeping, waiting with half-closed eyes and hungry talons for the final battle between the dragons and the humans.

It was Doomsday, and the world needed a Hero.

Not just *any* Hero, but a
Hero who could change the
course of history.

And there were those
abroad even now, very now,
in the palest hours of earliest
morning on the Doomsday
of Yule, who were out there
looking for one.

Two young Viking Warriors,
a boy and a girl, were sitting on
the back of a beautiful three-headed
Deadly Shadow dragon. Both had
ruins and rags for clothes. They were far, far from
home, these young Warriors, for the tornado howl of
the dragons' war had flamed their sweet, safe homes
into ash, and tossed them in the air, and blown them
all away to be scattered to the four corners of the earth
by the wild winds of the Archipelago.

Only a Hero could save them now, and they were
both afraid—very, very afraid—although the girl was
pretending not to be.

The girl, a ferocious little Bog-Burglar with hair
so tangled it was as if it had been whipped up
by a whirlwind, leaned over the side of the Deadly

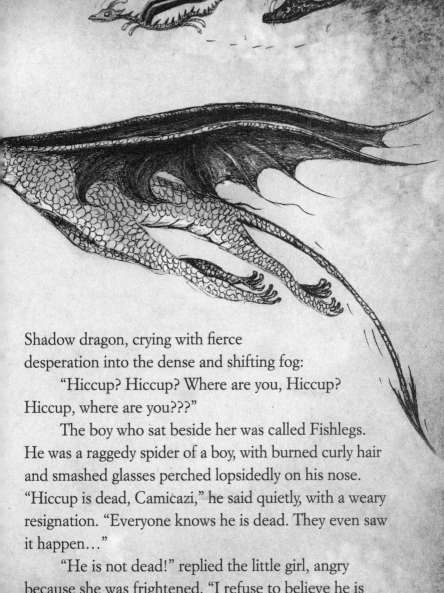

Shadow dragon, crying with fierce
desperation into the dense and shifting fog:

"Hiccup? Hiccup? Where are you, Hiccup?
Hiccup, where are you???"

The boy who sat beside her was called Fishlegs.
He was a raggedy spider of a boy, with burned curly hair
and smashed glasses perched lopsidedly on his nose.
"Hiccup is dead, Camicazi," he said quietly, with a weary
resignation. "Everyone knows he is dead. They even saw
it happen…"

"He is not dead!" replied the little girl, angry
because she was frightened. "I refuse to believe he is
dead! I know he is alive! I know it in my heart…"

"Hiccup? Where are you, Hiccup? Hiccup, where a-a-a-are you???"

There were *others* abroad, out hunting for a Hero.

Far away in the fog, the witch's Vampire Spydragon had escaped from drowning, and spread its cruel bat wings, red eyes gleaming, monkey face snuffling, hunting, hunting for a Hero. But the Spydragon was not hunting blindly in that misty darkness—it was hunting with exactitude and surety and precision. Two days before, it had bitten the Hero Hiccup with its very own jaws and

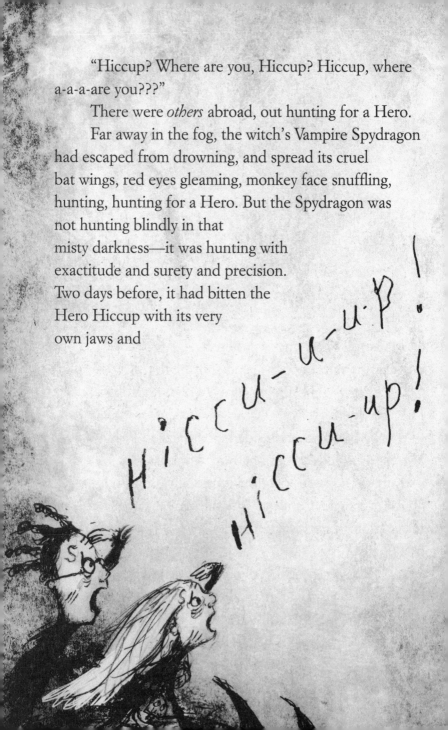

HiCCU-U-P!

HiCCU-up!

where are yo-o-u ???

where are yo-o-ou ???

where

left two of its favorite
teeth in the Hero's arm, and it
could hear those teeth calling to it,
somewhere down there in the foggy seas.

Tick-tock tick-tock, sang the teeth of the
Vampire Spydragon, *tick-tock tick-tock*, as they lay
there ticking in the Hero's arm, down there in the
darkness.

And up in the misty skies above, the Spydragon's
batlike ears swiveled to the sound: *tick-tock tick-tock*.

No, no, thought the Spydragon to itself. *The Hero
is only terribly wounded; he is not dead...But he is GOING
to be dead—oh yes, he is. I will make sure of that...*

The dragon Furious also knew that the Hero was
not yet dead.

And all through that fog, throughout the entire
Archipelago, the dragon Furious had sent out search
parties, hunting, hunting the Hero in the desolation of
fog and sea wilderness.

Hiccup, where are you?

Across the Sullen Sea they had flown all the night, with dripping fangs and bright cat eyes, north to the Frozen Isle of Nowhere, east to the Bay of the Broken Heart, south to the Flaming Forest, west to the Mystery and the Waterlands, flying like vengeful ghosts and spirits of the past, all of them crying in a bitter, relentless chant:

"Hunt the human...Hunt the human...Hunt the human..."

And…

"Hiccup? Where are you, Hiccup? Hiccup, where a-a-a-are you???"

One of those search parties was a little band of Sand Sharks. They had spotted the Spydragon tracking someone with his teeth, and they knew who that someone was, so they followed the Spydragon through the fog…

"Hiccup? Where are you, Hiccup? Hiccup, where a-a-a-are you?"

Oh, the world needs a Hero all right. For in a few small hours, the rest of that sleeping dragon army would awake, and then the inferno would begin.

But who would
get to Hiccup first on the last
day of Doomsday?

Would it be the friends with their
helpful hands and loving hearts, or would it be
the enemies with their fangs and fire?

Follow me, reader, if you dare. Take my hand, for
we can fly more swiftly than Vampire Spydragons, and
more invisibly than the Deadly Shadow; we can follow
the sound of ticking teeth faster than they can, and
trace the Hero back to where he lies, on the little isle
of Hero's End.

The little isle of Hero's End, where things end
and things begin…

Let me begin at the beginning, even though
this is the ending.

1. HOWEVER BAD THINGS SEEM TO BE, THEY CAN ALWAYS GET WORSE

On the last day of Doomsday, known as the Doomsday of Yule, Hiccup Horrendous Haddock the Third lay unconscious on a beach on the little isle of Hero's End.

It was a dreadful day indeed, bitterly cold, with the sun struggling to come up over the frozen horizon, and the Winter Wind howling like a hundred banshees, and the early-morning fog so dense and thick with the acrid smoke of war and burning forest that you could barely see your hand out in front of you.

The fog was a blessing, though, for it hid the blackened devastation all around. It hid the many dragons who had been out all night, hunting for our Hero. It hid the dragon Furious's mighty army, which was just beginning to wake up and move about in the nearby desolation of Wrecker's Bay.

And it hid the Hero himself.

Hiccup had always been an unremarkable-looking boy for a Viking Hero, with one of those ordinary faces that was difficult to remember. But now he was a truly pitiable sight, like a broken scarecrow that someone

has accidentally trodden on. Half in and half out of the water, strewn with seaweed, his clothes ragged and in ribbons about him, two black eyes, face clawed by dragons' talons, body coated in sea salt. He had been bitten on the arm by a Vampire Spydragon the other day, so his left arm had swollen up, and his whole left-hand side was a strange purple color.

An odd sort of Hero, for the worst crisis humanity has ever faced.

But he was alive, at least...*just*.

On Hiccup's chest there perched a very ancient hunting dragon called the Wodensfang, over a thousand years old, and as wrinkled and tattered as a crumbling brown leaf.

The Wodensfang had tried to haul Hiccup up the beach, gripping Hiccup's torn collar, and pulling as hard as he could with his little old tired legs, but the Wodensfang was only the size of a small, skinny rabbit, so the sad bedraggled body of the unconscious boy did not move so much as an inch.

"Oh dear, oh dear," moaned the Wodensfang desperately, warming Hiccup's heart with the heat of his own body and gently trying to wake him by blowing warm air into his face. "This really couldn't be worse... They're going to find us if we don't get a move on...

and I'm worried the tide might come in and drown you, just to add to our problems...Wake up, Hiccup, wake up! You *must* wake up!"

The boy's eyelids fluttered. In desperation, the Wodensfang spat a little seawater into his face. The boy spluttered and coughed.

"Oh thank the great Wings in the Sky!" exclaimed the Wodensfang, so agitated he hopped from foot to foot, rubbing his wings together like a grasshopper. "He's alive and he's waking up!"

He's alive!

The boy's eyes opened. Or rather, one of them did. The other was so swollen and bruised, he could barely open it at all.

"Oh, Hiccup," crooned the Wodensfang, "I am so sorry, boy, but you must get out of the sea immediately...The tide is coming in..."

Hiccup sat up with a groan, coughing, and put a hand to his forehead, which ached as if Thor the blacksmith was bringing down his hammer on it repeatedly from the inside and the outside with such ringing blows that Hiccup's ears sang with the pain.

"Where am I?" whispered Hiccup, coughing up seawater and struggling for breath.

"You're on the little isle of Hero's End," explained the Wodensfang. "Your ship sank,

Who am I??

with all the Lost Things on it, I'm afraid, so Alvin retrieved them and he has them now, which means we're in a bit of a hurry, actually—"

"Why was I on a ship?" interrupted Hiccup. "Who is Alvin? What are the Lost Things? Who are you? And, more importantly...

"...Who am I?"

The Wodensfang blinked at him.

"I beg your pardon?"

"Who am I?" repeated Hiccup.

"You don't know who you are?" squeaked the Wodensfang. *"Are you really telling me you don't know who you are?"*

Hiccup shook his head.

"Oh dear, oh dear, oh dear, oh dear!" moaned the Wodensfang. "However bad things seem to be, they can always get *worse*! The boy has lost his memory!"

I'm afraid that the Wodensfang was right. Hiccup had been hit on the head by the mast of the ship as it sank, and he had indeed lost his memory.

YOU DON'T KNOW WHO YOU ARE ?? ? ?

"I'm sorry," shivered Hiccup miserably. "I can't remember who I am, or why I am here, or anything at all."

He struggled to think, but it was as if the choking smoke and fog that was all around them had crept through his ears and into his aching head and turned everything upside down and into confusion.

All he knew was that he was cold, and sore, and something terrible had just happened, and he was in the middle of doing something very important.

"Oh, this is a disaster! Not to mention a *very* long story," said the Wodensfang, jumping anxiously from foot to foot. "And I cannot emphasize more how pushed we are for time. *I* am the Wodensfang, *you* are Hiccup Horrendous Haddock the Third, and you're a very great Hero!"

"Am I?" said Hiccup in surprise, looking down at his ragged, skinny little frame. "But that seems so unlikely!"

"Trust me," said the Wodensfang. "It's unlikely, but you are. You're not the normal sort of Viking Hero, admittedly, but you're very clever and you can speak Dragonese, and you're one of the only people in the world who can do that. How extraordinary that you don't know who you are, but you can still remember your Dragonese..."

"So I can!" said Hiccup in surprise, replying to the Wodensfang, indeed, in Dragonese.

"You're going to have to concentrate very hard here," fretted the Wodensfang, trying unsuccessfully not to panic, "because we're in a bit of a dire situation. Look over there!"

The Wodensfang, thoroughly agitated, pointed a shaking dragon wing to the northeast. Hiccup couldn't see out of one of his eyes, which was too swollen to open, but if he tilted his head slightly to the left, and slo-o-o-wly and painfully cracked open the bruised eyelid of his right eye, he could just about see out of that one.

"I can't see anything over there," said Hiccup. The fog was indeed so dense that you couldn't really see anything at all.

"Okay, you're going to have to trust me on this," squeaked the Wodensfang. "OVER THERE, on the Murderous Island, the dragon Furious has gathered together a multitude of dragons so enormous, so ferocious, that the world has never seen anything like it before. He has drawn them together, these wild and lawless creatures, with a single aim...

"And the aim of the dragon Furious...is the extinction of the entire human race."

21

There was a nasty silence.

Hiccup swallowed hard as all around him the smoke swirled, getting up and into his nose and making him cough, and the cold sea seemed to have seeped into his very bones, so that he shivered uncontrollably, and he could hear his heart beating: *thump…thump…thump…*

"*Doomsday…*" whispered Hiccup in slow horror, a single dim memory coming back to him, like a Sharkworm fin surfacing in the water, and disappearing again as suddenly as it had returned. "*Doomsday…*The last battle between the dragons and the humans…

"Are you quite sure about this?" said Hiccup, peering uncertainly into the smog.

"I'm absolutely sure," gabbled the Wodensfang in a quiver of anxiety. "And *you*, Hiccup Horrendous Haddock the Third, are the Hero who is the humans' and the dragons' last and only hope."

"I am?" spluttered Hiccup. "Me?"

He gave a strangled, disbelieving laugh and looked down at his battered body. He had legs like pieces of seaweed, and arms like chicken wings, and his left forearm seemed to have been attacked by something, because it had swollen up to twice the size of a normal forearm. It was also purple, along with the entire left side of his body.

"Heroes have to swordfight and throw axes and spears and stuff. What can *I* do against a dragon army like that?" Hiccup said in some desperation.

"Actually, you're a surprisingly good swordfighter—"

Hiccup flapped his floppy forearm at the Wodensfang. "Not right now I'm not! I can't hold a sword. What am I going to do, *flap* my opponents to death? Maybe I could *dribble* on them. That would be scary..."

The Wodensfang ignored this interruption.

"We need to get off this island as soon as possible. I've been watching the dragon rebellion sending out search parties, hunting for you all night and—oh! *Oh dear!*"

The little brown dragon gave a short, sharp exclamation, his big eyes opened wide, and he looked down at a small brown dart protruding from one of his skinny little shoulder blades.

"Oh! Oh my goodness, I've been hit!" squeaked the Wodensfang. Many species of dragon shoot little darts containing a mild poison that send their prey to sleep. Wodensfang pointed a wing up toward the grasses at the back of the beach. "Mayday! Mayday! Dragon rebellion search party!"

23

Hiccup whirled around. There was nothing to be seen in any direction on the beach, only that thick black smoke and the wind and the cry of seagulls.

Z-I-N-G!

Another little dart flew past Hiccup's nose, missing him by inches. It seemed to be coming from the bluff of the beach, behind them. There wasn't time to think; Hiccup had to react automatically.

Hiccup leaped to his feet and made the unwelcome discovery that not only was the whole left-hand side of his body an unusual color, his left leg was as numb as his arm and as floppy as a jellyfish.

He staggered forward, wobbling like a drunken sailor, fell over at exactly the right moment for another dart to miss him and go sailing over his head, skidded up to the Wodensfang, removed the dart from the little dragon's shoulder blade, and stuffed him in the ragged remains of his waistcoat.

"Are you all right?" stuttered Hiccup.

"I'm fine!" squeaked the Wodensfang. "A bit of a numbing effect but otherwise fine..."

Z-I-N-G! Z-I-N-G! Z-I-N-G!

Hiccup rolled behind a large nearby rock. The little darts were coming from up on the grassy edge of the beach, thought Hiccup to himself, his heart thumping with horror. He tilted his head and tried to peer over the edge of the rock through his one good eye, through the smoke and the fog…

And then he saw them.

Eyes.

Dragon eyes gleaming in the darkness.

Oh for Thor's sake.

He was being hunted.

I've been HIT!!!

2. YOU SEE? IT JUST GOT WORSE AGAIN LESS THAN FIVE MINUTES INTO THE STORY

"What's going on?" whispered Hiccup to the Wodensfang. "Who are these dragons? Why do they want to kill me?"

The Wodensfang's eyelids were drooping in a worrying way, as if he was about to lose consciousness. "I told you..." he squeaked. "Those are dragon rebellion dragons and they want to stop you from becoming King because you are the Hero who finds the Lost Things..."

"What?" yelled Hiccup, as...

Z-Z-I-I-ING!!!

... many more darts shot briskly past the rock they were hiding behind.

"Oh dear," gabbled the Wodensfang very, very quickly, for he could feel himself falling asleep. "It's a very long story, Hiccup, but it's so important that you understand everything...Where shall I start? A long time ago, on the island of Tomorrow, King Grimbeard the Ghastly killed his son Hiccup the

Hello Second because
he thought that his
son was leading a rebellion
against him, and imprisoned his
son's dragon, the dragon Furious, in a
forest prison—"

"We don't have time for the
WHOLE story!" shouted Hiccup as darts
sang Z-Z-ZING Z-ING ZING over their
heads. "Just tell me the important parts!"

"ALL the parts are important!"
squealed the Wodensfang in a total panic.

"I'm going to have to find somewhere
a bit safer for us to hide," said Hiccup.
"This rock isn't big enough—"

At that point, so completely out of the
blue that Hiccup nearly had a heart attack,
something wriggled at the back of his neck and
something said in a deep little voice:

"Where's the cookie?"

"AAARGGHHH!" yelped Hiccup,
flapping desperately at the back of his head,
under the understandable impression that
something was attacking him from behind
and had gotten him by the neck.

28

"Don't worry, don't worry," said the Wodensfang soothingly. "That's just another little dragon; you must have put him in your backpack to protect him when the boat sank, but don't worry, he's no danger; he's on *our* side...He must have just woken up..."

Sure enough, Hiccup was wearing a small, very bashed-up backpack, and out of the backpack buzzed a small, circular lapdragon that bore a remarkable resemblance to a happy little pig.

It was a Hogfly.

Hogflys are the stupidest, most good-natured dragons in the Archipelago, far more likely to lick your enemies than to bite them, and much more of a hindrance than a help.

"Woof, woof!" barked the happy little Hogfly enthusiastically. (The Hogfly was under the impression that he was a dog.) "Hello, Mother! Is it teatime? I can help! I can be tremendously helpful!"

"Oh dear...yes, I'm sure you can," said Hiccup, feeling a little hysterical, "but in the meantime just stay here with us behind this rock and try not to get SHOT."

It was a Hogfly.

"Back to
the story," said
the Wodensfang.
"Grimbeard the Ghastly
repented, and declared
there would never be a King
of the Wilderwest again, unless
the King could be a better King than
he was. He created an Impossible Task,
by hiding ten Lost Things. Only a true Hero
can gather the things together and become the next
King of the Wilderwest..."

Hiccup wasn't really listening to the story. He was peering over the rock to look up at the bluff of the beach.

Dark shapes were beginning to slink over the bluff and down onto the sandy beach. They dug into the sand until only the fins on the top of their heads were showing, and then the sharklike fins moved through the sand easily, as if it were water.

Every now and then the creatures would thrust their heads above the sand to fire their drugged darts...

This is ridiculous! thought Hiccup.

Here he was, with that funny little brown dragon saying he was this great Hero, and Hiccup could feel how weak he was,

how defenseless. He could barely move, let alone fight off a pack of sharklike dragons.

At this point, a memory popped up at him out of nowhere, like an uncontrollable jack-in-the-box.

Sand Sharks.

He knew what these dragons were: They were Sand Sharks.

He didn't know *how* he knew; he just knew.

And, as it turned out, he didn't just know a little bit about Sand Sharks.

He knew *everything* about them.

He knew that they are pack animals about the size of a dog or wolf. They can hunt prey much larger than themselves by using their darts to send their victims to sleep. Once they shoot a number of darts into their target, it falls unconscious, and they can swarm all over it, and kill their prey without it putting up a fight.

"*Most* unfortunately," squeaked the Wodensfang, desperately carrying on with the story, even though no one was listening, "although *you* of course found all the Lost Things, Hiccup, Alvin the Treacherous has stolen the things from you, and he is about to be crowned King, and once he is crowned, he will be told the secret of the Dragon Jewel, which has the power to destroy all dragons forever...Are you concentrating on this story, Hiccup?"

No, Hiccup was *not* concentrating on this story, funnily enough.

He was thinking about the rather more urgent problem of staying alive.

The Wodensfang was still awake, which suggested that it would take at least five or six of those darts to

put a sizable creature like himself to sleep. A little way away there was the broken hull of a wrecked boat, within rolling distance. If he could just get to the shelter of that boat without being hit by too many of the darts, then it would give him some time to figure out what to do…

But the Hogfly had other ideas.

"Oh look, those dragons are playing fetch!" squealed the Hogfly in excitement. "Fetch is my favorite game! *Much* better than hide-and-go-seek! And I'm SO good at it!"

Before Hiccup could stop him, the Hogfly dashed out from behind the rock and flew hither and thither, trying to catch the darts in his mouth.

"No!" warned Hiccup in frantic exasperation. "No, Hogfly, no! Don't try and catch the darts! They're drugged!"

But the Hogfly
didn't listen. "*Lovely
darts!*" sang the Hogfly, his
curly tail wagging in an absolute blur of pleasure.
"*Pretty little darts! COME to the Hogfly!*"

"*The darts are BAD, Hogfly, they're BAD!*"
screamed Hiccup, as the Hogfly launched himself at
three or four more. Excitement always made the Hogfly
buzz louder than normal, and he was so thrilled by this
new game that he could not hear Hiccup over the sound
of his own buzzing.

"*Bother!*" squealed the Hogfly, as he narrowly
missed another dart.

"*Nearly!*" screamed the Hogfly, as his little piggy
jaws snapped on thin air once more.

Luckily, not only was the Hogfly *not* as good at
the fetching game as he thought he was, he was in fact
supremely hopeless at it. But there were so many darts
flying around that it was really only a question of time
before he got hit by one.

"*Ooh, I really am going to get this one...*"
said the Hogfly to himself, narrowing his eyes as he
spotted a dart coming right at him, and positioning
himself cunningly so that he was right on target.

Hiccup transferred his weight onto his right

foot, and with all his strength he launched himself in a heroic HOP toward the Hogfly, flinging up his left arm in the nick of time so that the dart landed in his floppy forearm rather than in the Hogfly, and then landing facedown in the sand again.

"Mother's playing too!" squawked the Hogfly. "Good catch, Mother!"

The little dragon was so wild with excitement that he blew himself up and floated within an arm's length of where Hiccup was lying. Hiccup reached up, caught the passing Hogfly by his curly tail, and half-hopped, half-rolled his way forward, taking himself, the drowsy Wodensfang, and the inflated, overexcited little Hogfly into the shelter of the broken boat in a hail of arrows.

Z-I-N-G! Z-I-N-G! Z-I-N-G!

Three darts buried themselves into the shell of the boat as Hiccup ducked inside it.

BONG!

One dart landed on the Hogfly just before Hiccup got him into the broken boat, but in his puffed-up, inflated state, it just bounced off harmlessly.

The boat offered a bit more protection, but when Hiccup put his eye up to a small knothole in the hull, he could see the fins of the Sand Sharks already beginning to circle the shipwrecked boat. Was it Hiccup's imagination, or did they seem closer than before?

Panting with fear, Hiccup checked the Hogfly anxiously. "Are you okay, Hogfly?"

"I'm *fine*!" squeaked the Hogfly happily. "One did hit me but I was UP so it just went BONG right off me! Did you hear it? Did you hear it? BONG!"

Reassured, Hiccup turned his attention to the dart in his forearm. His whole left side was so numb already that it wouldn't make much difference.

Rather disgustingly, when he pulled the dart out, he noticed a couple of things already embedded in his arm. The things were white, and looked horribly like *teeth*. YUCKY.

"Wodensfang, do you know why I have two TEETH in my arm?" asked Hiccup, staring at the teeth in horrified fascination.

"Oh, yes," said the Wodensfang soothingly.

"I forgot to mention a *tiny* extra problem: You got bitten by a Vampire Spydragon."

A VAMPIRE SPYDRAGON? For Thor's sake… Hiccup put his swollen eye up to the knothole again. More and more Sand Sharks were slinking out of the grass on the bluff and sinking down into the sand, their fins creeping nearer, nearer to the shipwrecked boat…

Hang on a second! What was that, just the edge of the group? *That* wasn't a Sand Shark!

Two red eyes were glowing in the grass, almost like they were levitating, and around the two red eyes there slowly materialized a far scarier animal than a Sand Shark—a chameleon dragon with the head of a bat and the body of a monkey…

Vampire Spydragon, said Hiccup's brain.

That would explain why this hunting party had found him so easily. Vampire Spydragons hunt in quite a similar way to Sand Sharks.

But instead of using darts, they bite their victims with their teeth, leaving one or both of the teeth in the wound before letting them go. The poison in the bite then slowly paralyzes the prey, and a Vampire Spydragon locates its lame and helpless target by the tracking device of its own teeth, which tick like clocks inside the bitten body of the victim.

I'm sorry. It's yucky, but it's true.

"Oh for Thor's sake, oh for Thor's sake, this just gets worse and worse..."

"Back to the story," squeaked the Wodensfang, bug-eyed with alarm. "YOU have to get to the island of Tomorrow, Hiccup, and be crowned King instead of Alvin!"

"Forget about the story!" snapped Hiccup. "The story isn't important right now! You can tell me the story later—"

"Stories are *always* important!" shrieked the Wodensfang. "These dragons right here, right now are just a minor problem. I'm trying to fill you in on the big picture here—"

"These minor problems are going to *kill us*!" panicked Hiccup.

With shaking hands, Hiccup picked up a couple of stones that were lying underneath the boat, and threw them as far as he could in the direction of the attacking dragons. He could hear the dull thump as the stones landed uselessly in the sand.

"YOU HAVE TO LISTEN TO ME, HICCUP!" begged the Wodensfang, so desperate now that with an immense effort he dragged himself up Hiccup's waistcoat and planted himself on Hiccup's face, putting his wings on either side of Hiccup's cheeks, and staring into Hiccup's eyes.

Now he had Hiccup's attention. Something about looking into the hypnotic yellow eyes of a Sea-Dragon always commands attention.

"If Alvin the Treacherous is made King, he will use the power of the Jewel to destroy dragons FOREVER!" shrieked the little brown dragon, in a frenzy of anxiety. "So YOU have to stop Alvin! YOU have to go over to the island of Tomorrow, and YOU have to be made King instead of him! And then YOU can ride out and meet the dragon Furious and try to persuade him to call off the rebellion! That's why it's so urgent! *That's why we're in a hurry!*"

"Okay, okay..." said Hiccup, stroking the little brown dragon's back because he seemed so very upset. "I'll do it, I'll do it..."

"And it's QUITE TRICKY!" shrieked the Wodensfang. "Because you haven't got a BOAT, or any of the LOST THINGS, or any WEAPONS..."

"Don't worry," said Hiccup. "I'll do it..."

"The fact that Fate has led us to Hero's End is important, Hiccup. I can't tell you exactly why, but this is where Grimbeard the Ghastly was buried. The humans don't know you're alive yet, because Alvin killed your cousin Snotlout the day before yesterday and everybody thought it was you..."

The Wodensfang was sounding very tired now, and he was gabbling away as fast as he could, aware that he was about to fall asleep. "In a nutshell, trust NOBODY. They all want to kill you. The dragon Furious, Alvin—EVERYBODY'S TRYING TO KILL YOU..."

"I won't trust anybody," said Hiccup soothingly.

"And finally, Hiccup, when you get to Tomorrow you mustn't la—"

But the Wodensfang couldn't say any more. The sleepy substance in the Sand Shark's dart was making

the Wodensfang's eyelids droop and his forked tongue
flop in his mouth.

He tried again. *"You mustn't la—"*

But it was too late.

The Wodensfang collapsed with his eyes closed
before he could finish the sentence.

Which was unfortunate, to say the least, because
the sentence he was trying to say was: *"When you get
to Tomorrow you mustn't land on the beach,
because the dragon Guardians of Tomorrow
are guarding it."* And that was quite an
important sentence.

The Wodensfang was
quite right.

However bad things
seem to be, they can
always get worse.

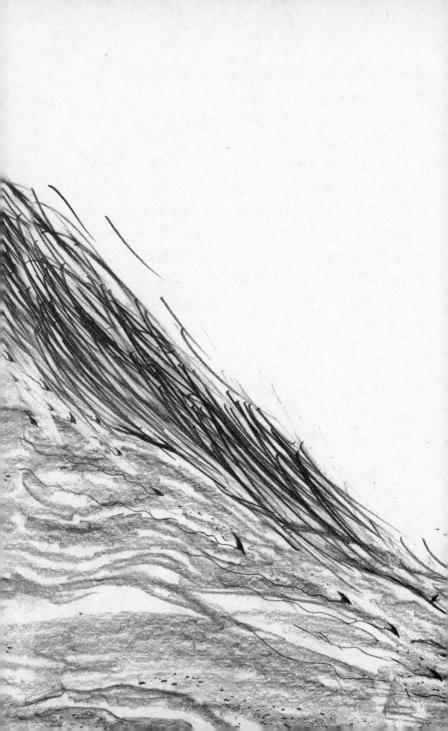

3. THE MINOR PROBLEM

Five minutes earlier, the Wodensfang had been trying to wake up the unconscious boy.

Now the positions were reversed.

"Wake up!" whispered Hiccup, gently shaking the Wodensfang and tickling him behind the ears. "Please... wake up! I don't know what to do!"

The drug in that dart hadn't killed the Wodensfang, but it was strong enough to send the little dragon very soundly to sleep, and he snored on, surprisingly loudly and snortily for such a small dragon, happily oblivious to the impending dragon attack.

Think POSITIVE, think POSITIVE.

On the *enemy* side: thirty Sand Sharks and one really creepy Vampire Spydragon.

On *Hiccup's* side: an unconscious Wodensfang, a half-numb Hero who could only hop or crawl and who was embedded with a rather revolting tracking device, and one very sweet but extremely stupid little Hogfly panting expectantly in front of him with his tongue hanging out.

Closer and closer crept the Sand Sharks.

Closer and closer crept the Vampire Spydragon.

The nearer the Vampire Spydragon got, the more Hiccup's forearm burned with pain, as if the teeth could sense the presence of their owner. They quivered inside Hiccup's arm, and their little serrated edges made this agony for Hiccup.

And then he could hear horrible sniffing noises on the other side of the boat's wooden hull. Oh for Thor's sake, they were so close now he could hear the dragons *panting*. He had to take one more look.

Just in the nick of time, Hiccup drew back from the knothole, for to his absolute horror, the gigantic eye of the Spydragon was peering into the boat from the other side.

Trembling, Hiccup waited for the eye to disappear, and then he looked through the knothole himself.

The Vampire Spydragon was right in front of the boat, so close that Hiccup could see its nose snuffling as the saliva dripped down its vampire fangs. It was making that dangerous *chuck-chuck* noise that a dragon makes deep in its throat when it is about to pounce…Its long, curling tail was wound with some kind of rope, and that rope was trailing behind it in the sand.*

Hiccup had to do something, *anything*, or they were doomed.

He had a sudden desperate idea. Those darts hadn't worked on the Hogfly when he was inflated…He could get the Hogfly to distract the Sand Sharks while he dealt with the Spydragon.

"Hogfly, I need your help here," whispered Hiccup urgently. "I want you to play a game of It…"

"Oh, I LOVE playing It!" squeaked the Hogfly enthusiastically. "Who's 'it'? Is it me or you?"

"The Sand Sharks are 'it,'" whispered Hiccup.

"Are they the ones singing that pretty song?" asked the Hogfly.

"That's them," said Hiccup. "But you must puff yourself UP, Hogfly…"

*The rope was left over from Hiccup's battle with the Spydragon in the previous book.

"Like *this?*" squeaked the Hogfly, concentrating very hard and swelling up like a balloon.

"Like that," said Hiccup. "And then I want you to go out there, and you mustn't let them catch you..."

"Okeydokey!" said the Hogfly, as circular and as purple as an enormous fat grape, if you can picture a grape with a curly tail and an eager little piggy face. "I LOVE playing It! I'm even better at It than fetch! They'll NEVER catch *me!*"

"Wait until I give the signal," whispered Hiccup, taking the unconscious Wodensfang out of his waistcoat and putting him into his backpack, so he'd be safe. Hiccup grabbed a large handful of seaweed and put it on his head, and smothered himself with sand and muck.

The Hogfly hid just below the rim of the boat, round as the moon, and giggling excitedly to himself. "They'll get *such a* surprise..." gurgled the Hogfly.

They'll get such a surprise...

Hiccup put his eye to the knothole. The Vampire Spydragon was crouched down low, ready to pounce...

"*Now!*" whispered Hiccup.

Over the top shot the Hogfly, squeaking, "Can't catch *me!*"

BONG! BONG! BONG! BONG! BONG! BONG! BONG! BONG!

The Sand Sharks let off their darts simultaneously, and every single one of those darts ricocheted off the circular body of the inflated

CATCH ME!!

little Hogfly and landed harmlessly in the sand.

The Vampire Spydragon started, paused in his pouncing, and turned his red eyes toward the extraordinary sight of the puffed-up lapdragon flapping speedily through the air.

"Oh, good *shot*!" the Hogfly twittered generously, dodging this way and that like a bashyball with wings. "But I bet you can't catch me *now*!"

BONG! BONG! BONG! BONG! BONG! BONG! BONG! BONG! BONG!

"Good shot again!" chirruped the Hogfly in good-natured surprise. "But now I'm going to make it a bit trickier for you all by doing *this*..."

BONG! BONG! BONG! BONG! BONG! BONG!

In that second when the Spydragon was staring at the Hogfly in astonishment, Hiccup crawled out from behind the shelter of the boat, heart thumping, his forearm singing with such pain that he had to bite his lip to prevent himself from crying out. Covered in sand and muck with the seaweed on his head like a rather jaunty hat, Hiccup squirmed forward in the sand as fast as he could slither, dragging his swollen side behind him.

The Sand Sharks had never come across anything like the Hogfly before. The more they shot a battery of darts at the Hogfly, the more the darts bounced off his spherical little body. It was baffling. They had shot so many darts that a cute little lapdragon as small as this one ought to be stuffed full with the adder's bite of the sleep drug and lying dead upon the sand, not flapping around above them making happy conversation.

"Oh, you guys, you're so good at this—you must have played this game before! But you won't be expecting...*that*..."

BONG! BONG! BONG! BONG! BONG! BONG! BONG! BONG!

"Oh!" exclaimed the Hogfly in surprise. "You *were* expecting that!"

"Die, you fat little lapdragon, *die*!" hissed the Sand Sharks, shooting even more darts at the Hogfly, and of course that had absolutely no effect on the Hogfly whatsoever, and the anger of the Sand Sharks led them to lose their heads, as anger often does, and they shot at him recklessly, getting too close to one another. The Vampire Spydragon watched, its red eyes mesmerized.

With the Vampire Spydragon's attention on the battle, Hiccup squirmed around to the other side of it. He gently picked up the rope trailing from the Spydragon's tail, and tied it around a gigantic rock covered in big fat mussels. He tied it with the firmest knot he could remember, which was the Unbreakable Fast Reef Tough Knot, a knot his father had taught him long ago.

How strange a universe is the human mind. Hiccup couldn't remember he had a father, but he *could* remember the Unbreakable Fast Reef Tough Knot.

He had just tied the last finishing touches to the knot when the Vampire Spydragon slo-o-owly turned its head away from the riveting spectacle of the Hogfly and back to the boat again.

Heart pounding, stomach churning, Hiccup crawled away as fast as he possibly could in the other direction, his forearm roaring with pain.

The Vampire Spydragon looked at the boat, realized its teeth were not there, and swiveled around to see Hiccup, who had frozen still as a statue, in the pathetic hope that the Spydragon would mistake him for a rock with a bit of seaweed on the top.

The sand-and-seaweed disguise wasn't very

effective, for the Vampire Spydragon recognized him immediately. The eyes of the Vampire Spydragon glowed red…

With a spine-chilling scream, the Vampire Spydragon leaped toward Hiccup, claws out, fangs down, muscles rippling with impressive athletic power.

Hiccup screamed and scrambled backward, and for one heartstopping moment it looked as if he wasn't far enough away…

But in mid-leap, the Spydragon got to the end of the rope and it yanked it back in the nick of time so that its jaws clanged shut on thin air, inches away from Hiccup's nose. Hiccup was so close to having his head bitten off that he actually smelled the bad breath of the creature as it snapped his mighty jaws shut.

"Yowwwwwww!" screeched the Vampire Spydragon in agony, for the rope tied around the rock pulled on its tail in the most painful way, and having your tail pulled, as everyone knows, is extremely uncomfortable as well as undignified.

"Yowwwww!" screeched the Vampire Spydragon again.

And then the Vampire Spydragon went mad.

Bucking this way and that, it tried to get away, and only succeeded in entangling itself further. It tore at the rope; it heaved in all directions with all its strength; it fought so hard that despite the pain in its tail it actually managed to move the stone a couple of inches. But the Unbreakable Fast Reef Tough Knot held fast.

This is where every Viking father since the dawn of time points out the importance of knowing your knots properly. "There will come a time," says the Viking father, "when you will thank your lucky stars that you have used an Unbreakable Fast Reef Tough Knot rather than a Slippy Slippy Slip Knot."

And it is absolutely true that when you have tied up a Vampire Spydragon by its tail to a rock, it is extremely important to use the right kind of knot.

However, it would be a better idea not to tie one up in the first place, and Hiccup was about to find out why. In fact, he was about to find out something new about Vampire Spydragons.

A rather strange expression came over the Vampire Spydragon's face, as if it were making some sort of momentous decision. And then it pulled forward on the rock with the utmost of its strength, screwed up its horrible bat-face, and crossed its glowing red eyes, so fierce was its concentration.

Uh-oh, thought Hiccup, looking over his shoulder as he half-hopped, half-crawled across the sand. *I've seen*

*that expression before on other dragons. It's dumping its tail.
I didn't know a Vampire Spydragon could do that...*

The Vampire Spydragon was indeed dumping
its tail.

A few dragons have this ability, but they only use
it in very extreme circumstances, for most creatures are
very fond of their tails and will hang on to them except
in the most dire emergency.

The Vampire Spydragon's long, curly tail detached
itself from the rear end of the Vampire Spydragon and
fell into the sand.

The Vampire Spydragon gave an evil smile. It was
no longer attached to its tail, so it was also no longer
attached to the rock.

It was free.

Free to get the horrible little tooth-burglar in its
jaws and...

It bounded forward like a great black tiger, muscles
gleaming, screaming with mad fury, head down low,
ready to pounce.

Oh no...

Oh no, wept Hiccup, hearing the soft, bounding
footsteps behind him, coming nearer, ever nearer.
Hiccup staggered onto his one good foot and hopped
down the beach as fast as he could, but let me tell you,

it is quite hard to travel very quickly
down a wet soggy beach when you can
only hop on one leg.

Oh no, oh no, oh no, oh no…

"Hogfly, help!" screamed the
hopping Hiccup.

The Hogfly was already at the Vampire
Spydragon's shoulder, buzzing with concern.
"Excuse me, Mr. Scary Bat-Dragon, but I
think you might have dropped

something?" squeaked the Hogfly, helpfully pointing his trotter back to the abandoned tail.

The Vampire Spydragon ignored the polite question of the Hogfly, and sprang after the hopping Hiccup, in great tigerish leaps, dripping jaws wide open…

The Hogfly flapped after it, shouting, "You've forgotten your *tail*, Mr. Bat-Dragon! You've forgotten your *tail*!" as loudly as he could, in case the poor bat-dragon was deaf as well as forgetful. The obsessed Sand Sharks were still sending a volley of darts in the Hogfly's direction, all of which sprang back off his bafflingly invulnerable roundness like stones thrown at a roof.

BONG! BONG! BONG! BONG! BONG! *BONG-ZING!*

The Vampire Spydragon stopped dead, mid-leap, with a startled exclamation of rage as one of the darts rebounded off the helpful Hogfly—BONG-ZING!—and stuck into the Spydragon's back leg. "Yowwwww!" yelled the Spydragon. The Hogfly caught up with the Spydragon, panting.

"That's right, sir, it's just over there!" squeaked the Hogfly, pointing back with all four trotters at the sad sight of the dropped tail.

But the Vampire Spydragon didn't appear to be listening.

BONG-ZING! BONG-ZING! Two more darts bounced off the Hogfly and stuck, quivering, into the bottom of the Spydragon, a bottom that was still feeling rather sensitive after the whole tail-pulling and tail-dumping incident.

"YARRROOOOOOOOOOOO!" squealed the Vampire Spydragon, jumping right into the air with all four legs outstretched. It stared down in disbelief at the darts. It could already feel its leg and its bottom going numb.

It forgot about Hiccup.

Its red eyes glowed.

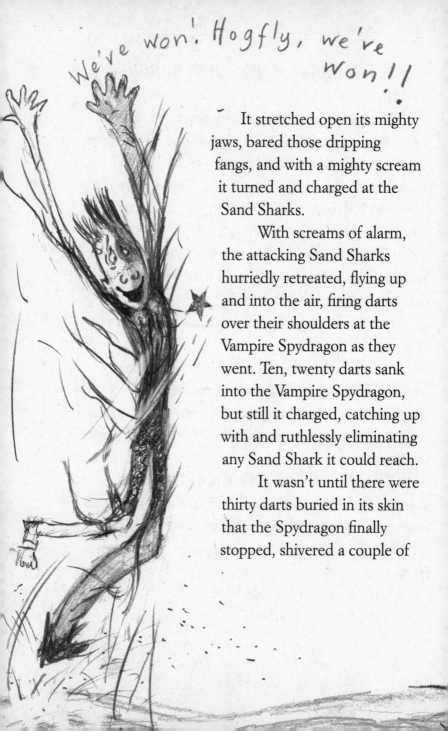

We've won! Hogfly, we've won!!

It stretched open its mighty jaws, bared those dripping fangs, and with a mighty scream it turned and charged at the Sand Sharks.

With screams of alarm, the attacking Sand Sharks hurriedly retreated, flying up and into the air, firing darts over their shoulders at the Vampire Spydragon as they went. Ten, twenty darts sank into the Vampire Spydragon, but still it charged, catching up with and ruthlessly eliminating any Sand Shark it could reach.

It wasn't until there were thirty darts buried in its skin that the Spydragon finally stopped, shivered a couple of

Have we?

times, and keeled over in the sand, heavily asleep.

The Sand Sharks disappeared into the sky, shrieking furiously.

All that remained on the beach were the sleeping Vampire Spydragon, the still bodies of about seven or eight Sand Sharks, the buzzing little Hogfly wondering where everyone had gone, and Hiccup Horrendous Haddock the Third, covered with sand and wearing a very silly bit of seaweed on his head for a hat.

"Oh my goodness," said Hiccup. "I don't believe this...Have we won?"

It appeared that they had.

"We've won!" said Hiccup, punching the air in triumph. "We've won, Hogfly, we've won!"

"Have we?" said the Hogfly, uncertainly, and slowly, slowly deflating, and landing on Hiccup's shoulder.

"I'm quite surprised," admitted the Hogfly, "because the others seemed to be doing quite well..."

"I'm quite surprised too," said Hiccup, making a fuss of the Hogfly by tickling him on the tummy. "All your brilliant It playing was ever so helpful."

Hiccup was impressed with himself. He had defeated all of those Sand-Sharks! And a Vampire Spydragon! All on his own with only a Hogfly to help him!

Maybe he really was the Hero that this Wodensfang said he was.

Maybe, wounded and unarmed and helpless as he was, he *could* do this.

But then his momentary joy evaporated as fast as the deflation of a helpful Hogfly.

For behind the departing shapes of the Sand Sharks, now as small as seagulls as they flew away through the fog and the smoke, the mist had thinned.

Hiccup could see right through to Murderous Island for the first time, and what he saw made his stomach flip over queasily, like it was doing somersaults on the deck of a ship at sea.

Suddenly Hiccup understood what the Wodensfang had been trying to tell him. These Sand Sharks, this Vampire Spydragon, they were just minor problems.

The REAL PROBLEM lay ahead.

Murderous Island had mountains that pointed straight up to the sky like witch's fingers, and that island was *teeming* with dragons.

Hiccup had never seen so many dragons.

There were thousands and thousands and thousands of them, smothering the island in such thick, dense numbers that you could barely see the rock beneath.

Dawn was breaking, so the dragons were beginning to wake up, rising above the mountains in great choking clouds, wheeling and screeching and fighting and hovering, like a swarm of angry locusts.

With the same ease with which he could speak Dragonese despite not knowing who he was, Hiccup found that he could identify the different species of dragon from their wing shapes, and their cries, and their ominous outlines, and they were the most terrifying species in the Archipelago.

They were like a vision from a nightmare.

Firestarters, Breathquenchers, and Poison Darters. Brainpickers, Tongue-twisters, and Flamehuffers with their long tongues lolling out. Rhinobacks, Razorwings, Riproarers, and Raptortongues. Saber-Toothed Driver Dragons and Polarserpents and Driller Dragons and Dreaders and Darkbreathers and…

There was such a bewildering number of dangerous and violent species that it was almost impossible to take in.

Oh for Thor's sake, weren't those Snub-Nosed Hellsteethers? And Savagers…and…Triple-Header Rageblasts…and the long, terrifying necks of Thor's Thunderers, shooting lightning from their nostrils…

And…Oh, by the

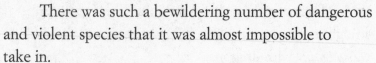

Great Curly Whiskers and Hairy Armpits of the Mighty God Thor! Wasn't that the gigantic form of a *Woden's Nightmare*, surfacing in the waters in front of the island? Woden's Nightmares were many-eyed giants that lived in the dark and wild depths of the Open Ocean and they never came this far into the inland seas. Their eyes shot lasers and they were, as far as Hiccup knew, invincible...

All around the great grim shape of the Woden's Nightmare in the water was the dreaded sight of the serrated fins of Sharkworms...

Hiccup could see the faint outlines of other islands in the Archipelago way in the distance, all of them in flames, smoking like they were volcanoes, and over every island there

hung a cloud of more dragons, more and more and more
of them, stretching on forever…

Oh for Thor's sake.

Every single word the Wodensfang had said was
true. *This* was the dragon rebellion. *This* was the last day
of Doomsday.

Hiccup may have just won a victory over a few
Sand Sharks and a Vampire Spydragon.

But the Sand Sharks were flying back to the
Murderous Mountains, back to the dragon Furious,
back to the dragon rebellion, and they would tell this
dragon Furious where Hiccup was.

And the dragon
Furious wouldn't send Sand Sharks to get
Hiccup this time, or even a Vampire Spydragon.

No, he would send Tongue-twisters,
Gorebreathers, Brainpickers—all the most fearsome
dragons in his dragon army, and they would fly across
the little strait of the sea to hunt for Hiccup, and on
an island this small there would be nowhere to hide,
nowhere to run to, and no way for a Hiccup, a Hogfly,
and an unconscious Wodensfang to fight back.

What had the Wodensfang said he had to do?

Hiccup tried to think back to the Wodensfang's story. It had been a little difficult to take in; there had been so much going on at the time…

Hiccup had to get to an island called Tomorrow.

He had to be crowned King instead of somebody called Alvin.

And then he had to persuade this dragon Furious to call off the dragon rebellion.

In one day.

And he didn't have a BOAT, or any LOST THINGS, or any WEAPONS.

The Wodensfang was right.

This was a problem.

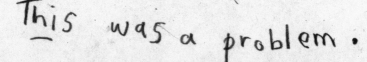

4. THE LARGER PROBLEM

Meanwhile, lying half-submerged in the waters of
Wrecker's Bay, just to the north of the island of
Tomorrow, there was the most gigantic dragon.

The dragon was very, very still, as if war
had turned him into a mountainside, a volcano
perhaps, for great yellow clouds of sulfurous
steam rose from his battle-scarred body,
gouged and scraped with many wounds and
burn marks.

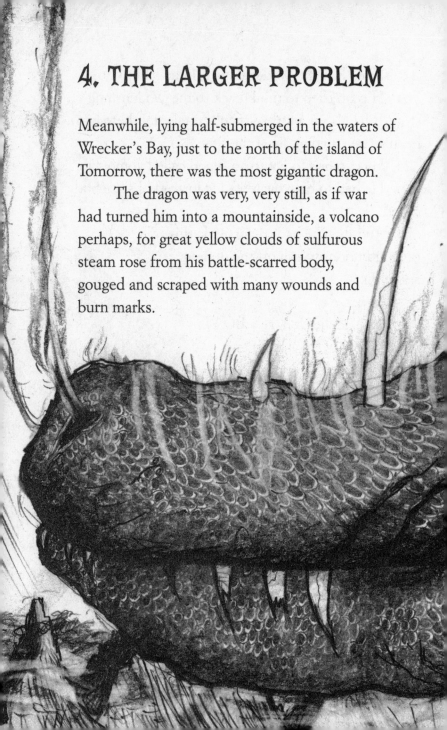

A great smoking mountain, he was. Nothing on him moved, not a whisker, not a muscle, not a ripple on his skin, not even a beating heart, to show he was alive and not made out of rock, just that steady smoking.

But what was that, up at the top of the dragon-mountain? A crack splitting in the rock…The dragon was opening his eyelids, just a tiny, tiny sliver, and you could see the buried fire in the eyes that lay beneath, seething and raging like lava in a hole.

War had changed this dragon, and not for the better.

This was the dragon Furious, and today on the Doomsday of Yule he would meet the new King of the Wilderwest in single combat.

The dragon had rested well in preparation for the battle, and now he was watching Hero's Gap, the little stretch of water between the Murderous Mountains and the island of Tomorrow, like a cat watching a mousehole.

The dragon Furious's gigantic eyes saw everything.

He saw the Sand Sharks returning from Hero's End, and he knew that they would tell him that Hiccup was alive.

Surely, thought the dragon Furious to himself, surely I still have nothing to fear, even if he *is* alive?

The boy had no Things! Not one! So if he were to set one Hiccupy *toenail* on the sands of Tomorrow… if he flew on the back of a dragon into one *inch* of Tomorrow's airspace…why, the sands of Tomorrow would begin to shake, and they would give birth to those dreadful monsters known as THE DRAGON GUARDIANS OF TOMORROW. They would rocket out of the sands, take the boy in their dreadful claws, and give him Death by Airy Oblivion…

So surely there was nothing to fear?

And even if, by some extraordinary and impossible chance, Hiccup survived the dragon Guardians, and got himself crowned without any Things, the Wodensfang had promised to betray the new King, even if that King was Hiccup, and steal the Dragon Jewel from him, and bring it to the dragon Furious before the fight.

No King would win without the Jewel. Not Hiccup. Not Alvin. Not anyone.

A King without a Jewel could be broken in half like a matchstick.

There was nothing to fear…

Nothing at all.

But the dragon Furious's gigantic eyes saw everything. And he remained uneasy.

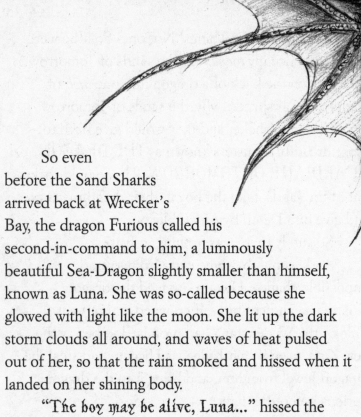

So even
before the Sand Sharks
arrived back at Wrecker's
Bay, the dragon Furious called his
second-in-command to him, a luminously
beautiful Sea-Dragon slightly smaller than himself,
known as Luna. She was so-called because she
glowed with light like the moon. She lit up the dark
storm clouds all around, and waves of heat pulsed
out of her, so that the rain smoked and hissed when it
landed on her shining body.

"The boy may be alive, Luna..." hissed the
dragon Furious.

The dragon Furious did not move his lips to
say this, for Sea-Dragons can communicate with one
another telepathically. Nothing of the dragon-mountain
moved, although his eyes may have glowed a little
brighter as the thoughts transferred themselves.

"Send your best and most ruthless dragons

through Hero's Gap to look for the boy. And Luna...do not go yourself."

"You do not trust me, King?" asked Luna, affronted.

"I do not question your loyalty, Luna, but it is harder to harden your heart than you think. Particularly against well-meaning humans like Hiccup," said the dragon Furious. "There is something *about* this boy..."

The dragon Furious's words rolled on in Luna's mind.

"Many dragons have refused to fight alongside us because of this boy. One Eye, for instance...and even those irritating little nanodragons will not join the rebellion, chattering rudely about how Hiccup once saved their King's life or some such nonsense...

"This is our last chance, Luna. The humans are growing in cleverness. In the next few centuries they will develop weapons of such power that they will wipe us out, because humans are incapable of sharing this world. But if we strike now, we shall have freedom for the dragons forever..."

"Freedom..." sighed Luna, with longing melancholy. "*Freedom*...Free to wander where we will in the open skies. Free to fly high, high, high in the airy winds, free to touch the moon itself, free to dive forever in the sweet black nothingness of the Open Ocean...ah...*freedom*..."

"Send your best dragons, Luna," growled the dragon Furious. "But stay here yourself."

Luna bowed her radiant head. She would send out a party of their most fearsome and pitiless dragons to destroy Hiccup before he got to Tomorrow: Hellsteethers, Tongue-twisters, Gorebreathers...Just in case.

The dragon Furious sank slowly below the waves until only his eyes were showing above the water, his gaze fixed on Hero's Gap.

The dragon had looked into the future, and the humans must be destroyed before they could destroy the dragons.

Watching, waiting.

Only a few more hours now.

He knew that it was Doomsday.

But Doomsday for *whom*?

On the high cliffs of Tomorrow, in the ruins of Grimbeard's City, the battered remains of the human army were waking up too. Human beings from the four corners of the Archipelago were gathered there, for they had all been burned out of their homes.

To the south and east, the Archipelago was in ruins, the landscape unrecognizable, island after island scorched black with fire, whole villages obliterated, hillsides with great bites taken out of them, and the dreadful stench of burning wafted across the Bay.

The Alvinsmen were there, of course, and the Danger-Brute, Hysteric, Murderous, Berserk, Villain, Visithug, Outcast, and Uglithug Tribes.

But even the Dragonmarkers had fled to follow Alvin. You could recognize them by the Dragonmark on their foreheads, and they were the Hooligan, Meathead, Bog-Burglar, Silent, Peaceable, and Quiet Life Tribes.

And then there were the Tribes that did not belong to either side: Wanderers, Swallows, former slaves, the Nowheres, and the Nothings, not to mention Humungously Hotshot and Tantrum the Heroes, and their Companions, the Ten Fiancés.

Even the Barbarians, the most ferocious fighters in the Archipelago, had been beaten back by the dragons.

The Barbarians carried highly trained cats into battle with them, who would leap from the Barbarians' shoulders and assault their opponents mid-swordfight. (A highly effective tactic, because it is enormously difficult to swordfight someone when a cat is attacking your head.)

A young teenage Heir called Barbara the Barbarian—a six-foot champion bare-knuckle fighter—and her black cat, Fearless, had held the dragon rebellion at bay for many long months that had turned into years. But she and her cat and her father and her exhausted people had sounded the retreat two weeks ago and joined the journey west to fight under Alvin's banner.

Stoick and Valhallarama, Hiccup's father and mother, woke after hardly sleeping. These great Heroes were Vikings, not used to the softer emotions, but on the hard ground, Stoick had placed his hand around Valhallarama's to comfort her, and they slept with the helmet of what they imagined to be their dead son between them.

Two days before, Hiccup's cousin Snotlout had heroically worn Hiccup's clothes, and ridden Hiccup's dragon into

"This is not my fault, is it, Valhallarama?"

battle. Half the Tribes of the Archipelago had witnessed Snotlout falling into the sea with an arrow in his chest, so Stoick and Valhallarama believed that Hiccup had died and gone to the Viking afterworld.

"This is not my fault, is it, Valhallarama?" said Stoick, wearily looking out on the obliterated landscape, holding his shaggy head. Somewhere out there was his lost Chiefdom, his ships turned to ashes, his old world gone forever. "Is this a curse come down on us all because I would not put the baby Hiccup out to sea to die, when we knew he was a runt? Are the gods punishing us because I loved my son too much to follow the tradition? Should Hiccup—though we loved him so—should Hiccup not have lived?"

For it was Hiccup who had released the dragon Furious and started the trouble in the first place.

Valhallarama put her iron hand on Stoick's shoulder. "We are Warriors, Stoick," she said gently. "We both know what war means, that our loved ones can pay the ultimate price by losing their lives, so wars should never be undertaken lightly.

"But the slavery of humans and of dragons was an abomination that could not

"We are Warriors, Stoick..."

continue," said Valhallarama, that great Hero, her stern clifflike face refusing to show her grief. "Hiccup was right to release the dragon Furious, and you were right not to follow tradition. There are some questions, some battles, some Hiccups worth losing a world for.

"And perhaps even when all ends in disaster, you cannot do the wrong thing, if you do it out of love."

"That is true, Valhallarama," said Stoick, taking some small comfort from this, and standing a little straighter, with some of his old Chiefly spirit. "I *did* do the right thing, didn't I? Our beloved Hiccup may have died and nothing will ever take that grief away, but he was a very great Hero, was he not?"

"He was," Valhallarama agreed.

"I can still see Hiccup now," sighed Stoick proudly, "in that terrible Prison Darkheart, standing in front of Alvin and shouting: 'Is it perfect to have humans and dragons dying in chains? Are creatures as beautiful as this to be made extinct for all time? Are we to say good-bye forever to the magic and the dreaming and the flying of our childhoods? I say NO!'"

Stoick punched the

They pressed their foreheads together

air in imitation of his son's glorious defiance. And then he shook his shaggy head in admiration. "What a son he was! What a very great boy...Yes, I am proud to die with his Dragonmark on my forehead, and I am proud to have been his father, although the gods only let him be with us for that very little while..."

The two middle-aged Heroes leaned in toward each other, creaking a little, for they had put on weight in recent years, and constant swordfighting can be wearing on the knees. They pressed their foreheads together, Dragonmark to Dragonmark, like two old trees leaning inward to support each other against the raging of the gale.

like two old trees leaning in to support one another from the raging of the gale.

And maybe they were thinking, *At least Hiccup did not have to open his eyes to a Doomsday such as this*.

The Vikings had promised to submit themselves to the will of the gods, but it was difficult to know what the gods could be thinking of as the humans prepared for the last great battle, up here in the ruins of Grimbeard's Castle.

Sadly, Bertha, Chief of the Bog-Burglars, sharpened her axe, looking back on happier times when she was striding waist-deep in the delightful bogs of home, her faithful Goreblaster swimming by her side.

Mournfully, Barbara the Barbarian stroked the proud back of Fearless, while her six bodyguards tested their arrows and dreamed of riding through the snowy wastes of Barbaria on the backs of their snowdragons, wind streaming through their mustaches, cats meowing happily on their shoulders, flying back, back in time to a village that no longer existed.

Even the Alvinsmen were out of sorts and unhappy with themselves. Madguts stroked his mighty, invisible Stealth Dragon, trying not to think of life without him. Yes, these humans HATED Alvin. But what could they do but follow him?

The armies of the dragons were everywhere, thick

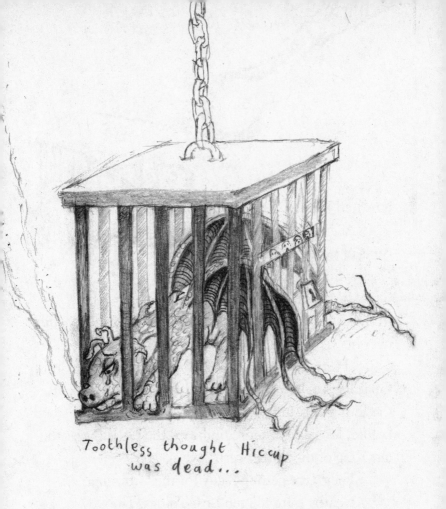

Toothless thought Hiccup
was dead...

and dark like locusts, turning the sky black with their
numbers, leaping out of the sea and crawling across the
ice floes.

Alvin was the humans' only chance now.

For Alvin had the Lost Things, so he was the only

one who could be
crowned King.

Alvin stood in the
ruins of Grimbeard's
Castle, that noseless, heartless,
pitiless Man of War, breath hissing through his
iron mask, sharpening his hungry hook, already gloating
over his victory.

"Hurry up, hurry up!" snapped Alvin as the Druid
Guardians of Tomorrow maneuvered the Throne onto
the four stout stumps where the Throne had once stood
before, long ago, when Grimbeard the Ghastly was the
last King of the Wilderwest.

They were getting ready for the Crowning.

Nearby were the ten Lost Things. The
ticking-thing, the shield, the Crown, the key-that-opens-
all-locks, the Dragon Jewel, the second-best sword, the
ruby heart's stone, the arrow, the Throne, and Hiccup's
little hunting dragon, Toothless: the smallest, naughtiest
little hunting dragon in the whole of the Archipelago,
swinging from the back of the Throne in a tiny cage.

Toothless, too, thought his Master was dead, so the poor little dragon was limp with his continual crying, his spines all flopped over with his misery, lifting up his head to the sky and howling like a little wolf.

"Can't somebody shut that dragon up?" said Alvin between gritted teeth, gripping his sword, the Stormblade, in a hopeful fashion. But there was nothing he could do—Toothless was one of the Lost Things, so until Alvin was crowned King, Alvin could not lay a finger on him.

Take THAT, you horrible Master-killing human nightmare!

"I promise you,
you horrible little newt-with-wings," swore Alvin, putting his face right up to the cage and leering at Toothless with his one grim eye, and pointing his hook at him, "that the very first act I shall accomplish as King is to wring your little froggy neck…"

"T-t-toothless will bite you all over first!" yelled Toothless in Dragonese. "You h-h-horrible Master-killing human nightmare!"

Toothless leaned through the bars of the cage and shot flames at Alvin's good hand. And then Toothless howled even harder.

"Aaarggh!" cried Alvin, sucking his finger. "If only I could kill you RIGHT NOW, you wretched little creature!"

"You c-c-can't!" sobbed Toothless, with some of his old defiance. "T-t-toothless is one of the Lost Things…and Toothless is the B-B-BEST ONE…"

"Don't you worry, little Juiceless," said Stoick, with ponderous, awkward sympathy, poking one of his fingers through the bars of the cage and stroking the trembling, miserable little dragon along his back. "Your Master Hiccup may be dead, but *we* will look after you…"

But how would Stoick be able to do that once Alvin was crowned King? How could he and

90

Alvin be ?

Valhallarama protect
Toothless, or the Silver
Phantom, or *any* of these
dragons who had remained
faithful to the humans' side,
and were now waking up and
wheeling above their human
masters' heads right here, right
now in Grimbeard's Castle?
These dragons were prepared to
go into battle with their masters,
to lay down their lives in order to
protect them. Was their loyalty
to be rewarded with their own
extinction?

Alvin's mother, the witch
Excellinor, bounded up on all
fours like a big white bony
dog, her long white hair
dragging behind her in the
mud.

"Patience, Alvin my sweetest," she purred. "You will not have to wait long for the pleasure of executing the little dragon-rat…and *any others* who may be annoying you…" She rolled her eyes significantly in the direction of the Dragonmarkers.

Alvin shook his bitten hand, cheering up immensely. "Once I'm King, and I've defeated the dragon Furious with the Jewel, I could start the executions immediately…"

He postponed his hook-sharpening for a moment to have a happy little daydream of all the people he would like to execute in the first half hour of his reign. (As it happens, his mother, the witch Excellinor, was rather high up that list, but luckily she didn't guess that.)

Only one little hour until he was crowned King.

One little hour, and then he would be told the Secret of the Dragon Jewel, so now that he came to think of it, he wouldn't even HAVE to wring Toothless's neck.

He could just use the power of the Jewel to destroy the dragons forever…

Tick-tock tick-tock tick-tock tick-tock went the ticking-thing, swinging from Alvin's belt, ticking down the minutes until Alvin was crowned King.

Would it be the humans or the dragons who survived?

Both camps were ready now. Both knew that before this day was over, numberless unlucky ones among them would die on the battlefield, just as they imagined Hiccup had done two days before, and they would not *all* be opening their eyes on another day tomorrow...

Watching, waiting.

Only a few more hours now.

They knew that it was Doomsday.

But Doomsday for *whom*?

There are some Questions, some battles, some Hiccups worth losing a world for...

5. GETTING TO TOMORROW

"We have to get to the island that the Wodensfang was talking about, Hogfly...The island that is called Yesterday or Tomorrow or something," said Hiccup, checking with trembling fingers to see whether the Wodensfang was awake. "And we've got to get there FAST.

"Wake up, Wodensfang! Wake up! *Please* wake up!" whispered Hiccup, desperately tickling the Wodensfang behind the ears, under the arms, but no, the Wodensfang snored on, extraordinarily loudly for such a small and elderly dragon. "Okay, he's not waking up. Hogfly, I'm afraid we're going to have to do this on our own. But that's okay, right? We can do it, can't we? Only we don't have much time..." said Hiccup, hurriedly putting the Wodensfang back in his backpack.

Hiccup's left side was feeling a little less numb, and his brain seemed to have cleared a little, like the mist lifting all around them. There is nothing like MORTAL DANGER to clear the mind.

Right.

He staggered swiftly toward the sleeping Spydragon, which was snoring almost as loudly as the

...we CAN do this...

Wodensfang. This was going to be painful, but Hiccup had to do it. He held his forearm up to the Spydragon's snoring jaws, averting his eyes because he didn't want to see what would happen next.

"Ow!"

The two teeth lifted out of Hiccup's forearm with a most repellent sucking noise and slid, like magnets, back into the two gaps in the Spydragon's mouth. Even if the

Vampire Spydragon woke up, it wouldn't be able to track them now.

"YUCKY," gulped the Hogfly.

Hiccup hurriedly wrapped the wound with a rag torn from his shirt, because it was bleeding quite a bit. He stooped to pick up some of the Sand Shark darts and stuffed them into his pockets, and then he half-ran and half-hopped up the beach. As he stumbled along, he tried to reassure the little Hogfly in case he was worried. "It'll be fine, Hogfly. I mean, look at how we dealt with those Sand Sharks. We can do this..."

The Hogfly did not look worried. He was practicing flying upside down.

"All we have to do is get to this Tomorrow place. I'm sure the dragon rebellion dragons won't be able to follow us there..."

But which island was Tomorrow? Maybe it was the big island just to the south of the Murderous Mountains, the only island in sight not covered in dragons.

"Is that the island of Tomorrow, Hogfly?" asked Hiccup, pointing.

"Ooh, are we playing a guessing game now?" asked the Hogfly, eagerly turning the right way up, and frowning in a puzzled way at the outline of the island. "It's a tricky one...I give up! Is it a pancake? Is it a teacup? Is it your grandmother's hat?"

96

"Oh brother," said Hiccup.

He staggered on, up the sand dune behind the beach. From the top, he could see the rolling ocean to the west, and another larger island to the north, flatter than this one, in the shape of the top of a question mark. He could also see the whole of the tiny island of Hero's End laid out in front of him.

And it was extraordinary.

The entire island was covered in shipwrecks.

Not just *one* shipwreck, but the wrecks of thirty or forty Viking ships, strewn out over the blasted landscape in front of him.

For when the dreadful gales of the Winter Wind of Woden blew unfortunate ships through Hero's Gap, those that weren't blown out into the cold Atlantic ended here, on the little isle of Hero's End.

"Maybe there's something we can use as a boat, something that isn't completely wrecked!" shouted Hiccup to the Hogfly with rising hope, and he stumbled unsteadily toward the broken ships, as the wind tried its best to pluck him out of the marsh and send him bowling over into the sea.

"Look for a ship that might actually sail, Hogfly!" shouted Hiccup to Hogfly over the shrieking wind.

Most of the ships had been sunk there for centuries, their tattered sails rotting into the marshes over hundreds of years. Some were more recent, but they all had great holes in the hull, or were split in two, and Hiccup knew they could not carry him across the narrow strip of water to Tomorrow.

"I've found one!" squealed the Hogfly, pointing both trotters at one.

"No, Hogfly, it has to be one that doesn't have a hole in it..."

"I've found another one!"

"No, Hogfly, it really, really *does* have to be one with no holes in it at all..."

A little farther on, Hiccup spotted the small upturned bottom of a rowboat; and hurrying toward it, he realized with mounting excitement that the boat was virtually intact, apart from a small section bitten out of it by some large sea creature.

Perhaps a Leviathorgan? Or a half-grown Woden's Nightmare, by the look of those tooth patterns... he thought to himself. And then: *Wow, I do seem to know an awful LOT about dragons. Imagine thinking about natural history at a time like this...*

The boat was small enough that Hiccup could turn it over by himself, and panting hard, he dragged it

over the marshes by the end of a fraying rope, every now and then sinking so deep into the soggy ground that he thought he wouldn't be able to get out again. A little later, he had gotten the little boat into the sea, and to Hiccup's passionate relief, it floated, a little lopsidedly.

Everything seemed to be going Hiccup's way. The wind had even changed direction, so it was now blowing a violent gale in the direction of the island he hoped was Tomorrow. That wind would blow him rapidly across the white-tipped waves and onto the island, Hiccup was sure of it—as long as the boat didn't sink…

He pushed away from the shore of Hero's End, bailing out the water slopping over the shattered, bitten side and steering as best he could with a broken oar he had found inside the boat. The salt was in his eyes, every bone ached, and his toes and swollen arm were so cold that he could barely feel them.

Ah, the final test was a test indeed, of heart and body and mind and spirit. Hiccup was so very, very weary, so cold, so confused, that some part of him wanted to give up, just lie down in the bottom of the boat and let it fill up with water and go down to the quiet, soft nothingness of the seabed, where the pain would be no more. But something within him made him keep on bailing that water, and moving the oar with

his numb and swollen arm. He had
to get to Tomorrow…He had to get to
Tomorrow…

He did not really know *why* he had to
get to Tomorrow, but still he made himself
move that oar, bail that water, with what
little strength he had.

His heart began to lift a little
halfway across the causeway. Maybe
he would make it after all. Maybe he
wouldn't be blown off course...

And then he looked up through his
slightly less bruised eye, and for a second,
as the fog shifted, he caught sight of a
little army of dragons flying swiftly toward

him from the direction of the Murderous Mountains, before the fog closed up again and swallowed them from view.

Gorebreathers. Tongue-twisters. Hellsteethers, his brain told him helpfully. *Armed with poisonous gases, arm-twisting tongues, jaws that leap out and get you...*

Those Sand Sharks must have told the dragon rebellion where he was, and this was the dragon Furious sending more dragons to kill him.

Hiccup was so well informed about dragons that he had noticed the exact flying speeds of each one, and had already calculated that they would intercept him before he got to the beach of Tomorrow, even though it was now so tantalizingly close. How could he fight these dragons, all on his own, with no weapons?

And it appeared that *one* of the dragons, at least, was nearer than he thought.

There was a confused roaring noise, and something swooped down out of the fog, and Hiccup only just flattened himself on the bottom of the boat in time to avoid being swept up by it.

Oh for Thor's sake! What was *that*?

Whatever-it-was was so well camouflaged that it was invisible, but as it rose up and away from Hiccup, its chameleon body slowly turned from the exact color of a foggy sky to its own natural color, a breathtaking sea-green.

It was a Deadly Shadow, and a *Triple-Header* Deadly Shadow at that. He could see each of his three heads outlined against the fog. Deadly Shadows are extremely rare, and exceptionally dangerous.

Fires electric lightning bolts as well as flames…one of the rarest and most frightening attack dragons in the Archipelago…

Hiccup picked himself up from the bottom of the boat, and gripped his pathetic broken oar in one trembling hand, swiveling around to see where it might attack from next. But there was nothing to be seen but fog, fog, and more fog.

"Woof! Woof! Woof!" barked the Hogfly warningly.

The Deadly Shadow swooped down again, and this time as he dived, Hiccup aimed at him with the oar but missed and fell over.

And as the dragon swooped that second time, just before he fell over, Hiccup saw two wild-looking human figures sitting on the Deadly Shadow's back, screaming at him. The smaller of the two had a lot of blond hair, and was yelling at the top of her voice, and brandishing a sword above her head.

The three heads of the Deadly Shadow appeared to be arguing with one another. Hiccup glimpsed two other dragons flying beside the Deadly Shadow: a black Windwalker dragon and a yellow hunting dragon whom Hiccup saw too briefly to figure out what species it was.

"Trust *nobody*," the Wodensfang had said.

These must be the humans that the Wodensfang said would be hunting him too...And they looked ferocious.

The third time the Deadly Shadow swooped, Hiccup was ready.

There was the same roaring noise, and as the highly camouflaged creature dived, and Hiccup could see the dim outline of gigantic outstretched claws, he ducked again before stretching up and WHACKING the claws as hard as he could with his splintered oar, which nearly split in two.

Then Hiccup took out two of the Sand Shark darts and threw them as hard as he could with his good hand, and one of them sank into the shining flanks of the Deadly Shadow, and the other one hit the smaller yellow dragon next to it.

The Deadly Shadow soared away into invisibility again, leaving the boat rocking so violently that it nearly sank, and water came pouring in over one of the sides, and poor Hiccup tried to bail it out with his cupped hands…

This was all rather unfortunate, to say the least.

For, of course, the three heads of the Deadly Shadow were Innocence, Arrogance, and Patience. (Patience was the middle head, because that was what he had to have.) And the people on the back of that Deadly Shadow dragon were Fishlegs No-Name and Camicazi, Heir to the Bog-Burglars. And the two dragons flying with them were Stormfly, Camicazi's little golden Mood Dragon, and the Windwalker, Hiccup's very own riding dragon.

They were Hiccup's very best friends in all the world, and with Hiccup, Wodensfang, and Toothless they formed the Ten Companions of the Dragonmark.

But, of course, Hiccup had no clue who they were.

Hiccup, where are you?

6. IT'S DIFFICULT TO RESCUE SOMEBODY WHO DOESN'T *WANT* TO BE RESCUED

Camicazi and Fishlegs had spent a long and weary night on dragonback, searching for Hiccup through the fog.

They may have looked a little crazed to Hiccup, but that was because they had been up all night without so much as a wink of sleep.

Throughout the night, they hunted through that terrible blinding mist, hiding when they suddenly came across the dragon Furious's search parties, looking, looking, looking for Hiccup. They had traveled all around the coast of Tomorrow, north to the isle of Grimbeard's Despair, south to Lava-Lout Island, shouting until their throats were cracked and sore:

"Hiccup, where are yo-o-ou?"

It had been a long night indeed.

What Fishlegs really wanted to be in life was a bard, so these kinds of "total war" situations weren't where he was at his best. Every now and then he would drop off to sleep on the Deadly Shadow's shoulder and have a little dream about happier times on the little Isle of Berk, with him and Hiccup sitting down in the

green grass chatting about poetry or something restful like that.

And then he would wake up with a start, and he was in the fog, and all the grass on Berk had been burned to a crisp, and his cheeks were streaked with tears, and Hiccup was probably dead.

The only thing that gave him any comfort was being on the back of the Deadly Shadow dragon. There is something vaguely soothing about the presence of an enormous invisible three-headed Deadly Shadow, who has sworn to stay by your side forever and protect you with his life.

"Face it, Camicazi," Fishlegs said very sadly at about five o'clock in the morning. "They brought his helmet back up from the sea. Hundreds of people saw him die. It's *impossible* for him to be alive."

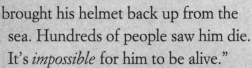

Unlike Fishlegs, Camicazi *was* a good person to have by your side in a "total war" situation, because she loved a good battle, and she was incurably optimistic. But even *she* was beginning to doubt that Hiccup

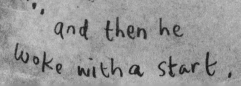

and then he woke with a start,

was alive, though she would rather have died than admit it.

"And then," continued Fishlegs in an even smaller voice, "even if he *is* alive, he can't land on Tomorrow because the dragon Guardians are guarding it, and he can't be made King because Alvin has all the Lost Things…"

"Come on, Fishlegs, has Hiccup taught you NOTHING?" replied Camicazi briskly. "There is no such thing as im-*possible*, only im-*probable*."

She rubbed her dirty nose on her sleeve.

"Besides, *of course* he isn't dead. He is our Hero, so he cannot be dead. And we cannot give up. *He* would not give up on *us*, would he?

"I remember what Hiccup said when he was tied up in chains, rescuing me from the Witch: 'I will NEVER give up fighting you even though it is too late…' he said, '…even though all is lost…even though it is impossible… never never never!'" And Camicazi punched the air, copying Hiccup, just as Stoick had done earlier. "Windwalker," she continued, asking the shaggy, gentle riding dragon

He is NOT dead, I know it in my heart

for the twenty-somethingth time, "are you sure you can't get a scent of him? Not even the faintest little whiff?"

The Windwalker was so tired that he kept on accidentally falling asleep on the wing, and dropping like a stone for thirty feet or so before Camicazi hollered at him to wake up and he had to put his wings out hurriedly to break his fall. He was just nodding off again, but at Camicazi's question, he opened his drooping eyelids, and shook his shaggy head, and a tear crept down his cheek.

So imagine the disbelieving excitement of the panicked, terrified, weary Companions of the Dragonmark, when all at once the Deadly Shadow's six eyes spotted something on the rocking water, and for one sleep-crazed second he thought it was a lobster pot, but no, it was a boat!

"It's Hiccup!" said Camicazi, raising her head at the Deadly Shadow's instant joyful snort. "It's Hiccup! He's *alive*!"

Fishlegs couldn't believe it. "Are you sure? I mean, Camicazi, are you *really* sure?"

"Yes! *Yes!*"

And the Deadly Shadow and the Stormfly trumpeted with joy, and the Windwalker did a happy little barrel roll in the air in his excitement.

But there wasn't much time for celebration, as the

very next moment, they spotted the grisly little army of dragons flying swiftly toward the tiny boat from the direction of the Murderous Mountains.

"Tongue-twisters!" said Fishlegs in horror. "Hellsteethers…Brainpickers…Razorwings…That is one *nasty* search party…"

"They must have been sent by the dragon Furious to kill the person in that boat!" shouted Camicazi. "That just *proves* it's Hiccup! Don't worry, Fishlegs. We're closer than they are. We can just swoop in and save him before they get there…

"COMPANIONS OF THE DRAGONMARK TO THE RESCUE!"

One of the great advantages of the Deadly Shadow is his ability to camouflage himself so effectively that he becomes invisible. All they had to do now was to pick Hiccup up off the boat, and put him on the back of the Deadly Shadow, and then they could all fade into nothingness, right in front of the enemy's eyes.

Imagine you have been searching, all night,

He's alive!!

for someone you know in your heart of hearts cannot be found…the only Hero who can change the course of history…the Hero who also happens to be *your* Hero, your best friend Hiccup…And suddenly, when you have lost all hope, you find he is alive!

No wonder they went a little crazy as they swooped down to save him.

"Hiccup!" roared Camicazi and Fishlegs in cracked, broken voices, wild with excitement, as the Deadly Shadow dived.

"Hiccup! Hiccup! Hiccup!" called Innocence, Arrogance, and Patience, and the three heads of the Deadly Shadow shot triumphant bolts of lightning in three directions over Hiccup's head, so thrilled were they to have found the boy at last.

But as the Deadly Shadow put out helpful talons to pluck Hiccup up to safety…

Hiccup threw himself into the bottom of the boat.

"What IS he doing?" said Camicazi, peering down in puzzlement. "Oh my goodness, he looks even more terrible than when we saw him last time. I do hope he's not badly wounded…" And then: "That is the MOST unseaworthy boat I think I have ever seen…Dive a bit more slowly, Shadow, and sort of *hover* above him, so he can see who we are…"

So the Deadly Shadow dived more slowly this time, and Camicazi and Fishlegs shouted down madly, "It's us, Hiccup, us!" with Camicazi waving her sword in a friendly welcoming fashion, but it appeared to make no difference, and on the third dive, the badly wounded Hiccup whacked the Deadly Shadow very hard on the leg, and peppered them with Sand Shark darts.

"OW!" yelled Arrogance as one of the darts caught him in the flank.

"Ow!" squealed Stormfly as she was hit in the wing, and Camicazi only just caught her as she fell out of the sky.

This wasn't quite how Camicazi and Fishlegs had imagined the happy reunion.

"Well his *throwing* has gotten better at least," said Camicazi, removing the dart from Stormfly's wing. "That was pretty accurate (for a boy, of course)…"

She tried to keep the hurt out of her voice, because when you have been up all night, searching for someone you love, and finally, oh heart-thumping joy, against all odds, you find them, you sort of hope that they will give you a big pleased-to-see-you *hug*, not attack you with oars and throw Sand Shark darts at you.

What in Freya's name was Hiccup *doing*? Why was he attacking them?

Didn't he recognize them?

At the very least, Hiccup ought to recognize Shadow, because there weren't that many three-headed Deadly Shadow dragons in the Archipelago.

To be precise, there was only one.

But they'd had a brief vision of Hiccup's terrified white face as he struck the Shadow with his oar, and it was quite clear he had no clue who they were.

"We can't dive again until he knows it's us," Camicazi decided. "We nearly sank the boat that time. He must be finding it hard to see with two black eyes. Stormfly, you fly down and tell him it's us…"

"HA!" huffed Stormfly, pointing at her numb wing. "I can't fly with only one wing, and I have to say, if ungrateful Heroes are going to go around throwing

painful darts at dragons who are trying to save them, they can jolly well save themselves."

"Okay, Fishlegs," said Camicazi, "you steer the Shadow, and I'll wing-walk and try and shout down to him…"

Camicazi leaped onto the Deadly Shadow's wing, and walked along it as sure as a cat, and shouted down at Hiccup, crossly waving her arms about:

"It's US, you LUNATIC HOOLIGAN, OPEN YOUR EYES! IT'S US! WE'RE TRYING TO HELP YOU! WE'RE TRYING TO STOP THOSE DRAGON REBELLION DRAGONS FROM KILLING YOU!" And Hiccup threw a whole load more darts at her, while Hogfly barked in an excitable fashion.

The truth is, it is extremely difficult to rescue someone who doesn't *want* to be rescued.

"Too late!" squeaked Fishlegs, pointing ahead.

The treacherous fog parted, showing that the search party of dragon rebellion dragons was getting way too close for comfort.

"Okay, okay," said Camicazi, thinking fast. "Time for Plan B. It's a shame because Plan A would have been a whole lot simpler…"

"We have a Plan B?" said Fishlegs in surprise.

"There's always a Plan B," said Camicazi. "Plan

B is, we change from being the Companions of the Dragonmark Rescue Party, to the Companions of the Dragonmark DIVERSION Party.

"We'll have to distract the dragon rebellion dragons so that Hiccup can get to the beach of Tomorrow. Those dragons won't dare follow him there because they'll be scared of the dragon Guardians."

This was completely true. Tomorrow was the only island that the dragon rebellion did not dare attack, because they were so frightened of the dragon Guardians.

"But what will *Hiccup* do about the dragon Guardians?"

"Well, Hiccup must have some clever plan to deal with those dragon Guardians, mustn't he? Because he's already heading to the beach," argued Camicazi, with a touching faith in Hiccup's intelligence. "Hiccup will know what he's doing."

"And what do you mean by *distract* the dragon rebellion dragons?" moaned Fishlegs. "Does distracting them involve going anywhere *near* them, or is it the sort of thing we can do safely, from a distance?"

"Wait for them to get a bit closer, Shadow," said Camicazi, crouched against the dragon's three necks, eyes sparkling with excitement, "and make sure you're completely invisible. Then, when they're within earshot, we're going to…"

She whispered something into the Deadly Shadow's six ears.

The Shadow could understand Norse, though none of his heads spoke it, and all three heads enjoyed a little trickery.

"Very good," hissed Arrogance, eyes alight with enjoyment.

"Nice touch," purred Patience.

"'Earshot' sounds quite *close*," said Fishlegs, putting his hands over his eyes.

The dragon rebellion dragons closed in on the ridiculous, half-sinking little boat, eyes gleaming with mischief.

"We have to wait…" whispered Camicazi, sitting invisible above them. "We have to wait until they can all hear us…"

"But they're getting really *close*…" moaned Fishlegs.

It wasn't just a silly little band of Sand Sharks attacking Hiccup *this* time.

Poison Darters, Riproarers, Tongue-twisters, Hellsteethers, Driller Dragons, Brainpickers, and many more of the most feared species of the Archipelago circled Hiccup in his tiny boat. The Hellsteethers softly rattled their teeth, with that dreadful warning rattle that turned Vikings' hearts to ice when they heard it surrounding their ships in the dead of night.

The many-eyed Tongue-twisters pushed out their disgusting lolling tongues, strong enough to twist off a man's arm; the Brainpickers slowly, slowly put out their dreaded picks; the Driller Dragons set their drills a-turning…

Three gigantic Thor's Thunderers slowly emerged from beneath the waves and stretched their long necks into the sky, like giant beanstalks growing out of the ocean. Up, up, up those beanstalks grew, long tentacles trailing beautifully from their necks, every one of those tentacles tingling with poison as strong as a man-o'-war jellyfish.

Softly, grimly, Darkbreathers broke the surface of the waves. Darkbreathers have lived so long in the darkness that it has entered their very souls and twisted them forever…

Luna had chosen her assassins well. There are some dragons that really *are* monsters. These were the kind of dragons who killed without thinking, without remorse, and almost for the pleasure of it.

They had a sense of drama too. Slowly they circled

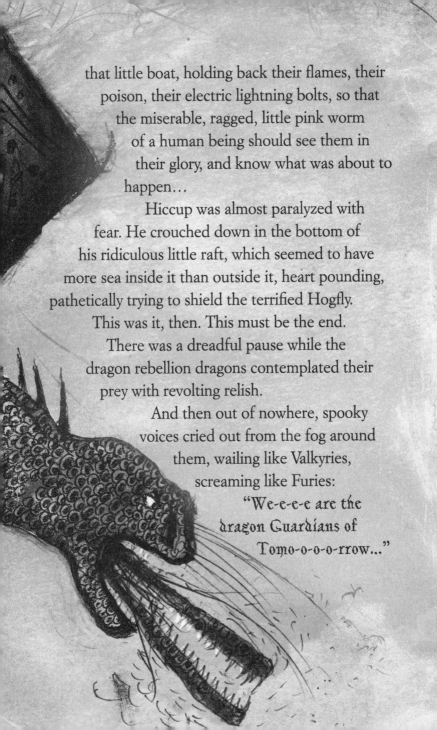

that little boat, holding back their flames, their
poison, their electric lightning bolts, so that
the miserable, ragged, little pink worm
of a human being should see them in
their glory, and know what was about to
happen…

Hiccup was almost paralyzed with
fear. He crouched down in the bottom of
his ridiculous little raft, which seemed to have
more sea inside it than outside it, heart pounding,
pathetically trying to shield the terrified Hogfly.
This was it, then. This must be the end.

There was a dreadful pause while the
dragon rebellion dragons contemplated their
prey with revolting relish.

And then out of nowhere, spooky
voices cried out from the fog around
them, wailing like Valkyries,
screaming like Furies:

"We-e-e-e are the
dragon Guardians of
Tomo-o-o-o-rrow…"

Camicazi had a good sense of drama too.

The voices belonged to Arrogance, Innocence, and Patience, of course, but the dragon rebellion dragons weren't to know that. The dragon search party found themselves struck by bolts of lightning that seemed to come from the very fog itself, followed by sheets of shooting flames, and a rain of very accurate arrows from Camicazi's bow shooting them in the legs, the shoulders, the sides…

You cannot blame the dragon rebellion dragons for assuming that they really *were* being attacked by the dragon Guardians of Tomorrow. After all, they were only within a hundred yards of Tomorrow's beach.

And even the Thor's Thunderers were frightened of the dragon Guardians.

The dragon rebellion horde, who only seconds earlier

had been regarding their prey with smug satisfaction, now responded with what can only be described as *total panic*. They screamed in horror and confusion and whirled around, trying to escape their dragon Guardian attackers and get away from Tomorrow as fast as they could.

There was absolute chaos in the stampede to get away. Thor's Thunderer tentacles flew everywhere, lightning bolts exploded at random, and darts and flames and spears and arrows rained down in waves, while the terrible tails of the panicking beasts lashed the ocean into a frothing, foaming, thunderbolting storm.

Hiccup looked upward with his jaw hanging open.

What in the name of Freya and Woden and all the other gods was going on? He wasn't going to wait to find out. He leaned over the side of the sinking boat and paddled it toward the beach of Tomorrow as fast as he could.

As the dragon rebellion dragons retreated, the Windwalker and the Deadly Shadow gave chase, shooting lightning bolts and screaming insults. Every now and then the Deadly Shadow got overexcited and chased a Darkbreather under the water before resurfacing again.

"BOG-BURGLARS FIGHT FORE-E-EVER!
Take *that*, you big-tongued, hairy-backed,
bully-alligators!" yelled Camicazi, reloading her bow
with delight. "Let me know when Hiccup has gotten to
the beach, Fishlegs…"

"He's nearly there," panted Fishlegs, spitting out
seawater and looking back at the shores of Tomorrow.
"Hang on…his boat's half underwater, but he's *almost*
there…Oh *dear*…now the boat's *sunk*…but it's all
right—he's swimming the last bit…He's standing up…
He's there! He's on the beach!"

"He's ON TOMORROW! WE'VE GOTTEN
HIM TO TOMORROW! Thanks to CAMICAZI THE
MAGNIFICENT, who has just saved the day ONCE
AGAIN!" crowed Camicazi, punching the air.

"Camicazi," said Fishlegs anxiously, screwing up his
eyes to see what was happening through the fog, "I really
hope you're right and Hiccup has a plan for what to do
about those dragon Guardians…He's just wandering
up the beach…"

Fishlegs was seized by a horrible thought. "He didn't recognize us...*He does know the dragon Guardians are there, doesn't he?*"

"Of course he does, and he'll have a plan! Hiccup ALWAYS has a plan," said Camicazi confidently.

Let us hope he *does* have a plan.

For the little figure of Hiccup had already staggered halfway up the beach.

7. ONLY THE ONE WITH THE KING'S LOST THINGS CAN LAND ON TOMORROW AND LIVE

Hiccup had no idea what was going on in the skies above him. The attacking dragons were fighting among themselves, with such violence that lightning bolts and darts and flames rained down around his sinking boat as he paddled desperately toward the white beach with his broken oar.

Nearer, nearer, nearer.

When he got within twenty yards, the boat sank entirely, and he had to swim the last part with only one arm, for the left one was now so swollen and numb he could barely move it. Thor, the water was cold. Hiccup almost passed out from the icy shock of it.

And then he nearly drowned in the last dozen feet of his journey, which would have been ironic.

The sea to the west of Tomorrow is a great ocean that stretches far to the west until you get to America, the land-that-does-not-exist (or you fall off the edge of the world, of course—whatever you happen to believe).

So the waves reaching this coast are gigantic, and come rolling in with great violence on a windy winter's day like this one.

As Hiccup swam in to the beach, a great wave took him, and tumbled him over and over for such a long time that his lungs were bursting for lack of air, before grinding him down on the sand. And as the water retreated, he staggered to his feet, gasping and retching and limping, wading thigh-high through the icy water before collapsing on the sand exhausted, trembling, and gasping for breath like a poor stranded fish. But even in his bedraggled, numb state, he felt a weary sense of conquest.

He had made it to Tomorrow! Although he still could not remember much of his life before waking up on Hero's End, something told him that he had been searching for a long, long time to get to this place, this spot, this wild and windy shore on the edge of nowhere. And he was here! He had made it!

Tomorrow. There was something hopeful about even the word.

Hiccup let himself enjoy the triumph of it for one victorious moment, before forcing himself to get up and stumble onward. He looked over his shoulder at the continuing commotion of the dragon rebellion dragons.

They might yet come after him. He had to get out of here…The little brown dragon Wodensfang had said he must find a ruined city where the King was going to be crowned…

He staggered forward, so bruised and battered that it was painful to make each step, but forcing himself to move nonetheless.

The beach stretched out for miles to his left and right, and there was something *about* that beach that made him feel very uneasy, and lurch even faster in his limping, rollicking gait.

Perhaps it was the way that, under his feet, the sand didn't feel entirely *firm*. It was shaking, just a tiny, tiny bit, and shifting—as if the very grains of sand were alive, like tiny wriggling worms. Hiccup looked down at the sand in horror as he shambled faster, and ever faster, trying to get to the top of the dunes and off the beach. There was something very peculiar going on.

"I think I might just go in your backpack if you don't mind," said the Hogfly nervously, diving into the backpack next to the snoring Wodensfang, and half-shutting the lid so that only his eyes were peering out. "That sand is a little SPOOKY…"

The sand was indeed a little spooky.

It appeared to be singing.

An unearthly, terrifying song that seemed to come from another world.

A song that hissed and hummed with menace.

Hiccup broke into a shambling run, panting hard and crying, and he had nearly made it to the edge of the beach when, to his absolute horror…

Three yards in front of him, a colossal figure stepped out from behind a rock.

Hiccup stopped dead with shock.

The figure was huge, and hooded, and his arms were crossed. He strode toward Hiccup, one, two, three steps, and threw back his hood.

His face was as stern and unyielding as a granite cliff, and he was blindfolded.

He drew a gigantic axe from his belt, and he held it directly above Hiccup's head, as if he could actually *see* Hiccup despite the blindfold.

"I am a Guardian of Tomorrow," roared the blind Axeman. "I, and my father, and my father's father, and my father's father's father, have guarded these shores for nearly a century from those who are unworthy.

"ONLY THE ONE WITH THE KING'S LOST THINGS CAN LAND ON TOMORROW AND LIVE.

"Who are you who dares to risk Death by Airy Oblivion by landing on our beach?"

Hiccup swallowed. "Death by Airy Oblivion" didn't sound good.

"I think my name is Hiccup," said Hiccup. Out in the bay between Hero's End and Tomorrow, the Deadly Shadow was flying as fast as he could toward the beach, for now even Camicazi was a little worried that Hiccup might not have a plan.

ONLY THE one with
the King's Lost Things
can land on Tomorrow
and LIVE!!

"Who is Hiccup talking
to?" shouted Camicazi.

"That must be one of
the human Guardians of
Tomorrow," said Fishlegs.
"There are hundreds
of them posted all
along the coast
of this island.
Oh dear,

133

oh dear, oh dear…Remember when we saw those dragon Guardians of Tomorrow ROCKETING out from underneath the sands yesterday? Isn't there some horrible saying like: 'Only the one with the King's Lost Things can land on Tomorrow and live'? Can you go any faster, Shadow?"

"We're flying…as…fast…as…we…can…" snorted Innocence.

"Are you saying you are he-who-would-be-king?" barked the blind Axeman.

"I believe so," said Hiccup uncertainly. "That is what I was told by this small brown dragon who said his name was the Wodensfang. I don't know if you know him?"

The Axeman shook his head.

Hiccup was gabbling slightly, because he was so frightened. "That same brown dragon gave me reason to believe that there may be some kind of ruined city on this island. Would you possibly mind showing me the way?"

The blind Axeman looked impassively down at him with his blank, blindfolded face. His axe was still raised, which wasn't a good sign.

"The thing is," said the Axeman, "we already have a man on the island who has passed the test. And when he is crowned in an hour's time, we Guardians will be released from ninety-nine years of bondage, ninety-nine years of imprisonment on this island. *Free!*" The blind Axeman's voice was hoarse with longing. "Free from this island cage…free to roam the seas and skies of the Archipelago and wander where we will…And I shall take off my blindfold and see the wonder of the world around me for the very first time, and gasp to see the beauty of the things that I can only smell and touch!"

"That's wonderful," said Hiccup.

"It *is* wonderful," agreed the Axeman.

"And I'm sure you deserve it," said Hiccup.

"You're a nice, polite boy," said the blind Axeman. "And politeness is underestimated as a good quality in a King. But if we have a King already on the island, it follows, just as night follows day, that *you* cannot be the King as well.

"Show me the things," said the blind Axeman.

Hiccup swallowed again. His teeth were chattering, but whether from cold or fear, he did not know.

"Yes, I'm afraid I don't *have* any of the things right now," he admitted. "But the little brown dragon—the one I was just telling you about—he told me there was a man called Alvin the Treacherous who stole all these

Things from me, so even though he got here first, I am in fact the rightful King…"

The blindfolded man stared down at Hiccup, if a blindfolded man could be said to stare, his axe still raised. Hiccup was uncomfortably aware of what an unlikely, un-Kinglike figure he must make, as if he were offering a drowned rat to be the King—although, of course, the blindfolded man couldn't see him anyway.

"So Alvin the Treacherous stole the Lost Things from you?" repeated the blind Axeman.

"That's right," said Hiccup. It sounded like a rather feeble excuse, out there on the wild and windy beach of Tomorrow, with an axe being held above your head.

"And *you* are the rightful King?" asked the blind Axeman.

"That's what the Wodensfang said," said Hiccup.

The blind Axeman put his axe back in his swordbelt.

Hiccup felt faint with relief. "Thank you," he said, gratefully. "Now if you could just show me the way to the ruined—"

"I'm sorry," said the Axeman regretfully. "Truly sorry, for you are only a boy, and a nice, polite boy at that."

The Axeman lifted his arms up so that they spread out like bats' wings, and he shouted up to the stormy sky: "BUT...

"Only the one with the King's Lost Things can land on Tomorrow and live..."

This didn't look good.

"COME, GREAT POWERS OF DEATH AND DARKNESS! COME, MIGHTY PROTECTORS OF TOMORROW ACROSS THE AGES! COME, DRAGON GUARDIANS, AND TAKE THIS UNWORTHY BOY AND GIVE HIM DEATH BY AIRY OBLIV-I-I-ION!"

"NO!" screamed Camicazi, as the Deadly Shadow flew as fast as he possibly could toward the beach.

All around Hiccup the sand began to bubble.

-O-O-O-O-O!!! / /

He looked around himself, appalled.

That sand…that sand that earlier had seemed alive, now gave birth to creatures of indescribable horror. Who knows what they were: dragons or monsters or something worse.

They were so huge and
so swift and so deadly, it
was impossible to see them.
They burst from the sand
like some alien force, shrieking

otherworldly vengeance, and they took hold of the screaming, terrified Hiccup, and they shot up into the air like great grim shooting stars, carrying him up, up, UP, to drown him in the upper atmosphere.

This was Death by Airy Oblivion.

"Nooooooo!" shrieked Camicazi and Fishlegs and Windwalker. "No! No! No!"

Windwalker put his paws over his eyes.

No…surely not…

8. I BET YOU THOUGHT THAT THIS WAS NEVER GOING TO HAPPEN...

"Nooooo!" howled Hiccup, and he could feel his ears popping, and a fierce grip around his arms and body.

I'm going to die... thought Hiccup. And as he rocketed upward in a tornado of sand, he was aware of being lifted toward the eyes of the creatures carrying him up, up, up, but he had to close his own

Me hafta care for

Toothless!

eyes, so bright
was their gaze.
In the throes
of death, we cannot
lie—we have to speak the
truth—and Hiccup shouted
something that came right from
the very heart of him, even though
he had lost his memory, and he could
not even remember who Toothless was.

Look! That's Hiccup, isn't it?

These were the words he screamed:

"Me hafta care for Toothless!"

Which of course means, "I have to save Toothless!"

Hiccup's stomach lurched as the unknown monsters that were carrying him changed course for a second, plunging crazily downward like a rocket, suddenly and erratically changing direction, and Hiccup felt himself slipping.

He was indeed a little slippery, for he was covered in slimy mud from the ground at Hero's End, and greasy with seaweed from the beach here on Tomorrow—so the creatures had probably relaxed their hold for a moment, trying to get a better grip, perhaps?

Who knows?

But Hiccup slid, like a little slimy worm, out of the creatures' clasp and down, down, down toward the marshy bog of Tomorrow.

Camicazi, Fishlegs, Windwalker, and Stormfly were watching, screaming, from the back of the Deadly Shadow. They saw the terrible creatures emerging, and the beach turning into a scene of horror, with Hiccup swept up in a whirlwind of sand so choking that it was almost impossible to see any longer...

But then they saw, distinctly, the creatures shooting back down again, madly, like unimaginably huge fireworks that have lost control, and zigzagging low over the bogs. Something dropped from their claws into the bog, something small and raggedy and insignificant.

"Oh for Freya's sake," gasped Camicazi. "That's Hiccup, isn't it? Isn't that Hiccup?"

Down on the beach, the blind Axeman sniffed the air, thick with sand. "I don't believe it," he whispered. "The dragon Guardians have made a mistake...They never make mistakes..."

His freedom and his chance to see the world might be taken away from him, if the dragon Guardians had made a mistake...

"BROTHERS!" roared the blind Axeman. "RISE UP! THE DRAGON GUARDIANS HAVE MADE A MISTAKE, AND THERE IS AN INTERLOPER ON THE ISLAND!!!!"

He took a great stick from his waistband

and rapped it on the ground in a weird tattoo, stamping in time to the beat a message in code to his fellow Guardians.

The western beach of Tomorrow had looked entirely deserted.

But at the cry of the blind Axeman, all along the beach, the human Guardians of Tomorrow revealed themselves.

There were hundreds and hundreds of human sentries secretly posted all around the island's coast.

They stepped out from behind rocks; they burst out of the grasses on the cliffs; they sat up from shallow graves they had dug themselves on the beach, as if the very sand itself were giving birth to them: tall, hooded, grim men and women, all blindfolded.

Half of the Guardians remained at their posts, guarding the island's borders; the rest drew their axes, and set off at a brisk trot toward the interior of the island.

"Quick!" whispered Camicazi. "Hiccup needs us, if he's still alive. Shadow, you can get past the sentries in all this chaos..."

The Deadly Shadow stretched out his three necks, and flew low and straight over the heads of the shouting human Guardians. Fishlegs held his breath, expecting

148

a cry at any moment from the troops below—but no cry came. It looked like Camicazi was right.

Normally even a Stealth Dragon could not get through the double defense of the human and dragon Guardians of Tomorrow.

But the sentries were busy searching for Hiccup, and the launch of the dragon Guardians from the beach had created a bewildering, blinding sandstorm that mingled with the fog and the smoke.

The dragon Guardians had rocketed up into the airy atmosphere, and it would take them at least five minutes to turn around and dive, like unimaginably enormous peregrine falcons, back down under the sands of Tomorrow.

So in the middle of all that disturbance, the Deadly Shadow sailed right over the top of the entire Guardian army and into the airspace of Tomorrow without being detected.

Fishlegs and Camicazi got their first good look at the island of Tomorrow, laid out beneath them like a child's map in a fairy tale.

It was a good-sized island, covered, like all the islands of the Archipelago, with marsh and bog and bracken, and thickly forested in the south. Although the ruined city of Tomorrow was in a state of splendid decay, it was still the largest city that Fishlegs and Camicazi had ever seen. No fewer than fifteen castles were built around the edge of a large natural harbor, and thousands more buildings were laid out in a ruined rabbit warren that was sinking slowly back down into the marsh, broken windows peering only inches above the level of the bog.

Where there once had been houses, shops, stables, a bustling, thriving city—the center of the Kingdom of the Wilderwest—was now only the tumbledown rubble of stone and wall and roof, where the wind whistled sadly and the melancholy cry of the seagulls echoed through the ruins.

Right on the top of the highest cliff, the largest building of all could be seen: the great ruined wreck of the Castle of Grimbeard the Ghastly himself.

It was here that the great human party of cheering Alvinsmen and mourning Dragonmarkers had assembled for the Crowning.

They had halted, and were staring at the sky, looking at the awesome sight of the dragon Guardians rocketing ever upward, with the sand raining down on them in a drenching storm.

"What's happening? What does this mean?" snapped Alvin, in a sudden panic that his Kingdom might be snatched away from him at the last minute.

The Druid Guardian, head of the human Guardians of Tomorrow, turned his blindfolded face to the heavens and sniffed the air. He knelt down on the ground, and listened to the sound of the pounding feet of his fellow Guardians searching the island.

His Master... Could it be his Master?

"Intruders…" whispered the Guardian. "Intruders on Tomorrow…How extraordinary…"

Poor little cried-out Toothless, his spines all flopped over with misery, lifted up his head and opened up his eyes, and gave a little whine of hope. His Master…Could it be his Master?

Alvin whitened. He forgot he was not King yet, and hauled the Druid Guardian roughly to his feet. "Quick! The Crowning! We must hurry up with the Crowning!"

The Druid Guardian shook him off angrily. "The Crowning will not be hurried. My dragon and human Guardians will have dealt with these intruders…"

"Alv-i-i-innn…" warned the witch Excellinor, her mouth stretched in a warning grin. "Patience, my sweetest…*Patience*, my darling…"

Alvin recalled himself with an effort. He mentally added the Druid Guardian to his executions list. And then he swallowed his irritation and groveled cringingly.

"I am sorry, Your Worshipfulness…I forgot myself for a moment…I am so keen, you see, to assume the responsibilities of Kingship…and get you your freedom, of course…"

"Freedom…" whispered the Druid Guardian longingly.

Who was he to quarrel with the will of the gods? And if the will of the gods came in the unpalatable

form of Alvin the Treacherous, why, then, it would at least grant him his freedom and his eyesight, right at the end of his life, to see the world for the very first time…

The Throne of the Wilderwest had been carried by two strong men up to the dais in the center of the room, and for the first time in a century, the Throne was back in its rightful place, looking out over Grimbeard's Kingdom.

The Druid Guardian cleared his throat and threw up his arms, to begin the sacred words of the Crowning Ceremony.

Two minutes earlier, Hiccup had landed up to his waist in a large bog.

He could hear the screams and shouts of the Axemen from the beach, and sheer terror gave him the strength to struggle out of the bog and fling himself into the cover of some nearby bracken.

He would be hunted now—he knew it—and he tried to force himself to calm down and think clearly.

He stuck his head out of the bracken for a second. To the east was the city of Tomorrow. He could see the little figures of the Alvinsmen and the Dragonmarkers standing among the ruins of a great castle on the highest ground. That must be where the little brown Wodensfang had said the Crowning would take place, and he had to get there before they crowned the wrong King.

But in between him and the castle, there was a sea of ferns that seemed to stretch out forever. He would never make it in time…

He dropped back down into the

This was ridiculous...
He had no idea who he was, or what he was doing.

cover of the undergrowth again, as the shouting behind him grew louder.

As he crawled forward through the wet bracken on his hands and knees, he began to shake with hysterical laughter. This was ridiculous…He had no idea who he was, or what he was doing. He ached all over; it looked like he was being chased by thousands of men and dragons, and all he really wanted to do was lie down in the undergrowth and go to sleep.

But something within him made him push on, moving one swollen knee forward after the other, even though he knew what he was doing was impossible, even though he knew he was defeated before he had even begun.

And perhaps that is what heroism truly is. Who knows?

For Hiccup could hear the shouting of hundreds of Guardian Axemen, wading through the bog behind him. It could be only minutes before he was discovered, for they could run far faster than he could crawl.

But as Hiccup pushed forward, by some extraordinary miracle he stumbled across a long tunnel, made by a creature who wanted to travel secretly through the bracken without being spotted by predators wheeling in the skies above.

Fernwinders, his brain told him.

Wingless, medium-sized dragons that carve tunnels through the forests of ferns in the Archipelago so they can charge across the islands at surprising speeds.

There was a trembling and a shuddering and a sound of running feet, and Hiccup rolled out of the way just in time as a dragon about the size of a large dog stormed past him with mad, panicked eyes.

Those huge monsters that had erupted from the sands must have unsettled the Fernwinders, for the bracken was now alive with them, charging through the undergrowth like terrified little rhinoceroses.

Hiccup was ready for the next one that careered through the tunnel he was lying in, and as the creature plunged past in a snorting, puffing, rocketing rush, Hiccup flung himself at the Fernwinder's retreating tail and just managed to grab hold of one of the spiny fins. The Fernwinder squealed in protest, and swung his tail wildly to try and free himself from Hiccup's grasp, but he did not halt his terrified progress, and leaped on through the tunnel, with Hiccup hanging on for dear life.

That was a mad, hectic sleigh ride of a couple of minutes, with Hiccup bumping after the charging Fernwinder, the breath being knocked out of his poor battered body as he was dragged frantically through the undergrowth. But he could hear the cries of the Guardian Axemen growing fainter, and he desperately hung on, trying not to scream with each crunching jolt as the maddened Fernwinder took him deeper and deeper into the bracken.

"Faster! Faster!" squeaked the Hogfly in delight, peering out of the back of Hiccup's backpack as they careered through the ferns.

Twisting around corners, the Fernwinder stampeded on, with Hiccup dragging after him like a broken doll, until the creature's tail gave a final frenzied swipe, and Hiccup could hold on no longer, and spiraled to a bruising halt. Panting hard, Hiccup picked himself up, and *very* cautiously poked his head above the fern canopy. His spirits rose with excitement this time, rather than fear.

The Fernwinder could have taken him anywhere on the island. He could have been farther away than ever from his destination.

But by sheer, blind, dumb luck, he had been dragged *toward* the castle rather than away from it. He was only a couple of hundred yards away now.

This could not be luck. It had to be Fate.

Ignoring the pain, Hiccup forced himself on, on, on, half-limping, half-crawling through the clinging mud and brambles.

On, on, on.

On,, oh... on,,

the stumbling, shambling wrecked figure of..
Hiccup Horrendous Haddock
the Third

9. THE PROPHECY OF GRIMBEARD THE GHASTLY

In Grimbeard's Castle, the ceremony for the Crowning of the next King of the Wilderwest was under way.

Inside the great ruined walls, the surviving remnants of the Tribes of the Archipelago were gathered: burned, hungry, wounded, and exhausted by this terrible war against the dragons.

The necessity for that Crowning could not be more self-evident.

For Grimbeard's City had been built at the exact place where Grimbeard himself would have the best view of his Kingdom. To the north, the towering peaks of the Murderous Mountains. To the west, the ocean stretched out forever. And to the south and east, every single island of the Archipelago was in flames. Even those villages that the dragon rebellion had taken months ago burned afresh, for the dragon Furious had sent his armies out to relight the fires as a signal to the

humans, on this Doomsday of Yule, that the Day of Reckoning had arrived.

It was as if the whole world was on fire.

The great dragon himself was stretched out in Wrecker's Bay, so unimaginably enormous he made the Bay look like a shallow pool. He could see them gathered there in their ruined Castle, puny little human ants.

"See, you pathetic human worms," hissed the dragon Furious. "See, and be afraid."

The dragon Furious spoke in a voice so low and powerful and at such an extraordinary frequency that it caused great waves to roll out across the Inner Ocean. It was so loud that all could hear it: the people of the Archipelago in the Castle, Fishlegs and Camicazi on the back of the Shadow Dragon, even Hiccup, stumbling as fast as he could through the bracken.

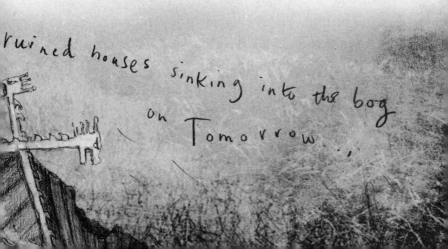

ruined houses sinking into the bog on Tomorrow...

The dragon spoke in Norse, for Sea-Dragons can speak Norse when they so choose.

"This is the Doomsday of Yule, and on this day, destruction awaits you all! CROWN your pathetic new King of the Wilderwest, put him on your silly human Throne, and then bring him out here to face *ME* in single combat...And once I have destroyed him, I shall not rest until I have destroyed every last human being breathing on this earth!"

The dragon lifted up his great head, and lightning poured out of his mouth in an upward storm, and the sky lit up with an extraordinary bright light, as all across the Archipelago the dragons answered his cry.

On the clifftop, the Dragonmarkers and the Alvinsmen held up their arms and hid their faces to shield them from the blinding brightness of the light as the whole world in front of them turned into a sea of flames, burning with the brightness of mini suns.

The numberless dragons of the dragon rebellion joined in that terrible, unearthly screaming, a sound of WAR so dreadful that the mountains echoed with it, and the ground actually shook with the multiple stamping of the dragons' feet as if it were the beginning of an earthquake. It was a sound that sent the hair

on every Viking's head a-quivering, for a people
accustomed to war knew what that sound meant.

Oh dear, thought Hiccup as he scrambled like
a mouse through the bracken. As the echoes of this
terrible noise died away, a dreadful silence came over the
massed Tribes of Vikings standing in the ruined Throne
Room of what had once been the Castle of Grimbeard
the Ghastly, as if for the very first time they'd realized
that the end was near.

This was their last hope, this Crowning of the
King, the last throw of the dice for a people trapped and
surrounded on the island of Tomorrow, and the Dragon
Jewel seemed a small protection against the coming
apocalypse.

Of one accord, the Tribes began to sing the Last
Song of Grimbeard the Ghastly, the song he sang just
before he went into the west on his ship *The Endless
Journey*, never to be seen again.

> *"I sailed so far to be a King but the time
> was never right...
> I lost my way on a stormy past, got wrecked in
> starless night...
> But let my heart be wrecked by hurricanes and my
> ship by stormy weather,*

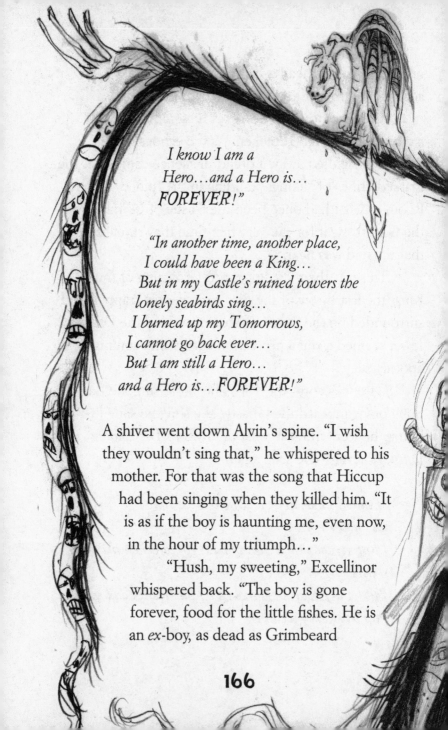

I know I am a
Hero…and a Hero is…
FOREVER!"

"*In another time, another place,*
I could have been a King…
But in my Castle's ruined towers the
lonely seabirds sing…
I burned up my Tomorrows,
I cannot go back ever…
But I am still a Hero…
and a Hero is…FOREVER!"

A shiver went down Alvin's spine. "I wish
they wouldn't sing that," he whispered to his
mother. For that was the song that Hiccup
had been singing when they killed him. "It
is as if the boy is haunting me, even now,
in the hour of my triumph…"

"Hush, my sweeting," Excellinor
whispered back. "The boy is gone
forever, food for the little fishes. He is
an *ex*-boy, as dead as Grimbeard

166

HEAR YE!
Listen to the Prophecy
of GRIMBEARD the GHASTLY

the Ghastly himself…Enjoy your victory."

The Druid Guardian stepped forward.

"Give me the King's Things," rasped the old man.

Alvin held up the King's Lost Things.

All were mouse-quiet now. Even the dragon rebellion was quiet, as if the dragons, too, were trying to listen to what was going on in the ruined Castle. It was as if they all knew that hundreds of years of dragon and human history had been leading up to this moment.

The Druid Guardian examined the

Things. He held up the Dragon Jewel so that its amber caught the light. The Jewel, so small that it could easily fit into a human fist, seemed a tiny protection against the coming apocalypse.

He took Toothless out of the cage in which he was cowering and stroked him gently. "Dragons should not be in cages," murmured the Druid Guardian softly. "Be proud, little dragon, and hold your head high, for you are the first Lost Thing…"

Poor little Toothless cheered up a little at this human kindness. He licked the Druid Guardian's hand gratefully. "And T-t-toothless is the B-b-best One," whispered Toothless, straightening his back with some of his old cheeky arrogance, and hopping onto the Druid Guardian's shoulder.

The Druid Guardian unrolled a great tattered scroll of paper, so ancient it was nearly falling into papery dust in his hands, and proceeded to read from it, although Toothless could not work out how he could do that, for the Druid Guardian was blindfolded. Toothless tried to peer under the Guardian's blindfold, but no, he wasn't cheating.

"Hear ye! Hear ye! Listen to the prophecy of Grimbeard the Ghastly, read by me, the Druid Guardian, on this, the Doomsday of Yule!"

THE PROPHECY OF
THE KING'S LOST THINGS

"The Dragontime is coming
And only a King can save you now.
The King shall be the
Champion of Champions.

You shall know the King
By the King's Lost Things.
A fang-free dragon, my second-best sword,
My Roman shield,
An arrow-from-the-land-that-does-not-exist,
The heart's stone, the key-that-opens-all-locks,
The ticking-thing, the Throne, the Crown.

And last and best of all the ten,
The Dragon Jewel shall save all men."

"My prophecy," whispered the witch Excellinor, eyes shining. "The prophecy passed down from age to age and witch to witch…See, Alvin, my darling? I whispered that prophecy to you when you were a tiny babe…I rocked you to sleep with it…See how right your mother was?"

"One hundred years ago today," croaked the Druid Guardian, "in this very spot on Tomorrow, Grimbeard the Ghastly's son Hiccup Horrendous Haddock the Second and his dragon, the dragon Furious, were leading a peaceful dragon petition to plead with Hiccup the Second's father to end the misery of slavery. Grimbeard was tricked into mistaking the petition for rebellion. He killed his very own son by his very own sword, the Stormblade, and the blood of his son was spilled on the seat of this very Throne."

The listening humans shivered at the sadness of this tale.

"That was the beginning of the curse upon the Throne and the island of Tomorrow. The dragons were beaten, and the dragon Furious captured and bound in inescapable chains in the depths of a forest prison. And Grimbeard the Ghastly, realizing he had been tricked, stood in the ruins of his burning Castle, holding the body of his beloved son, and he swore that the next King of the Wilderwest should be a better man than he was.

"So Grimbeard created an Impossible Task.

"He scattered ten of the King's Lost Things to the four corners of the earth. He hid these Things in the very crooks and crannies of the Archipelago," croaked the Druid Guardian. "Many of them were guarded by the most terrible monsters that Grimbeard could find, or hidden in riddles. Only a true Hero could gather the Lost Things together and lift the curse, and become the next King of the Wilderwest.

"Only a very great Hero indeed would have the strength, the cleverness, the fighting power, and the wisdom to collect all these Things together, and claim the Throne.

"Only a Hero this great is worthy of being the next King of the Wilderwest.

"And looking at the perils that surround us," said the Druid Guardian, wryly gesturing to the forces of the dragon rebellion surrounding them all. "You can see that we need a very great Hero indeed.

"So who is this Hero?" called out the Druid Guardian in ringing tones. "Who is he who has found these Things, who is a greater man than Grimbeard the Ghastly, and who is the true King of the Wilderwest?

"If he is here, he should now step forward and announce himself!"

I am the

Hero who has found the Things!!

Swollen with pride, Alvin the Treacherous stuck out his chest, and stepped forward, nearly falling over, for his horrible mother pushed him forward more violently than was strictly necessary.

Alvin had lived his whole life for this moment. He had tricked and stolen and murdered and betrayed.

And he had paid a terrible price for this moment, losing along the way his eye, his arm, his leg, his hair, his nose, and...*oh dear*—his *soul*.

All for the sake of this one precious moment.

And it was worth it.

"*I* am the Hero who found these Things, and collected them together!" shouted Alvin the Treacherous.

The Alvinsmen cheered, a ragged, proud cheer.

Valhallarama and Stoick the Vast shook their heads at these lies, but they said nothing. What could they do; what could they say? Valhallarama had spent her whole life searching for the Lost Things, but they never came to her, search though she may, and great Hero though she was. She had failed.

Both parents had not been able to protect their son at the last.

They had both failed.

So they were mute, holding hands, heads bowed.

"*I* am a greater man than Grimbeard the Ghastly! *I* am the true King of the Wilderwest, and I am here to claim my Throne, my Crown, and my birthright!" cried Alvin, leaping eagerly onto the dais.

The Druid Guardian lifted up the Crown, ready to place it on Alvin the Treacherous's gloating head.

But just before the Druid Guardian could crown Alvin, they were interrupted.

"Wait…" came a very faint voice from the back of the ruined hall.

Valhallarama's head lifted.

"Wait…" said the voice, fainter still.

The entire hall of Dragonmarkers, Alvinsmen, Guardians, Alvin, and the witch all turned their heads to see where that voice was coming from.

There, in the aisle of Grimbeard the Ghastly's ruined Castle on the island of Tomorrow, stood the ragged remains, the stumbling, shambling, wrecked figure of…

Hiccup Horrendous Haddock the Third.

"Wait…" came a very faint voice from the back of the Hall.

10. WHO IS THE KING?

Five minutes earlier, Camicazi and Fishlegs were sitting on the back of the Deadly Shadow dragon, searching for Hiccup, when suddenly they spotted him running out of the bracken. Although the human Guardians saw Hiccup too, they were inexplicably attacked by a Deadly Shadow dragon firing lightning bolts at them, so the human Guardians flattened themselves in the undergrowth, and Hiccup was able to make it into Grimbeard's Castle without being caught.

Camicazi and Fishlegs, Windwalker, Stormfly, and the Deadly Shadow landed on the edges of the ruined Castle just as Hiccup staggered down the remains of the central aisle leading to the Throne.

He was almost unrecognizable.

Two colors, half-purple, half-white; clothes ripped to ribbons by talons and seas and winds; one whole side of his body swollen so much that he could barely stand, let alone stumble lopsidedly forward.

A wrecked scarecrow of a boy.

Alvin let out a gasp of horror. For one dreadful moment, he really thought this boy was a ghost, the spirit of the Hiccup he had killed, come back to haunt him from Valhalla.

Vikings lead frightening lives, so they are not afraid of much, but they ARE afraid of ghosts. And the ghost of a boy you had murdered in cold blood was likely to be a ghost who was not happy, a ghost who was coming back for vengeance…

So no wonder Alvin turned white and clutched his cowardly neck as if to protect it.

"AAAARRRGGHHH!" screamed Alvin the Treacherous. "THOR AND WODEN AND ALL THE GODS SAVE ME FROM THIS PESTILENT GHOST OF A BOY! I REPENT! I REPENT! ONLY SPARE ME, SWEET GHOST! IT IS ALL MY MOTHER'S FAULT!"

"Steady, Alvin, steady," hissed the witch Excellinor, eyes narrowed, sniffing the air as if she could smell out whether the boy was real or not.

She placed her bony hand over her son's face to stifle his terrified screams, so violently that she nearly suffocated him. "Steady, darling…Don't betray us, now, when we are so near…"

"Who is this?" demanded the Druid Guardian. "Who dares to interrupt the solemn ceremony of the Crowning of the next King of the Wilderwest?"

Hiccup limped forward, trembling.

"It is I," said Hiccup, dragging his numb leg behind

Face in the mud, Hiccup contemplated just staying there,

him. "It is I, H…H…H…"

For one dreadful moment, his mind was a total blank. He couldn't even remember the name the little brown dragon had called him. Something beginning with "H"?

All the faces of the huge, hairy barbarians turned toward him with expressions of gobsmacked incomprehension.

No one recognized him.

This is ridiculous, thought Hiccup. *What am I doing? Look at me, I'm a wreck! How can I claim that I am the true King of the Wilderwest when I don't even know who I am? I'm a fool…The little brown dragon called the Wodensfang was just tricking me…*

"Wodensfang, are you awake?" hissed Hiccup, but the Wodensfang snored on, and Hiccup would have to do this alone.

"What am I called, Hogfly?" Hiccup whispered desperately. "Something beginning with 'H'?"

"Handshake? Hollybush? Human being?" the Hogfly whispered back, peeking out of the backpack, rather overawed by the number of people and dragons gathered here in this ruined Castle, standing

in dumbstruck silence, as Hiccup stumbled
down the central aisle, wavering drunkenly from one
side to the other.

"It's…me…" stuttered Hiccup. "H…H…H?"

And then he fell over.

Face in the mud, he contemplated just staying
there.

What was the point in carrying on?

But then, with tears pouring down his cheeks,
Stoick rushed down the aisle, and picked up the ragged
remains of his son, hugging him as though he would
crush him entirely.

"It's Hiccup! My son Hiccup! Hiccup Horrendous
Haddock the Third! He's alive!"

"Hiccup!"

"It's Hiccup!"

"Hiccup Horrendous Haddock the Third!" cried
the Dragonmarkers, and joyfully, Valhallarama swooped
down and clutched him to her iron chest, crying
"HICCUP!" with such astonishing pride and joy in her

voice that Hiccup, blinking, bemused, was scarcely able to believe it.

All these people he did not recognize…All these kind, unfamiliar faces cheering him, delighted to see him, *proud* of him. How could this be possible?

Drooping and shivering on the Druid Guardian's shoulder, Toothless blinked at Hiccup as if he were a vision from a dream. And then he gave a squeal of excitement, and…"H-h-hiccup! M-m-master!" he squeaked, and he cartwheeled through the air, throwing himself at Hiccup with such eagerness that he nearly knocked him over again, and licking his face lovingly all over so that Hiccup could barely breathe.

"You're A-A-ALIVE!"

And Toothless jumped up and down on Hiccup's already thumping and aching head, shouting:

"He's alive! He's a-a-alive! He's alive! HE'S ALIVE! HE'S ALIVE! HE'S ALIVE!"

The Vikings cheered until their throats were hoarse at this extraordinary, delightful, *incredible* twist of fate. The Hiccup boy was alive! Even the Alvinsmen stretched out to feel the boy's fingers, his arms, his chest, to check if he was warm and breathing.

How could this be? They had all seen with their very own eyes the boy fall from the back of

MY HOGFLY!

the Windwalker into the sea with an arrow in his chest.

Very Vicious the Visithug had his own little surprise. Like many tough men, he had a soft spot, and in his case the soft spot was a dear little Hogfly who had gone missing a couple of days earlier. When all the world around him was falling to pieces, the thing that Very Vicious was really mourning was the loss of his dear little Hogfly, and he had been wearing a black armband in remembrance of the creature, who he presumed had been killed in one of the recent battles.

"MY HOGFLY!" boomed Very Vicious joyfully, opening wide his tattooed arms. "HE'S ALIVE!"

The Hogfly had the memory of a goldfish, so he had forgotten that Very Vicious ever existed. But now he remembered, and he popped out of the rucksack and flapped toward Very Vicious, and the terrifying

Warrior Chieftain grunted with excitement at the return of his pet, tickling him behind the ears and making soft cooing un-Warriorlike noises such as: "Did da liddle Hogfly miss his big Hairy Master, den?"

There were others less pleased with this unexpected turn of events.

"He's alive!" cursed the Witch.

"But how can that be?" swore Alvin the Treacherous, regaining his composure now that he realized that this was not a ghost after all, but the wretched Hiccup boy who had eluded death yet AGAIN, curse him. "It's impossible!"

"There's no such thing as im-POSSIBLE, Alvin," sighed the witch. "Only im-PROBABLE…"

"But we murdered him!" stormed Alvin.

"Now, now, Alvin," cautioned the witch, with an eye on the Druid Guardian. "*Murder* is such an ugly word…It was collateral damage, an unfortunate side effect of the total war scenario…"

"He was DEAD!" yelled Alvin, with a strong sense of injury.

"Alive or dead, no matter," said the witch. "The boy is nothing. A runt…an accident…a detour! One of Grimbeard the Ghastly's red herrings! The boy changes nothing!"

"HICCUP! HICCUP! HICCUP!" chanted the Dragonmarkers, and the jubilant Valhallarama and Stoick deposited Hiccup in front of the Druid Guardian.

"We would like to present our son, HICCUP!" roared Stoick the Vast. "Our son, HICCUP, who is the true King of the Wilderwest!"

The Druid Guardian put out his skinny hand and felt the son Hiccup, his scrawny little chicken-bone arm and the other swollen one, the raggedy remains of his Fire-Suit...

"His name is Hiccup, is it? Ah, that is a name to conjure within this Castle."

"The name of the boy is not important!" howled the witch.

"So, Hiccup," said the Druid Guardian, ignoring the witch. "You come here claiming to be King, and yet you carry none of the King's Things. You know the penalty for those who come with false claims to the Kingship..."

"DEATH!" interrupted Alvin eagerly. "The penalty is DEATH!"

"What have you to say for yourself?" asked the Druid Guardian.

"Don't ask him!" hissed the Witch uneasily. "You

183

mustn't let the little rat *talk*! He's a clever little rat, and you must never let him *talk*!"

Hiccup swallowed. What could he say? He had known that this would be a sticking point from the moment the little brown dragon told him the problem back there on the beach of Hero's End.

How could anybody who didn't have any of the King's Things claim the Crown?

Besides, he had no idea who he was, let alone how to make an argument that he should be the rightful King of this Wilderwest country.

But...

*There is no such thing as im-*POSSIBLE*, Alvin.*
*Only im-*PROBABLE*.*

The witch's words tweaked a memory in Hiccup's brain, like tugging on a little piece of string in a knot that will not unravel.

The wrinkly old man standing just two feet away from Hiccup—hadn't he said those words to Hiccup some time before? Long, long ago? Who *was* that dear old man smiling at him so sweetly, willing him to do well? Hiccup was sure that he recognized him, sure that he remembered other things that old man had said to him...

The only thing that limits us are the limits to our imaginations...

The little green dragon jumped up and down on Hiccup's shoulder. "T-t-tell them, Hiccup! Tell them why you should be King! Tell them who you are!" The little dragon gently turned Hiccup's face toward him so that Hiccup could look straight into his eyes.

"But I can't tell them who I am," whispered Hiccup. "I don't even know who you are..."

I'm Toothless...

Toothless's little face fell incredulously. "What do you mean, you don't know who I am?

"I'm *T-t-toothless.*"

As soon as Toothless said the words, Hiccup remembered.

It was as if the words pulled the final string on the knot, and the door to his memories swung open.

He remembered another time, another place,

another Quest when Toothless was his hunting dragon for the very first time, and had stared into his eyes with that hypnotic gaze of his.

Toothless.

His very own hunting dragon.

He looked into those hurt greengage eyes and whispered back, *"Toothless..."*

Toothless!

Cheeky, irrepressible Toothless, the naughtiest, sweetest, most maddening dragon in the whole of the wide Archipelago...He hugged the delighted little wriggly dragon with a smile of happy recognition.

He looked around the crowd, and he remembered them all...

Stoick, his father.

Valhallarama, his mother.

Old Wrinkly, Baggybum the Beerbelly, Humungously Hotshot the Hero, the Ten Fiancés, Alvin the Treacherous, the witch Excellinor, and right at the back of the ruined hall, the Deadly Shadow dragon with Camicazi and Fishlegs making thumbs-up signs to his back...All companions or enemies, on so many of his past Quests, all gazing at him with furious or loving eyes, hoping or dreading that he could somehow alter the inevitable, change the course of history, catch the axe of doom before it fell, as he had once before on the isle of Hysteria.*

He remembered his name, too. HICCUP.

His name was Hiccup. That was the job of a Hiccup, wasn't it?

To change the course of history.

And then with a sharp jolt, when Baggybum's eyes were upon him, Hiccup remembered that Baggybum's son Snotlout had died only two days ago, and Baggybum did not know it. Hiccup gave a groan as he was swamped and engulfed by the pain of that memory returning...

Snotlout: laughing, arrogant, fearless, fact-of-life Snotlout had, with unimaginable bravery, laid down his life in order that he, Hiccup, should live and become the King.

The very least that Hiccup could do was to make absolutely sure that Snotlout's sacrifice was worth it.

He HAD to do this.

Hiccup swallowed.

He did not have the King's Things...

But...

Somehow the crowding burst of memories reminded him of the ten great Quests that had brought him the ten Lost Things, although at the time he hadn't even realized he was collecting them, or that he was on a Quest at all.

---

*This happens in Book 4: *How to Cheat a Dragon's Curse*.

"You are right," said Hiccup at last. His voice trembled, because surely this would not be enough. "I do come here with empty hands. I have none of the King's Things. All I can tell you now is what I learned in the finding of them."

"He's *talking*!" squealed the witch, in a panic. "Don't let him TALK! You can't let the clever little rat talk his way out of this one…"

"Here are just some of the things I learned from the Quests to find the things," said Hiccup, ignoring her.

"One, the search for the fang-free dragon taught me that fear and intimidation might not be the best way to train dragons.

"Two, the sword: that sometimes second-best is best.

"Three, the shield: that sometimes freedom must be fought for.

"Four, the ticking-thing: that when you fight for your friend, you are also fighting for yourself.

"Five, the ruby heart's stone: that love never dies.

"Six, the arrow-from-the-land-that-does-not-exist: that you must make things right in the Old World before you go looking for the New, and sometimes the things that you are looking for are right here at home.

"Seven, the key-that-opens-all-locks: that accidents happen for a reason.

"Eight, the Throne: that power can corrupt.

"Nine, the Crown: that you have to keep on trying even though you are beaten before you even start.

"And ten, the Dragon Jewel," finished Hiccup. "You need to know what it is to be a slave before you can be a King."

There was a long, long silence.

How strange it was that all these Quests, which had seemed so unconnected at the time—wild goose chases even, some of them—twisting and turning this way and that like Hiccup's lost boat, *The Hopeful Puffin*, wobbling across the ocean in eccentric fashion.

How strange it was that when they were all added up together, you could suddenly see them for what they were.

The education of a King.

"That's quite clever, that is," said a lone Quiet Life.

"It's not clever at all! The important point here is that Hiccup cannot be the King because he has NO THINGS!" hissed the witch. "We've been through all this before...

"Hiccup may have acquired the things in the first place, but FATE has decreed that ALVIN should be the King for excellent reasons. Look out there at our beautiful world, burned to a crisp!"

The witch pointed a knobbly finger at the burning Archipelago. "The dragons are determined to wipe us out, and only Alvin has the courage to use the secret of the Jewel to defeat them. This boy is weak...He would try to bargain with the dragon Furious..."

"The dragon Furious is not a monster!" shouted Hiccup. "Maybe I could win him around! And even if all ends in failure, is it not worth even *trying* to save the dragons that we love?"

The Druid Guardian turned to the waiting, watching crowds. "What say you, peoples of the Archipelago?"

Barbara the Barbarian answered for so many of the humans gathered there.

"Once we would have followed you, Hiccup," she said. "In Prison Darkheart, many of us made that pledge, and later I took the Dragonmark along with many others. I hoped by your deeds, your Quests that I had heard of, that you would be the Boy of Destiny who would take us all into a new and glorious era...

"But nearly another year of war has passed since then. We have lost everything. The dragons have killed our loved ones, destroyed our homes, uprooted whole mountains," said Barbara. "They will not stop until we are all dead. And even though I am a Viking...

"I confess, I am afraid."

Barbara spoke for all of them. They were Vikings, but they were afraid. Not just of losing their own lives, but of losing their whole world.

"In order to do what you want to do, Hiccup," Barbara finished with a kind of weary desperation, "Destiny would have to be on your side in a very big way. Perhaps Alvin's way is the only way now. And perhaps that is why Destiny has given Alvin the King's Things."

Do not be too hard on the peoples of the Archipelago, dear reader. You cannot know how *you* would react in the same situation, if put to the same terrible test. They were homeless and hungry, and the testing fires of war had burned them so ragged that they were not themselves anymore. They had lost all hope and arrived at a place of despair. And once you are in that place of despair, it is harder to get out of than you might think.

The tired peoples of the Archipelago did not want the extinction of dragons. They loved their dragons. Until you have ridden on the back of a dragon, and felt the wind through your hair, and seen the world laid out beneath you in miniature, you haven't really lived. But...

Even though they were Vikings they were beginning to be afraid.

"ALVIN FOR KING!" roared a Danger-Brute.

Barbara the Barbarian and her black cat, Fearless.

"ALVIN FOR KING!" replied an angry Bashem-Oik, and even the gentler Tribes—the Quiet Lifes, the Meatheads, the Peaceables—they did not cry out for Alvin, but they did not speak against him, either, because they were hungry and tired and desperate.

The look that the Druid Guardian gave Hiccup was affectionate, if a terrifying blindfolded man could ever be said to look affectionate.

"You have learned well the lessons of the finding of the things, boy." There was a yearning in the Druid Guardian's voice as if he would choose Hiccup, if he were free to choose. "In times of peace, you might have made a wonderful King. But in times of war, Kings have to make difficult choices, have to do disagreeable things in order to protect their people…"

I have said this many times before, because important truths must be said more than once: Maybe we are lucky that we are not Kings and Heroes, because we do not have to make the choices that Kings and Heroes have to make.

"I have to crown the King that Destiny and Grimbeard the Ghastly have chosen," said the Druid Guardian. "I have to have CONCRETE EVIDENCE that Grimbeard intended you to be the King. And you see, when all is said and done, you have no Things."

"You don't understand," said Hiccup urgently. "I HAVE to be the King. I HAVE to do it. You see, Snotlout—"

"Step aside, boy," said the Druid Guardian.

"Is that all you're going to do?" raged Alvin. "Why don't you send down your dragon Guardians to *kill* him?"

The Druid Guardian pushed Hiccup aside, and held wide his bat-wing arms.

"COME, GREAT POWERS OF DESTINY AND DARKNESS!" he cried.

11. GRIMBEARD'S LETTER

"Excuse me!"

There was a scuffling at the back of the hall. The Guardians were trying to prevent a skinny boy who looked like a daddy longlegs from rushing up the aisle.

"Excuse me, Your Magnificence!" shouted Fishlegs, struggling in the Guardians' grip.

"Who is this who dares to interrupt our solemn Ceremony for the second time?" demanded the Druid

Excuse me, Your Magnificence

Excuse me, Your Magnificence!

Guardian, a little crossly. "I'm trying to crown a King here, for the first time in a hundred years!"

"This is nobody! Nobody at all!" screeched the witch. "He is just a runt like the Hiccup! We shouldn't listen to him…"

"My name is Fishlegs No-Name, and I have CONCRETE EVIDENCE that Hiccup is the King, in the form of a letter written by Grimbeard the Ghastly *himself*, written in his very own hand!" shouted Fishlegs.

Suddenly it seemed as if Destiny might be listening and taking a hand in the affairs of the humans after all. A letter written by Grimbeard the Ghastly, written in his very own hand!

"You *do*?" gasped Hiccup.

"Let the boy approach the Throne!" ordered the Druid Guardian.

Trembling, Fishlegs came forward. He took out the ragged remains of a letter from the tattered lobster pot that he had converted into his Running-Away Suitcase.* A letter that had been torn by dragons' talons, burned by volcano lava, drenched in Slitherfang saliva, and been through all of Fishlegs's and Hiccup's adventures with them, but somehow,

---

*A letter that is printed in full at the very end of Book 2: *How to Be a Pirate*, so exactly TEN BOOKS AGO, if you are an observant reader of these stories.

I dream of an Heir who shall be
a dragon whisperer, a swordfighter,
a man who talks with monsters and
who will harness the power of Thor's
thunder itself...

like Fishlegs and Hiccup themselves, it had survived, a little raggedy and burned at the edges, but more or less intact.

"Hiccup was going to leave this letter where we found it in the underground cavern with Grimbeard's treasure," Fishlegs said, "but I secretly took it with me in case we ever needed to prove that Hiccup was the true Heir to the Hooligan Tribe."

Fishlegs adjusted his glasses so that he could see out of the non-smashed parts. "This is the relevant part here," he said, reading from the letter. "Grimbeard the Ghastly says:

"A 'dragon whisperer' can only really refer to Hiccup, because Hiccup is the only one here who can speak Dragonese."

It was impressive evidence; there was no doubt about it.

"This boy Hiccup speaks Dragonese?" exclaimed the Druid Guardian in surprise.

The listening crowds were moved, in spite of their fear, in spite of their hunger, in spite of their desperation. They swayed and whispered like a restless sea. Grimbeard the Ghastly had been dreaming of an Heir who was a dragon whisperer, a swordfighter?

Was Hiccup really the Heir that Grimbeard had been dreaming of? That would change everything! Maybe there was a chance for a boy-who-would-be-king, if Destiny was on his side?

"Oooh, that is quite something…" gasped the crowd. "It's a good point…Hiccup does speak Dragonese…That's a very unusual skill…"

"Don't be impressed!" hissed the witch. "Alvin can speak Dragonese just as well as the Hiccup-boy. And Hiccup hasn't *harnessed the power of Thor's thunder*; apart from anything else, that wouldn't be possible…"

"Yes he has!" argued Fishlegs hotly. "One time when Norbert the Nutjob chased Hiccup up the mast of the ship we were sailing, Hiccup got one of Thor's lightning bolts to strike Norbert's axe of Doom at absolutely the right moment!"*

Harnessing Thor's thunder! That was quite something, wasn't it?

"Well if *that* is all harnessing Thor's thunder is, anyone could do it!" raged the witch. "All you have to do is go out in a storm carrying something pointy!"

But nobody was listening.

"I remember, that lightning bolt was when Hiccup

---

*You can read about this in Book 7: *How to Ride a Dragon's Storm*.

went to the land-that-does-not-exist and rescued us from slavery!" called out a little Wanderer named Bearcub from the back of the crowd. "I was there! That was when Hiccup saved my life!"

"And mine, he saved mine too!" shouted his elder sister Eggingarde, and a chorus of other Wanderer voices. "And mine! And mine! And mine!"

"Oh no!" hissed the witch, looking around anxiously at the crowd. *Oh no...Not again...* "Oh no..."

But it was too late.

There was a murmur of appreciation from the listening crowds of Vikings, and they began to whisper to one another...

"That's *clever*, that thing about the lightning bolt. Very clever..."

"Wasn't that when Hiccup won the Inter-Tribal Swimming Race? He was the only person to keep swimming for *three whole months*, and the *last* person to do that, of course, was Grimbeard the Ghastly himself..."

"Do you think it could be a *sign*?"

"OF COURSE it's a sign..."

"It's not a sign!" squealed the witch. "It's not a sign of anything apart from the fact that both Grimbeard and Hiccup must have CHEATED!"

201

"And I have MORE concrete evidence," said Fishlegs.

"Can't somebody shut this boy up?" snapped the witch.

"The map to find the Jewel is drawn on the back of Grimbeard the Ghastly's Last Will and Testament. Hiccup saved that Will and Testament from the burning of Prison Darkheart," said Fishlegs. "And I took the precaution of looking after it for Hiccup. I think there's a clue there too…"

"Grimbeard the Ghastly's Last Will and Testament!" gasped the Druid Guardian. "Why didn't you mention this before? Read it to me, boy!"

Fishlegs held up the paper so that all could see it.

Oh no…
oh
not
again…
oh no…

"'I leave to my True Heir, this my favorite Sword. Because the Stormblade always lunged a little to the left. And the Best is not always the most Obvious...'" read Fishlegs. "And over the top of that, Grimbeard has written: 'Courage: What is within is more important than what is without (this is not The End, I promise). Here is the map. And the map can lead you to the Dragon Jewel.'"*

"Ooh, that's interesting," said everybody, for they all loved a riddle. "The Best is not always the most Obvious...That CLEARLY refers to Hiccup because *he* is obviously not the Best..."

---

*The Will first appears in Book 2, but the second message is written in invisible ink, and only appears with the application of Vorpent Venom in Book 9: *How to Steal a Dragon's Sword*.

"And look! Alvin has the Stormblade! Which isn't Grimbeard's favorite...which means that Alvin is not the King..."

"Look!" said Barbara the Barbarian. "My black cat has chosen Hiccup! Do you think this could be a sign too?"

And indeed, Barbara's black cat had jumped off Barbara's head, and was curling around Hiccup's legs, purring.

"The King will not be chosen by a CAT!" raged the witch. "Of course it isn't a sign!"

But she was raging against an unstoppable tide.

This is how legends begin...

Hiccup's recalling of how he had found the King's Things had reminded the Vikings of the past, and they began to swap tales of when Hiccup had saved their lives.

"Hiccup saved *my* life three times, when I was captured by the Romans, the Berserks, and the witch..." boasted Camicazi.

"He saved *mine* when we were on that cliff face at Flashburn's School of Swordfighting!" called out a young Hooligan.

And others called out: "Me too! Me too! Me too!"

"And ours when we were about to be fed to the Beast of Berserk," said the Ten Fiancés.

"Hiccup saved us when the Green Death was terrorizing the Isle of Berk," cried a Meathead.

"And Hiccup saved US when we were trapped on the isle of Hysteria by the Doomfang…" shouted a Hysteric.

"And he saved ALL OF US when that plague of Exterminators descended on the Archipelago during the long, hot summer when the volcano exploded…" yelled a Hooligan.

There is a moment in the affairs of humans that is rather like the turning of the tides, or the changing of the wind. One minute everything seems to be going full-flood and full-blast in one direction. And then something happens, a single voice like Fishlegs speaks in what sounds like the voice of Destiny, the world hangs in the balance, there is a moment of pause…and then more voices speak, and more and more and more, and suddenly the wind has changed, the tide has turned, and everything is moving with tumbling, gathering, unstoppable force, absolutely the other way.

These poor people had been brought through despair and hunger, to the brink of following the unspeakable Alvin. But Grimbeard's letter, the Last Will and Testament, Hiccup's survival—suddenly these had given them hope once more.

And it has to be said, the Vikings are the kind of people who feel things very strongly, very passionately one second…but, like the changeable Archipelago winds, are perfectly capable of changing their minds and thinking the exact opposite the next.

"Quick, Alvin! Think of something good you've done recently!" hissed the witch. "Something that might make you popular!"

"Well…um… last week I stopped whipping the slaves for a bit," suggested Alvin. "My whip-hand was giving me blisters…"

"Haven't you ever saved anyone's life?" raged the witch.

"I've been too busy saving my *own* life, Mother," Alvin pointed out. "And in some pretty spectacular ways, even if I do say so myself…"

All around the ruined Castle of Grimbeard the Ghastly, the Vikings told one another of Hiccup's good deeds, and somewhere along the way, the tales were elaborated on by the storytellers, and Hiccup was given superhuman and superhero qualities, as is the way of storytelling and storytellers since the beginning of time.

Very Vicious the Visithug had been one of Alvin's most faithful followers, but even *he* jumped up on a ruined pillar and bellowed at the crowd, holding up his panting Hogfly in his cupped hands, like it was a precious relic:

"HICCUP WENT TO VALHALLA TO BRING ME BACK MY HOGFLY!"

Which wasn't strictly true, but it struck a chord with the public mood. A Boy of Destiny who could go to Valhalla and bring back a Hogfly? Why, that might be a boy who could pull off a miracle and finish this war without ending the dragons!

"If Hiccup really is a Boy of Destiny," they said to one another, "if he really is the Heir that Grimbeard dreamed of, maybe Hiccup *can* save the dragons for us…Maybe he *can* bargain with the dragon Furious…If he can magically come back from the dead, like he just did, perhaps he can do anything?"

"Hiccup was dead…" said a loyal Alvinsman, shaking his head in disbelief. "I saw the arrow go right into his chest myself."

It wasn't the truth, but the storytellers only heard what they wanted to hear, and the story was more important than the truth, so they went right on telling what they wanted to believe.

"Hiccup has been to Valhalla, and come back to walk among us, and anyone who can do that, well…I will follow him to the ends of the earth. HICCUP FOR KING!"

"HICCUP FOR KING! HICCUP FOR KING! HICCUP FOR KING!"

"NO!" shrieked the witch, beside herself with fury as she howled and bit and raged at the stampeding, applauding, clamoring crowd. "This isn't REALISTIC! YOU do not decide, you rabble! Where do you think you are, the REPUBLIC OF ROME? This is a dictatorship! This is Destiny! The scary old man with the blindfold gets to decide who the King is, not YOU! Not ANY OF YOU!"

"HICCUP FOR KING! HICCUP FOR KING! HICCUP FOR KING!"

"Silence! For if you offend the scary old man with the blindfold, he shall call up his dreadful dragon Guardians of Tomorrow and they shall take you all into oblivion and grind your bones to *dust*!" swore the infuriated witch.

"HICCUP FOR KING! HICCUP FOR KING! HICCUP FOR KING!"

"Well, Druid Guardian," cried Valhallarama of the White Arms. "What is the will of the people? I told the people of the Archipelago when they gathered once before, in Prison Darkheart, that they do have a choice of Kings, and I ask them the question once again. Should it be Alvin the Treacherous, who offers slavery and the destruction of dragons forever? Or should it be my son, Hiccup, who offers the hope of a new and better world?"

"This isn't ABOUT the will of the people now!" screeched the witch. "You can't sway *this* court of opinion, Valhallarama, by putting on some silly little Slavemark and claiming it is the Dragonmark!"

"Does Hiccup have the Dragonmark?" asked the Druid Guardian eagerly. "Did you know that *Grimbeard* took the Dragonmark at the end of his life as a sign of his repentance?"

"Oh stop it with these silly little signs!" snapped the witch, absolutely purple with irritation. "You should know better than to look for black cats and superstitions! This is Fate! This is the future of the humans! It's about the will of the GODS!"

"HICCUP FOR KING! HICCUP FOR KING! HICCUP FOR KING!"

The Druid Guardian held up his arms. "The witch is right," he said. "This IS about the will of the gods... SILENCE!"

The peoples of the Archipelago stood silent in the Castle.

The Druid Guardian held up the Crown, offering it up to the gods above as if it were a sacrifice.

209

Alvin stood on the Druid Guardian's right and Hiccup on his left.

"COME, GREAT POWERS OF DESTINY AND DARKNESS!" called the Druid Guardian up to the stormy heavens. "COMETH THE MAN, COMETH THE HOUR. BUT HERE I HAVE TWO HEROES, AND I CANNOT CROWN TWO KINGS. TELL ME, SWEET GHOST OF GRIMBEARD THE GHASTLY: WHO IS THE TRUE KING OF THE WILDERWEST? WHAT IS THE WILL OF THE GODS? GIVE ME SOME SIGN OF YOUR INTENTIONS!"

There was a long, long pause, while the storm clouds above raged and crackled. The humans in the ruined Castle held their breath, and out in the circle of Wrecker's Bay, it seemed as if the dragons did too, a great quiet descending on the world as all leaned in to listen to the Druid Guardian's verdict. The Druid Guardian swayed as he stood there in that silence, swayed and trembled as if he were receiving some message from the gods and the ghost of Grimbeard the Ghastly through the crackle and flash of the storm. The dragon Guardians were speaking to him. All the dragons around Hiccup had buried their heads in their chests, and had their paws over their ears, suggesting an extraordinarily high frequency that only the dragons and the Druid Guardian could hear.

The Druid Guardian muttered to himself, in reply to the dragon Guardians: "Really? Well, bless my soul... How interesting... Your eyes are better than mine... I bow to your superior judgement..."

It seemed an age before the Druid spoke.

But before he did, something happened, and who knows whether this was the final thing that tipped the balance? It certainly LOOKED spectacular.

The crowd had their concrete evidence. Now they just needed a sign from the gods that they were making the right choice.

And they got one.

There was the Druid Guardian, standing with one hand on Alvin and one hand on Hiccup, like an ancient pair of scales. And then Hiccup slowly, slowly rose up, and levitated in the air, magically, with no visible means of support, as if he were being picked up by the hand of a giant invisible god...

A miracle!

Hiccup flying upward without wings!

The gods had spoken!

That wasn't what was *really* happening, of course.

Thousands and thousands of tiny little

nanodragons had flown out of their secret hiding places in the bracken and the grasses and the heather all around the Castle, and descended upon the tattered Fire-Suit of Hiccup Horrendous Haddock the Third.

They clung to that Fire-Suit with their thousands and thousands of tiny little legs, and then they rose up into the air, carrying Hiccup with them.

"Ziggerastica..." whispered Hiccup to himself, in astonishment, as he looked at his Fire-Suit suddenly alive with minuscule, humming little nanodragons. Ziggerastica was the King of the nanodragons, and as it happens, Hiccup had saved Ziggerastica's life once. But Hiccup had not seen the little King for a number of years, so it was a little spooky that his numberless minions were appearing out of nowhere at this critical moment, apparently to assist him.

"You pay no attention to us, but we pay attention to you," buzzed the nanodragon swarm all together in tiny little malevolent voices,

as if they were
answering Hiccup's unspoken
question, and somehow even
when they were helping him,
they managed to do it with
an air of menace.

To the
watching crowds,
who could not
see the humming
nanodragons
carrying Hiccup

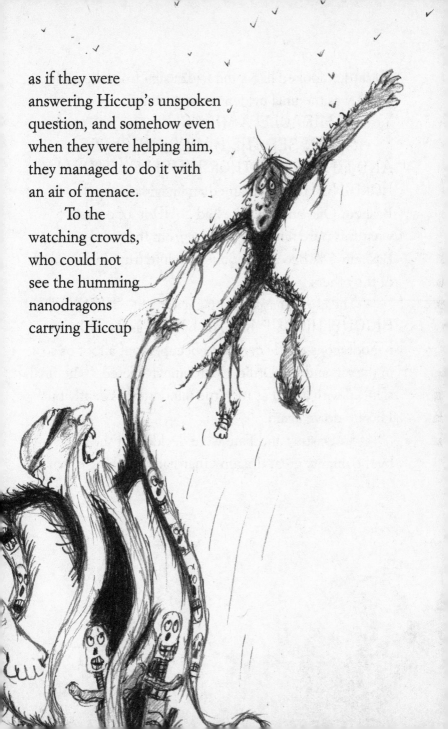

upward, it looked like a miracle, a sign from the gods, and it was the final evidence they needed.

"A MIRACLE! A MIRACLE!"

"I CAN SEE THE HAIRY KNUCKLES AND FINGERS OF THOR HIMSELF ACTUALLY HOLDING HIM!" screamed an imaginative Bashem-Oik, and once he had SAID it, of course, what was pure fantasy springing from the mind of the Bashem-Oik become at once absolute truth in the minds of the others.

The crowd gasped with excitement. "HICCUP! HICCUP! HICCUP IS THE KING!" as the little nanodragons gently dangled Hiccup about a foot or so in the air, and the Druid Guardian whispered, "The final sign…" with a sigh as the little nanodragons gently put Hiccup down again.

So Destiny and Fate were decided, at the last, by the mighty great dragon Guardians speaking down

It was Ziggerastica, Great High Despot of the Northern Grasses, Terror of the Bracken, Scourge of the Heather and Kingmaker Extraordinaire!

ominously from the sky, and the tiny little nanodragons speaking up sneakily from the grasses.

Which seems appropriate somehow.

At last, the Druid Guardian spoke the fateful words in a strange ethereal voice, as if receiving instructions from another world.

"HE WHO WEARS THIS CROWN SHALL BE THE KING FOREVER...

"HE WHO WEARS THIS CROWN SHALL LAY DOWN HIS LIFE FOR HIS PEOPLE...

"HE WHO WEARS THIS CROWN SHALL RULE ABSOLUTELY...

"THE NEW KING OF THE WILDERWEST SHALL BE..."

The Druid Guardian trembled, and then he turned to face Hiccup.

"Hiccup Horrendous Haddock the Third.

"Because what is within is more important than what is without…The Best is not always the most Obvious…

"…and sometimes the Will of Grimbeard the Ghastly, and the will of the gods, and the will of the people are the very same thing.

"We have found ourselves a King," said the Guardian quietly.

Alvin staggered as if somebody had shot him.

The witch screamed, "NOOOOOOOO!"

12. THE CROWNING OF THE KING OF THE WILDERWEST

Rustling by Hiccup's earhole was the unmistakable red-and-black spotted form of Ziggerastica, King of the nanodragons, looking rather older than when Hiccup saw him last, but every bit as self-important.

"The dragon Furious seemed to think that his great size meant that he could tell ME what to do, O Boy-with-No-Muscles-at-All!" snorted Ziggerastica. "I, Ziggerastica, Great High Despot of the Northern Grasses, Terror of the Bracken, Scourge of the Heather, and Kingmaker Extraordinaire! How DARE he presume to tell ME to revolt!"

"That was unwise," Hiccup whispered back.

It was indeed.

It is always a mistake to underestimate the little people of the world, for it is often they who tip the balance.

"I REVOLT against his revolution!" declared Ziggerastica

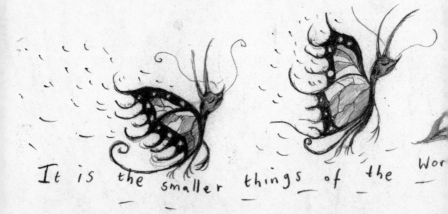

It is the smaller things of the Wor

proudly. "These ENORMOUS dragons think they are so important...But if there is a revolution to be declared, that revolution should be declared by the center of the universe, and the center of the universe is ME!

"I trust he will have learned his lesson," snapped Ziggerastica with a self-satisfied sniff, before declaring condescendingly, "Yes I know, I'm MARVELOUS..." as Hiccup tried to thank him. And he disappeared with his humming hordes just as mysteriously as he had come, like a wasp swarm lighting for a moment on a tree, buzzing there for a second, and vanishing.

Leaving only the words:

"It is the smaller things of the world who decide the fate of the Archipelago *once again*!"

...buzzing in the air.

The watching crowds were so overexcited that they noticed none of this.

once again!

who decide the fate of the Archipelago

Alvin staggered from the dais, and was crying on his mother's shoulder like he was a little boy again. "He cheated, Mother, didn't you see? He used little dragon accomplices…"

"I know, darling, I know," hissed his mother through gritted teeth. "But you should have cheated BETTER…"

The Druid Guardian held up his hand.

"SILENCE! HE IS NOT THE KING YET! THE KING NEEDS TO TAKE HIS VOWS FIRST, BEFORE HE CAN BE THE KING!"

Trying to look like a King despite the ridiculously swollen left half of his body, Hiccup limped up onto the broken dais, his tattered Fire-Suit flapping in the wind.

The Druid Guardian handed Hiccup, one by one, the ten Lost Things of Grimbeard the Ghastly.

"Hold up your hand, Hiccup," he said.

"Will you swear to be the King forever? Will you swear to lay down your life for your people? Will you swear to rule absolutely, but with fairness, and justice, mindful of the independence of your subjects?"

Hiccup looked out over the massed and silent crowds. He looked at the wild, stormy sky above, the

Archipelago in flames, and then far, far in the distance, the thousands upon thousands of dragons waiting for the final battle in Wrecker's Bay.

For the first time he realized, deep in his bones, what being a King would mean.

Once, back where these memoirs started, Hiccup had been afraid that he might be Chief of the Hooligan Tribe one day. How far he had come, for how much greater was *this* responsibility. All of these tough, huge adults looking at him with expectant eyes, wanting him to make the right decisions. He would be responsible for their lives in the upcoming battle.

After what had happened to Snotlout, Hiccup knew what this meant now, that real people, people who were close to him, might die in true life.

This is what war means.

And it would all be Hiccup's fault if anything went wrong.

Around his neck hung the Black Star of Courage that Snotlout had given him. Well, Hiccup needed courage now, and he held on to that star for dear life.

He swallowed hard.

"Peoples of the Archipelago," said Hiccup Horrendous Haddock the Third. "Two days ago my cousin Snotlout laid down his life for me."

Baggybum the Beerbelly gave a choking cry as he understood what had happened to his son.

"Snotlout put on my clothes," said Hiccup steadily. "He wore my helmet and rode my riding dragon to face the witch and Alvin's people; he took the arrow that was meant for me; he died the death that should have been *my* death. It was the bravest thing I have ever seen and...

"...he is the greatest Hero who I have ever known."

The crowd murmured in shock.

"Impossible!" hissed the witch. "Snotlout was a coward...treacherous worm. He hated you! He betrayed you to us!"

"He put his honor before his pride, which is one of the most Heroic things that any of us can ever do," said Hiccup. "Snotlout proved himself to be one of our greatest Heroes. He died with the Dragonmark on his forehead. I drew it there myself."

Baggybum the Beerbelly heaved with sobs, destroyed with grief but proud that Snotlout had proved himself a Hero at the last. He had regained his son, and lost his son, all in the course of a minute.

"Brave boy!" shouted Gobber the Belch, wiping his eyes, overcome with emotion. "The brave, brave boy! I knew he had it in him! SNOTLOUT HAS SHOWN US ALL THE WAY!"

"SNOTLOUT THE HERO!" cried a Visithug, and the crowds cheered Snotlout to the ruined rafters. "SNOTLOUT THE HERO! SNOTLOUT THE HERO! SNOTLOUT THE HERO!"

"Why did Snotlout do this for me?" asked Hiccup. "He did it because he believed that I could be the King. He said, and I will never forget this: 'You aren't the King that we wanted, but maybe you are the King we need.' And then he gave me his sword to be forever at my service.

"So you see why I have to do this, why I have to be the King.

"I take this Crown in honor of Snotlout.

"In honor of Snotlout, because he believed in me, and because his sacrifice must not be in vain. When I am King, he will live on in me. I will carry him with me every step I take, every decision I make.

"And before I take these vows, I will say to you all what I said to Snotlout.

"I wish I could offer you a King who is greater than I am. I can't turn into someone else; I can only be me. But I have discovered that I am stronger than I thought I was. I think that I can do this. I think I can be King. And if Snotlout believed I can, then maybe *I* believe it too."

Hiccup turned to the Druid Guardian.

223

He held up his hand.

He took the vow.

"I promise to be the King forever. I promise to lay down my life for my people. I promise to rule absolutely, but with fairness, and justice, mindful of the independence of my subjects.

"And I promise you this, peoples of the Archipelago." Hiccup's voice shook. "I will build a new and fairer Wilderwest, where dragons and humans can live together, where slavery is no more, a land fit for Heroes…I promise that I shall do this, or die in the attempt!"

"HOORAH!" roared the Vikings in a trumpet of applause, for they had forgotten who they were for a second, and now they remembered. They were Heroes. Heroes of the Dragonmark.

The Druid Guardian put the Crown on Hiccup's head.

"By the powers of the Guardians, both dragon and human, by the will of Destiny and Thor, and Grimbeard the Ghastly, and the peoples of the Archipelago, I crown you KING OF THE WILDERWEST."

The Crown was quite a bit too large, so the Guardian sort of rested it lopsidedly on Hiccup's ears. Thor, it was heavy. And then the Druid Guardian motioned for him to sit upon the Throne.

Hiccup refused.

"I'm so sorry," he said. "I'm happy to become King, but I *will not* sit on that Throne. It is clearly cursed."

Hiccup had a point. There had always been something malevolent about that Throne. Maybe it was the brown stain of Hiccup the Second's blood, still faintly visible on the seat. Who knows? But it seemed a good moment to start a new tradition.

"I shall sit here on this large Stone instead," said Hiccup.

"Excellent!" said the Druid Guardian. "You're going to make a wonderful King."

Hiccup sat down on the large Stone.

"Hear ye! Hear ye!" cried the Druid Guardian, hanging the Dragon Jewel around Hiccup's neck. "As I tell the King the *secret of the Dragon Jewel*!"

The crowd leaned in to listen.

"The secret of the Dragon Jewel is this," said the Druid Guardian. "The Jewel contains two dragons caught fighting in the amber. One of those dragons is suffering from a sickness that is so dangerous to dragons that it would wipe out the entire dragon population, were it ever to escape."

The crowd murmured sadly.

"So the way to use the Jewel against the dragons is to *break* it," continued the Druid Guardian solemnly, "and set the sickness free, to do its dreadful work."

Grimly, Hiccup looked at the Dragon Jewel. This was a dark secret indeed. He couldn't see any dragons caught within the amber, but perhaps they were nanodragons too small to see...

The Druid Guardian raised his arms to the crowd.

"I GIVE YOU THE FIRST KING OF THE WILDERWEST IN ONE HUNDRED YEARS... **KING HICCUP THE THIRD!**"*

"KING HICCUP THE THIRD!"

"HICCUP THE KING!"

"HICCUP, HICCUP, HICCUP THE KING!!!"

"THE KING! THE KING! THE KING!"

"HICC-UP! HICC-UP! HICC-UP!"

"HICCUP THE KING! HICCUP THE KING! HICCUP THE KING!"

The joyous cries of the crowds echoed even out across Wrecker's Bay, and came to the ears of the listening dragon Furious.

How had the boy done it?

Well, if the Fates would make him King, then...

The Dragon was ready for him.

Stoick the Vast was the first to approach the

---

*Strictly speaking, Hiccup was not the third King Hiccup but the second, because Hiccup the Second was never a King. However, in the excitement of the moment, the Druid Guardian got it wrong.

Stone. Creaking, for in middle age Stoick's magnificent belly had overspilled his breeches a little and his knees were perhaps not quite what they were, he knelt before his son.

"Father, what are you doing?" said Hiccup, and embarrassed and distressed, he tried to pull his father to his feet, and when that didn't work (Stoick was rather heavily built) Hiccup knelt down beside his father, until the Druid Guardian gave him a stern look, and said gently:

"You are the King now, Hiccup."

Slowly Hiccup sat back on the Stone.

"My sword is at your service, King," said Stoick the Vast, bowing his head as he knelt to his son, following the ancient code of the Kings of the Wilderwest.

"Oh…oh dear…" stuttered Hiccup, thoroughly rattled, but remembering in the nick of time to bow formally back, and give the traditional response.

"I am honored to accept it."

Valhallarama of the White Arms, that great Hero, knelt beside her husband. She, too, bowed her head.

"My sword is at your service, King."

"Er…Thank you, Mother," stammered Hiccup. "I mean, I am honored to accept it."

All around the ruined Castle of Grimbeard the Ghastly, these enormous hairy Vikings fell to their knees. These stern, grizzled, tattooed Warriors, Mogadon the Meathead, Dangerous the Tenth, Boily of Bashem, Barbara the Barbarian, Very Vicious the Visithug, the Vicious Twins, Bertha of the Bog-Burglars, all fell on their knees before Hiccup, and bowed their heads before him.

Father, what are you doing?

Hiccup's eyes filled with tears as he saw it. It was almost unbelievable. He looked out on a sea of kneeling people, great Warriors all, battle scarred, so much older, larger than he was, all bowing down before him.

All bowing down before him, a scraggly spiderweb runt of a boy, Hiccup, who once nobody thought would be Chief of the Hooligan Tribe, let alone a King!

With one great bellowing voice, they cried out:

"Our swords are at your service, King!"

And Hiccup replied, trying to stop his voice from trembling, trying to sound as Kingly as possible, "I am honored to accept it."

Toothless sat up proudly on Hiccup's shoulder. Hunting dragon to a King! He always *knew* he was an important dragon. He always *knew* he had royal connections. Stormfly would find him irresistible now...

"THREE CHEERS FOR KING HICCUP THE THIRD!" bellowed Gobber the Belch.

The Vikings leaped to their feet, or were helped up if they were on the fatter side, and threw their helmets in the air, and shouted:

"HURRAH! HURRAH! HURRAH!"

So that was how Hiccup Horrendous Haddock the Third became the thirteenth King of the Wilderwest. And only those who have been following Hiccup's memoirs up until now will know how very, very unlikely it is that it would end this way. That this gangly, thoughtful, imaginative, string bean of a boy would end up the Heir to Grimbeard the Ghastly.

Who would ever have thought it?

It has taken us twelve long Quests, and twelve long books to get to this point.

But there it is.

That is what happened, against all odds and unlikely as it may seem.

I told you this was the story of becoming a Hero the Hard Way.

But this, *of course*, is not the end of the story.

The Crowning of the King might make a good ending, but Hiccup had been crowned King in difficult circumstances, right in the middle of a dragon and human war, exactly at noon on the Doomsday of Yule.

So this is not the end of this particular story; indeed, in some ways, it is more like a beginning, and if you thought the first half of the Doomsday of Yule was hard, wait until you get to the second half.

However, it seems like a good moment for a pause, so that we can enjoy the unlikeliness of this triumph, and because we have spent quite a long time getting here.

END OF THE FIRST PART OF THE DOOMSDAY OF YULE

There is only one question left now in this Quest.

Can Hiccup save the dragons?

T-t-toothless has ROYAL BLOOD, Stormfly.

Why, hello there, Toothless...

13. A VERY SHORT CHAPTER THAT BEGINS WELL...AND ENDS BADLY

The reign of King Hiccup the Third began full of hope.

The coronation of a new King is always an exciting moment, and the Vikings had come from such a position of despair that there was quite a festive atmosphere in that ruined Castle, despite the waiting dragon army.

King Hiccup sat on his Stone, looking out on his new Kingdom, feeling rather grateful for the *rest*, and being able to put his feet up for a moment after a difficult morning. He was trying to put off the thought of meeting the dragon Furious so he could enjoy this moment, and he was thanking Fishlegs and Camicazi for trying to rescue him earlier in the little strait of water between Hero's End and Tomorrow.

"I don't know how to explain it; I just didn't have a clue who you were…"

"Humph," huffed Camicazi. "Well, I call it very ungrateful, and Stormfly will never forgive you because you hit her bang-smack on the bottom and Mood Dragons have long memories. But your **THROWING** has improved; actually, it was really quite good (for a *boy*, of course)…"

Stoick and Valhallarama, as the mother and the father of the King, were receiving the congratulations of all the other Vikings.

"Oh yes," boasted Stoick, "we always knew Hiccup was something special...different of course, but in a good way...*Some* people say that he takes after his father, but I don't know about that..."

Toothless was saying carelessly to Stormfly, "Oh, yes, T-t-toothless not surprised my Master turned out to be King because everybody says Toothless of royal blood...Not a Common or Garden at all, but a Toothless D-d-daydream, who are a bit like M-m-monstrous Nightmares only *cuter*..."

"Hmm," said Stormfly thoughtfully, looking him over to see if he was turning purple, which is what Mood Dragons do when they lie.

And a bright red and bashful Fishlegs was showing Barbara the Barbarian the letter they had found in the Underground Cavern, while saying in an offhand manner: "Oh yes, I go on all of Hiccup's Quests. I'm his best friend, you know; he's all the family I have, apart from this enormous Deadly Shadow dragon here. I know, quite cool, isn't he..." and trying not to itch at the same time because he didn't want Barbara to realize he was allergic to CATS.

But Barbara may have realized, because she brought out her foghorn and blew on it several times, making such a loud noise that the cat's fur stood up like the quills on a sea urchin and she immediately bounced back onto Barbara's shoulder.

Even the Alvinsmen seemed pretty pleased with the way things had turned out. Very Vicious was showing off the Hogfly to everyone, bellowing proudly: "He's the FIRST Hogfly to go to Valhalla and come back again, and I'm going to make him a Warrior and Hero of the Tribe," while the Hogfly licked him lovingly and Boily of Bashem snorted, "You can't make a lapdragon a WARRIOR, Vicious…"

Only Alvin and the witch seemed depressed, the witch snapping out useful things like, "I can't believe you couldn't think of ONE good deed that you did in twenty years. It didn't have to be a big one, Alvin; they were using anything. You could have just helped an old lady across the water or something…"

"I could help YOU into the water if you like, Mother," said Alvin bitterly, looking over the edge of the cliff in a hopeful fashion. "Just one little push…"

"And then the Druid Guardian shouted out: "THE KING NEEDS TO PREPARE FOR

241

THE BATTLE WITH THE DRAGON FURIOUS IN SINGLE COMBAT!"

"…yes, but the problem *was*, Camicazi, when you shook your axe in the air I just assumed you were **ATTACKING** me rather than waving hello…" Hiccup prattled on before Camicazi dug him in the ribs and hissed, "The King…He's talking about *you*, Hiccup."

"Oh!" exclaimed Hiccup, jumping in surprise. "So he is…"

…while thinking, *I am NEVER going to get used to this…*

As Hiccup rose to his feet, he was not looking forward to the single combat. He was absolutely terrified. Just the thought of the dragon Furious brought him out in a cold sweat. But in his heart of hearts, beneath his terror, he not only felt hopeful, he even felt *confident*.

The dragon would be frightened of the Jewel. The strength of the Jewel's power made Hiccup strong, and now that he knew its dark secret he would be able to bargain with the dragon Furious and save the humans without destroying the dragons.

And then he felt a rustling in his backpack, and the Wodensfang woke up.

The Wodensfang's little brown face appeared over

the top of Hiccup's backpack,
and his little brown nose twitched
as he tried to take everything
in, and his dazed, bleary eyes
blinked at the enormous
company of people gathered
excitedly
in the ruined hall.

"Dear me," croaked the
Wodensfang. "Where am I
and what on earth is going on?"

Did I miss anything?

And then he looked up, and saw the Crown on
Hiccup's head, did a double take, blinked twice, and
gave a whoop of joy.

"Oh my goodness! My dear boy! YOU DID IT!
YOU'RE THE KING! YOU DID IT! YOU REALLY,
REALLY DID IT!"

The Wodensfang fluttered out of the backpack on
his old brown wings. He capered around Hiccup, and
embraced him tearfully.

"I can't believe I MISSED it all! This is
marvelous! This is glorious! Oh happy, happy day! I
have to admit, I thought that the whole thing would
be completely impossible...HOW did you do it? What
did you do about the Sand Sharks? How did you get to

243

You
DID
it!
You're
the
King!

Tomorrow without a boat? How did you stop the dragon Furious from killing you before you got there?"

"It's a long story," smiled Hiccup. "But thank you, Wodensfang. I really couldn't have done it without you, even though you were only awake for the first five minutes; that was a vital five minutes..."

"Where did you find the Jewel?" asked Wodensfang eagerly.

"What do you mean, where did I find the Jewel?" said Hiccup, confused. "We found the Jewel ages ago, back in the Amber Slavelands. You were there, Wodensfang." And he pointed to the Dragon Jewel around his neck.

"No, I mean the *real* Dragon Jewel," said Wodensfang.

Hiccup had a very nasty feeling in the bottom of his stomach, the sort of tickly butterfly sensation that he got when he knew he was about to receive some very bad news.

But ... But... But ... why are you still wearing the fake Dragon Jewel?

The real Dragon Jewel? What did the Wodensfang mean?

"Wodensfang," said Hiccup with trepidation, "what on earth are you talking about? There is only one Dragon Jewel and that is this one."

Now it was the Wodensfang's jaw that fell open.

"DON'T TELL ME YOU HAVEN'T FOUND THE REAL DRAGON JEWEL YET?" squeaked the little brown dragon. "Oh dear! Oh dear! Oh my ears and whiskers!"

The Wodensfang quivered in the air in astonishment and disbelief.

"*This* is not the real Dragon Jewel!" he squeaked. "THIS IS

245

ONE OF GRIMBEARD'S RED
HERRINGS!

"*This* is a FAKE!"

Hiccup's heart sank right down
into his ragged, furry boots.

Oh dear. Oh dear. Oh dear oh
dear oh dear.

N-O-O-O

D
O
N'T

TELL

ME

YOU

HAVEN'T

FOUND

THE

REAL

DRAGON

JEWEL

YETII

,,

14. THAT GRIMBEARD THE GHASTLY REALLY WAS A VERY TRICKY MAN

"What ARE you talking about?" said Hiccup, looking at the Wodensfang in a dazed sort of way. "*Not the real Dragon Jewel?* Of course this is the real Dragon Jewel! It even has Grimbeard's initials, G.G., written quite clearly on the back of it!"

The witch could not understand Dragonese but she sensed a problem, and she bounded over, on all fours. "Is something wrong?" she hissed eagerly.

The Wodensfang switched to Norse. "This isn't the real Dragon Jewel! Oh dear oh dear oh dear! This is just terrible! I just ASSUMED that you must have found the Dragon Jewel if you were crowned King, because otherwise the Druid Guardian wouldn't have crowned you!"

"Don't blame *me*!" huffed the Druid Guardian, with a strong sense of injury.

"I do blame you!" squeaked the Wodensfang. "The real Dragon Jewel is unmistakable. In the real Dragon Jewel, there are two little dragons suspended in the heart of the amber, each with a tail in the other one's

UH - OH.

That isn't the REAL Dragon Jewel...

mouth. Look! No dragons!" He pointed a wing at the fake Dragon Jewel hanging around Hiccup's neck.

"Well, I can see that *now*," said the Druid Guardian crossly. "But before I crowned the King I was blindfolded. The Jewel's setting was correct. I checked with my dragon Guardians, and they told me I was crowning the right person…And just to make it absolutely clear, Thor actually lifted Hiccup up into the air with his mighty hand and—"

"Oh noooooooooooooooooo!" wailed the Wodensfang. "How could this be happening?"

Hiccup had a most unpleasant sick feeling in the bottom of his stomach. Suddenly it was all sounding

248

horribly like just the sort of thing that Grimbeard the Ghastly *would* do. In fact he was skilled in this regard. It would be just like Grimbeard to have two Jewels, in the same way that he had two swords and two treasures, one real one, and one decoy.*

Oh Grimbeard and his red herrings…

I have definitely said this before, but Grimbeard the Ghastly was the trickiest trickster since the great trickster god Loki put his Particularly Tricky Hat on.

Hiccup gasped with sudden realization. "There was a herring painted on the top of the map to find the Jewel! I always wondered what it meant…"

"And T-t-toothless *told* you it was a red one!" exclaimed Toothless, adding confidentially to the rest of the company: "T-t-toothless knows ALL the colors…"

And if you, dear reader, look back to the tenth volume of Hiccup's memoirs, *How to Seize a Dragon's Jewel*, you will discover that Hiccup is completely right. Painted on the top of the map of the Amber Slavelands is a very large red fish, and that fish is indeed a member of the herring family.

Fishlegs took out the map now.

And there it was. It wasn't a teeny weeny little herring, either, drawn discreetly in one of the corners. It was a whopping great *monster* of a herring that stretched

---

*See Book 2: *How to Be a Pirate*.

all the way from one side of the map right to the other, and to make it even more obvious, the herring in the picture was *winking*.

Not a little, secretive wink. A great, big **THIS IS ME, GRIMBEARD THE GHASTLY, MAKING ONE OF MY NASTY LITTLE JOKES** kind of wink.

How could I not have noticed that? breathed Hiccup. *It's completely OBVIOUS now that you know it's there…and I'm supposed to be GOOD at riddles.*

"Wodensfang," said Hiccup in Norse, patiently but between gritted teeth, "if you knew that this wasn't the real Jewel all along, why on earth didn't you tell us this earlier?"

"I couldn't tell you before," explained the Wodensfang, "because I promised Grimbeard the Ghastly that I wouldn't interfere with Destiny and the finding of the things because otherwise it wouldn't be a proper test. The *King* must find the things. *I* should not intervene. I am only speaking now because for some inexplicable reason you seem to have been crowned King anyway…"

"Everything was in order!" said the Druid Guardian crossly. "After one hundred years, do you think the dragon Guardians and I are going to make a mistake?"

"And I was so sure you were going to find the

250

real Jewel, Hiccup, back there on Hero's End," moaned Wodensfang. "Or rather, that *it* would find *you*, like all the other Things found you. I mean, *Grimbeard was buried on Hero's End*! It seemed like DESTINY had taken you there on purpose! Are you quite sure you didn't find it there?"

"Well, I'm so sorry, but I was rather busy at the time," said Hiccup, "dealing with a whole load of Sand Sharks who were trying to kill us, remember? And I also didn't know I was SUPPOSED to be looking for a Jewel, because I thought we had already *found* the Jewel. Understandably, you have to admit..."

"Well, *that* shouldn't matter!" said Wodensfang. "The things usually make their way to you without you looking for them. Did you not stumble over any large, grim-looking graves or anything? Are you quite sure it didn't fall into your pocket without your realizing it?"

Hiccup turned his pockets inside out. He patted himself all over. He even, in his desperation, took off his shoes and felt inside them.

"Quite sure," said Hiccup.

No Jewel.

"Well, this completely ruins my plan," said the Wodensfang.

"What was your plan, Wodensfang?" asked Hiccup dejectedly.

"I made a bargain with the dragon Furious a number of months ago when we were in the underground hideout..." said the Wodensfang.

"Oh!" said Toothless suddenly. "I remember this! Toothless h-h-heard you talking to the dragon Furious! But Toothless thought that was a dream!"

"Yes," said Wodensfang, "Toothless overheard me speaking telepathically to Furious because Toothless is a young Sea-Dragon just coming into his powers..."

"Toothless is a *Sea-Dragon*?" said Hiccup.

"T-t-toothless is j-j-jolly well *not* a Sea-Dragon!" retorted Toothless crossly. "Toothless is a Toothless Daydream! Everyone knows that!"

"Yes, well, Toothless is a Sea-Dragon at the beginning of his life, and I am a Sea-Dragon at the end of his life...but I can't go into that now," said the Wodensfang. "The point is, we were running out of time to find all the things, so I made a bargain with the dragon that if he called off his rebellion until the Doomsday of Yule, I would bring him the Dragon Jewel before the single combat..."

"Wodensfang!" gasped Hiccup. "You weren't thinking you would betray me, were you?"

"Of course I wasn't!" said the Wodensfang hurriedly. "I was going to take the dragon Furious the FAKE Dragon Jewel, so I could fulfill my promise, and then *you* would have ridden into single combat with the REAL Dragon Jewel, and everything would have been fine!"

Sometimes, talking to the Wodensfang made Hiccup's head go around and around, even when he wasn't being attacked by Sand Sharks at the same time.

He was having some difficulty taking all this in.

"Wodensfang," said Hiccup at last. "I've made some crazy plans in my time, but trust me, you have just come up with the *worst* plan in the history of plan-making.

"Even if, by some magical coincidence, I *had* managed to find a Jewel on Hero's End—a Jewel that I didn't even know I was looking for—and if you brought the dragon Furious a FAKE Jewel instead of the real one, let me tell you right now, Wodensfang, the dragon Furious would have KILLED you."

"The life of a little old dragon has never been of much importance when the fate of the world hangs in the balance," said Wodensfang. "Anyway, it may have been a bad plan, but it was, at least, a plan. Without the real Dragon Jewel," said the Wodensfang, "I am very much afraid we are doomed."

The Vikings hadn't understood the Dragonese parts of Hiccup and Wodensfang's conversation, but there had been enough parts in Norse for them to realize what a bad situation they were in.

There was a long silence, only broken by Toothless saying thoughtfully to no one in particular, "Actually, T-t-toothless might make rather a GOOD Sea-Dragon..."

"Is there any way of knowing where the real Jewel might be now?" asked Hiccup, speaking Norse again in desperation.

"It could be anywhere at all in the wild and windy wastes of an endless Archipelago," said the Wodensfang gloomily. "And we have run out of time to find it."

The Wodensfang was right. This was a disaster.

They could not win against the dragons now.

Without a Dragon Jewel, they all knew that they were lost. They looked at each other with hollow eyes. Oh dear, oh dear, oh dear...Everything suddenly got very dark.

The witch Excellinor showed her black gums in a very nasty grin. "Well, well, well," she gloated. "This *is* an interesting twist in the tale. Grimbeard the Ghastly certainly knows how to test a King! Now the boy has to go out and face the might of the dragon Furious in single combat without a Jewel, and I rather think that the result of *that* battle is a foregone conclusion..."

She made a very unpleasant sound, like frog bones rattling in a tin, which was the sound she made when she laughed, which was not something she did often.

"See how the web turns and twists," she grinned. "NOW I understand why Destiny might have wanted the Hiccup to be King. So that Hiccup could go out and take Alvin's place, just as Snotlout took Hiccup's place yesterday. Hiccup is going to die instead of Alvin! Heh heh heh...*Isn't* Fate artistic?"

Stoick and Valhallarama were white with horror. Their hands crept instinctively toward each other.

"But does this mean...does this mean that Hiccup still has to go out there and face the might of the dragon Furious in single combat all *on his own*?" Stoick stuttered. "Without a Jewel to protect him? But that will mean...that will mean..."

"Certain death," said the witch with relish.

15. PREPARING FOR THE FUNERAL—SORRY, SINGLE COMBAT

"No!" Stoick roared.

"Never!" Valhallarama bellowed.

"Now, now, Stoick and Valhallarama," tutted the witch. "Don't you think you're being a little overprotective? The boy has to grow up *sometime*. After all, he IS a King now…"

"And you heard the vow that he just made," taunted the witch. "What was it? It was so sweet…'I promise to lay down my life for my people.' Surely you would not have him break such a solemn promise so early in his Kingship? After all, a promise is a promise, if it is made in blood."

Ah, Grimbeard the Ghastly, this was to be a stern test indeed for the newly crowned King.

All the gaiety of the triumphant humans had gone now. And preparing Hiccup for the single combat took on more of the aspect of dressing someone for his own funeral.

How could they prepare a reed of a lad like Hiccup, who was wounded on top of everything else, to fight a dragon the size of a mountain in single combat?

It was quite touching to see the great, muscled, hairy Warriors fussing around the boy like anxious walruses, as if they could do something, anything, to help him with this fight. They offered the boy their advice, their favorite weapons, their superstitious objects... as if by all this kerfuffle, they could cover up the fact that this was completely hopeless, and the boy was doomed.

"King Hiccup," said Humungously Hotshot the Hero, "every dragon has his weakness, and I would advise you to aim at the skin above the dragon Furious's heart, where he has a scar already."

Gobber the Belch bustled forward. "Remember your spear-throwing lessons, my boy? You just take this spear of mine, and aim it at that weak spot and...bingo! One dead dragon-the-size-of-a-mountain!"

Gobber enthusiastically thrust his spear into Hiccup's hand, but unfortunately it was so heavy that Hiccup could barely lift it, let alone throw it.

"I'll lend you my cat, if you like," suggested Barbara the Barbarian. "It seems the least I can do."

"You will need my Fire-Suit, Hiccup," said Stoick, swallowing hard to contain his emotion. "Your own is far too ragged to give you any protection in case... in case..." He did not finish the sentence, and instead helped his son into his own Fire-Suit as if he were a five-year-old, for Hiccup's arm was too swollen to dress himself. The sleeves and legs were far too long, but Stoick rolled them up.

And then other Warriors pressed forward, offering helmets and breastplates and visors, until the new King was so wrapped in armor that he could barely move, and he insisted on taking some of it off.

"I have to be able to *breathe*, guys," said Hiccup gently. "I know you want to be helpful, but I can't carry ALL of your armor, because Windwalker would fall out of the sky."

"I would give everything in the world to go out there instead of you, Hiccup," said Stoick, choking over his words.

It is a father's worst nightmare to watch his son go out and face the death that he would gladly have taken instead of him. But Stoick knew his son must go without him, and he also knew in his heart of hearts that the end had come. However, at the very least, he would know his son went out into battle with his love, and the best armor he could give him.

Valhallarama offered Hiccup her own advice. It was stern advice indeed—but Valhallarama was made of stern stuff.

"Do you remember the letter I once sent to you, Hiccup?"

Hiccup frowned, thinking back in time.

Once, when he was a very young boy, he had gotten himself in some terrible scrape or another, and he remembered crying in front of his father, because he wanted Valhallarama to help him, and yet again she was not there.

"She's an amazing woman, your mother," Stoick had said, and he shook his head solemnly, with great pride. "She's doing great things out there, Hiccup. You should be very proud of her."

"But why isn't she here with us?" asked the little Hiccup, only five years old. "She's doing important Hero-work," explained Stoick patiently. "Some Heroes have to work alone. She's a very great woman, your mother." Stoick beamed with pride and shook his head. "Quite extraordinary she married me—the most beautiful woman in the Archipelago married me!"

Then much later, when he was about ten years old and trapped in the dungeons of the Danger-Brutes, in desperation, Hiccup had written to the Hero mother that he longed for, missed so much, cried for, for so many nights. "Save me, Mother!" the letter had said. He had given the letter to a passing mail dragon. The reply came one week later, burned and ragged, when the mail dragon returned. A starving, despairing Hiccup had opened it up eagerly.

This is what the letter said:

Stop expecting other people to save you.
YOU are the Hero.
Save yourself.

(If you want another answer, try another woman.)

Your loving mother,
Valhallarama

At the time, Hiccup had not appreciated that letter. He had been so upset he had torn it up into little pieces and thrown the pieces through the bars of the window, and watched them fall down, down, into the sea.

But Hiccup *had* escaped from the dungeons of the Danger-Brutes without his mother's help.

And now, perhaps, he understood a little better.

Valhallarama put her hands on her son's shoulders. Her stern, bright blue Warrior eyes looked straight into Hiccup's.

"I cannot change the Warrior-soul in me," said

Valhallarama. "My armored arms cannot give you the soft hugs I see other mothers give their sons. But this is, nonetheless, good advice, Hiccup, if you care to take it. YOU are the Hero. Save yourself."

"Where is the King's riding dragon?" called the Druid Guardian.

The Windwalker flew down and knelt before Hiccup, his raggedy wings trembling.

"You do not have to come with me, Windwalker, if you are afraid," said Hiccup.

"Of course I must come with you, Master," whispered the Windwalker. "You cannot ride into battle without your riding dragon."

"You're definitely not coming with me, Toothless," said Hiccup firmly. "You stay here, where it's safe."

"Toothless j-j-jolly well IS coming with you!" said Toothless indignantly. "T-t-try and stop me!"

Hiccup sighed. Toothless had never been the most obedient of dragons at the best of times and he could see that there was absolutely nothing he could do to stop Toothless from following him.

"And actually..." said Toothless carelessly, "you might need another GINORMOUS S-s-sea-Dragon with you to protect you, just in case things get a l-l-little dangerous, you know..."

You do not
have to come
with me if
you are afraid...

He could see himself now, Toothless, the Terror of the Archipelago, the Horror of the Oceans, storming through the seas in all his splendid toothless glory, while smaller more insignificant dragons fled in front of him, squealing: "No, Toothless, no...Please, have mercy, mighty Toothless..."

"What about us?" said Camicazi. "Fishlegs and I are allowed to come with you, aren't we, as the Companions of the Dragonmark?"

"I'm afraid not," said the Druid Guardian. "The King can take his hunting dragon and his riding dragon, but the King must go alone, because otherwise we are breaking the laws of single combat."

"Remember," wheezed Old Wrinkly, "little grandson, remember…" As he embraced Hiccup, the old man tapped a bony finger on Hiccup's heart. "What is within is always more important than what is without."

Hiccup put a hand on Camicazi's and Fishlegs's shoulders, and said good-bye to them last.

"Thank you," he said simply. "You have both been the truest and the best friends that a person could ever have, and I would never have gotten here without you."

Stoick helped his lopsided son climb up on the back of Windwalker.

Hiccup settled himself steadily and turned to face his subjects, on their feet now, all with drawn swords and solemn faces, for quietly, while the King was being made ready for the single combat, they too had been getting ready for the final battle. They knew that after Hiccup faced his doom, they would face their own.

But there was a sort of relief, in a way, for even though they might lose that battle, there is a joy in knowing that you are fighting on the right side.

Hiccup swallowed, so petrified he could barely move or speak.

He was terrified…but he was ready. He was prepared for this.

He was setting out, on the back of the Windwalker, just like Snotlout had two days before.

Snotlout had shown the way a Hero should face certain death.

Hiccup felt the Black Star to give himself courage.

Tick-tock tick-tock tick-tock tick-tock tick-tock went Grimbeard the Ghastly's ticking-thing at Hiccup's waistband, ticking down the minutes to Hiccup's doom.

He was a King now, even if only a King for a brief moment, and he knew that a King had to make a speech.

"Thank you, peoples of the Archipelago," said Hiccup, "for the gifts that you have given me. When I carry them into battle, I will be carrying you with me too. I am honored to lay down my life for you all, if that is what Fate decrees should happen. I promise you that I will fight this combat with all of my heart, and I ask you just one thing. Could you sing for me, as I ride into battle? If you all sing together, I will hear it while I am out there, facing the dragon, and it will help to give me courage...

"I will feel that you are fighting by my side...

"I am proud to be a King of this Wilderwest, but I am prouder still to be a Hero. For long after Kings are forgotten, and their names have turned to dust, the good deeds and the actions of the Heroes live on in glory. As the old song says: A Hero...IS...FOREVER..:"

Hiccup nudged Windwalker with his knees and, trembling and shaking, the brave

black dragon leaped into the sky. As he leaped, the crowd began to sing.

And although the peoples of the Archipelago spent a lot of their time fighting, burgling, and ransacking, they were a surprisingly musical lot. It was a shock to hear the tattoed, muscly, burned, and ragged characters open their mouths, with the words ringing out, every note pure and true, singing the words of Grimbeard's Last Song, just as Snotlout had sung it two days before.

> *"I sailed so far to be a King but the time was never right...*
> *I lost my way on a stormy past, got wrecked in starless night...*
> *But let my heart be wrecked by hurricanes and my ship by stormy weather,*
> *I know I am a Hero...and* A HERO IS...FOREVER!"

And the witch, whispering to herself with glowing eyes: "And a promise is a promise, if it is made in blood..."

16. SINGLE COMBAT

Wrecker's Bay was the scene of this final battle between
dragon and human.

 The Combat Ring looked like the setting of a play
in a great theater, where the audience stood on the edges
waiting to applaud, or to boo, and eventually, if Fate

decreed, to storm the stage and put their own lives to the test.

Hiccup and the Windwalker flew on, into the ring of fire to face the Dragon Furious, with Toothless and the Wodensfang flying on either side, so close that their wing tips touched the Windwalker's wings as if they were holding hands.

Tick-tock tick-tock tick-tock tick-tock went the ticking-thing.

Once (oh, it seemed a long time ago now), in the first of Hiccup's adventures, he had faced another Sea-Dragon that he thought had been called the Green Death, but in earlier times had been known as the dragon Merciless. Hiccup had walked out to see that dragon alone, and the dragon had lit the grass around him so that he was standing in the middle of a ring of fire.

This was another ring of fire entirely.

This time, as if to mark the occasion, the dragon rebellion had, it seemed, set the whole *world* on fire. The cliffs of Wrecker's Bay, all on fire. The islands of Silence, Villainy, Hysteria, Grimbeard's Despair, all on fire. Hiccup was surprised that there was any vegetation left to burn, but it appeared there was. All on fire.

To the west, the island of Tomorrow, with the

humans, lined up like little ants, watching solemnly from the clifftop. To the east, the victorious dragons of the dragon rebellion, and beyond them the wasted islands, blackened or in flames. Above, the hovering dragon Guardians, watchful, their eyes flicking like cats from one side to the other, as if trying to decide which side to go for.

Down below, buzzing in the grasses, the little unobserved nanodragons making their own judgements on the play, ticking in their little tiny voices:

"You do not see *us*, peoples of the Archipelago, but we see *you*..."

They were all there; pretty much all the people and dragons that Hiccup had ever known over twelve long adventures, and they would all play their part, big and small, in this coming battle, for a Hero, even a King-Hero, does not fight alone.

But until the single combat was over, stern Viking law said that only the dragon Furious and the human King could enter the Combat Ring.

The winner of that single combat would either decide to end the war entirely, or they could give the signal for the war to continue.

The stakes were high.

If Hiccup won, he would end the war.

But if the dragon won, he would declare the final

battle, and the waiting humans and dragons on the sidelines would storm out, screaming most terribly, and Wrecker's Bay would become a bloody, terrible scene as the two armies fought each other to the death.

It was already haunted by so many ghosts of the past, that Bay, for that was where the Winter Wind of Woden blew unfortunate ships that had been wrecked on the terrible reefs, and it wasn't always clear whether it was the wind howling through the holes in the reefs or the wailing of the human and the dragon ghosts who had lost their lives here once.

Now it was haunted by future ghosts as well as past ghosts. The silent watching audience could see them all in that moment, the ghosts of Heroes and Dragons past, present and future, flying together in the Bay in their minds' eye.

"T-t-toothless the Sea-Dragon has SPECIAL POWERS," said Toothless to himself as the little Hiccup party set out. "He will grind that F-f-furious's bones to dust with his...with his..." Toothless had no idea what his special powers would be, but he ran through all the delightful possibilities in his head. Invisibility, lasers, superspeed...

It was difficult for Windwalker to fly through the air toward where the dim black outline of Furious lay in Wrecker's Bay, for the air all around the dragon was so burningly, burningly hot, that at times Hiccup had to pull down the visor of his Fire-Suit and Windwalker had to draw down his third eyelid, which was see-through. The wind was blowing strongly, and so poor Windwalker felt as if he were trying to fly against a burning jet stream of fire, and any second, he felt as if his raggedy wings might blow inside out, sending him plummeting downward.

"It's hot," complained Toothless. "T-t-toothless LIKES it hot; Sea-Dragons love it toasty warm..."

Hiccup had a sudden longing image in his mind of happier times, of Toothless playing in the hearth fire in the old Chiefly hut on Berk, racing up and down the chimney with squeals of delight...

"...but this is too hot, even for a great terrifying Sea-Dragon like T-t-toothless..." said Toothless sadly.

"Yes, Toothless," replied Hiccup, who even in the protection of his Fire-Suit was drenched in sweat, his body burning up as though he had a raging temperature. "It's definitely too hot."

Every instinct in Hiccup was telling him to turn away, go back—but he could hear the distant voices of the peoples of the Archipelago singing those old Archipelago songs, and willing him on:

"I've heard that the sky in America
Is a blue that you wouldn't believe,
But my ship hit a rock on these boggy shores,
And now I'll never leave…"

And the songs gave him courage, and calmed him, as if the dear familiar owners of those voices were flying right beside him.

As he approached closer to the might and the heat of dragon Furious, Wodensfang began to fly more slowly, more uncertainly, his breath catching in his little throat. He had known the dragon Furious for so many years…old friend, old enemy. But now it was as if the dragon had turned into something else, something older than the hills around, and something more implacable.

The nearer, nearer Hiccup, Windwalker, Toothless, and Wodensfang came to the dragon Furious, the hotter they became, as if they were flying into the very fires of hell, and even underneath his Fire-Suit, Hiccup's face burned as if he had stuck it in the oven.

Hiccup had not been this close to the dragon Furious since the time he first met him, buried in briars and chains in the forest on Berserk, and you could still see the remnants of that forest captivity in the trees that had grown through the dragon's spines, the chains trailing from him.

Even back then he had been a truly terrifying sight, enough to make you sweat with fear when you saw him.

But the dragon had changed. War had changed that dragon, and something about the *way* he had changed made Hiccup's heart sink down into his boots and his stomach churn like a nauseous sea.

The maddened melancholy of Furious's great yellow eyes had become bleaker, and wilder, and deader, like the cruel implacable eyes of a great white shark. Although he was still—so still—you could feel the anger reeking off him like the clouds of steam that rose from his shining, blackened sides, and almost *smell* his fury in the heat of the air.

His skin was peeling off, like the little peelings of charcoal that fly into the air when a bonfire is roaring at its hottest, and all around, those little black flakes were whirling upward.

His great steaming, roasting body was covered in battle scars; and spears, axes, and swords were buried in his flanks and neck like ornaments, forming a little spiky coral crust.

Toothless was so terrified that he forgot he was a Sea-Dragon, and he couldn't really think of any special

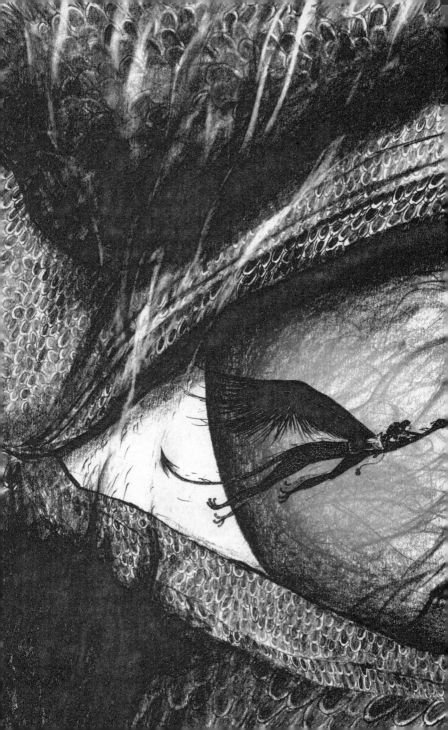

powers to give himself that would be up to this situation. So he gave up flying entirely and buried himself in Hiccup's waistcoat, while Hiccup forced himself nearer, nearer, although every instinct, every nerve in his body, was screaming: "Turn around! Go back! Pull on Windwalker's reins and turn him back the other way!"

Was the dragon Furious alive or was he dead?

The dragon was crouched down, still as if turned into rock, only the tip of his tail swaying as they approached, yellow eyes unblinking, but in their depths, moody firestorms brooded and crackled. Wodensfang could not meet the raging, seething intensity of the dragon's gaze.

There came a point when Windwalker could fly no farther. He just would not go on, but hovered in the steaming heat, his sleek black sides shaking so wildly with terror that it was as if he had some shivering fever.

And then the dragon suddenly opened his jaws with such unexpected violence that Hiccup nearly fell off the Windwalker's back with the shock of it.

The dragon Furious opened his mouth and let out a great wild, mad shriek, like the alien scream of a goshawk, and you could see, buried in the roasting, smoking chasm of his throat, the ghostly outline of a Viking ship's burning mast, stuck there like a fish bone. Who knows who they had been, those poor human souls, whose ship had been swallowed in one hungry gulp, and who had disappeared forever into the fiery furnace of the belly of the beast?

War has driven him crazy, thought Hiccup, feeling the sick taste of panic in his mouth. *How can I even dream of talking to a creature like this? How can I appeal to his reason when he has gone* so far beyond *reason into a wild alien place?*

The dragon shrieked, shrieked, and shrieked again, and the drilling sound of it burrowed so madly into Hiccup's brain that he had to cover his ears, and even then his eardrums vibrated and throbbed with pain.

For a second it seemed as if the dragon would not be able to speak at all, so mad with fury was he, that it was as if he had forgotten all language. He leaped forward as if to tear Hiccup apart on the spot, but then threw himself violently back the other way and thrashed about, shrieking on and on, until Hiccup thought he might go mad with the noise of it.

But eventually, the dragon seemed to be making an effort to control himself and find some memory of speech, thrashing and foaming at the mouth and making strange strangled guttural noises until he finally fixed on something approaching words. He spoke in Norse, even though he knew Hiccup spoke Dragonese, and there was something dreadful about that, for it was as if he were trying to keep Hiccup as a stranger, something alien to him…

Because he knows he is going to kill me, thought Hiccup with dull terror.

The dragon spat out each foreign Norse word as if he hated it, as if the human word was something poisonous and revolting in his mouth.

"So, Wodensfang, you have betrayed me…" said the dragon Furious. "You promised you would bring me the Dragon Jewel before the King came to meet me… Where *isss* this Jewel?"

Shaking, Wodensfang flew above Furious's head, hovered for a second with the Jewel in his claws…and then, guiltily, sadly, he dropped it.

Wodensfang dropped the little Jewel and the mountain moved. Out shot the Dragon's mighty fist, and the claws of Furious closed around the Jewel, as a hand might close around a speck of dust.

And now the steam around the dragon seemed to grow thicker and more intense as the Dragon brought the Jewel up to those seething, burning eyes so he could inspect it. His pupils narrowed to great unbelieving slits in order to better focus on the tiny bead of a Jewel. And then those great eyes raised slowly again to gaze with spearlike fury at the guilty, raggedy, flapping little Wodensfang.

A dreadful, ominous noise began to rumble in the dragon's throat, as if the dragon really were a volcano and he was going to explode.

"I know! I know!" squeaked the Wodensfang. "It is not the real Dragon Jewel, but give me a chance to explain!"

The steam rising from the dragon's back began to hum. The dragon did not open his mouth, but his eyes glowed with a strange light, and he spoke to the Wodensfang through his thoughts alone, for Sea-Dragons can communicate with one another like that. And those thoughts were SAVAGE.

"What...is...*this*???" The dragon's mouth did not move, but his words came alive in the Wodensfang's brain like hissing, angry serpents, and the Wodensfang's eyes glowed too as he received them.

"Thisss is not the Dragon Jewel.

"Thissss—as you must well know, Wodensfang, for you have known the Dragon Jewel well for a thousand years—*thisssss*...

"...is a FAKE."

"Yes," replied the Wodensfang nervously. "I know. I have to admit, it is, indeed, a fake..."

"BETRAYAL!" screamed the dragon Furious's thoughts. "TREACHERY! You have double-crossed me, Wodensfang!"

The dragon Furious turned his eyes upon the Wodensfang and drew in his breath to obliterate him.

"Yes," said the Wodensfang, brave once more. "I did, I am, and I will. But also," said the Wodensfang, "no, I didn't, I'm not, and I won't.* I have betrayed the enemy that you are now, but not the friend that you once were.

"Yes and no!" squeaked the Wodensfang. "No and yes! It is all Grimbeard the Ghastly's fault. The fake Jewel was one of his red herrings. He always did have a nasty sense of humor..."

"If *this* is not the real Dragon Jewel," hissed the dragon Furious's thoughts, "where isss the real Dragon Jewel? Be careful how you answer me, Wodensfang. Tell me the truth..."

"We do not know where it is," admitted the Wodensfang. "It could be anywhere at all in the vast and empty wastes of an endless Archipelago."

Furious finished the Wodensfang's thought for him.

"So it does not really matter if this is not the real Jewel. For although I do not now have the Jewel, neither does Hiccup. And you have run out of time to find it."

---

*For Sea-Dragons are used to talking to one another in this complicated way, living as they do in the past, present, and future simultaneously.

The seething madness in the dragon Furious's yellow eyes calmed a little at that.

The Wodensfang was very afraid to say the next sentence. But bravely he said it anyway:

"You see, I have always hoped, Furious, that you would not carry this through to its bloody ending. That you would let this Hiccup try one more time to bring the humans and dragons together."

The dragon hunched down, his eyes fixed on the little speck of Hiccup hovering in front of him in the smoke and the fire and the black rain of his smoking skin. He had grown very still again, as if he had turned to stone, with only the tip of his tail swaying very gently from side to side.

The dragon's thought-voice was now very cold and bleak, and he spoke with absolute finality.

"Then your hope will be in vain, Wodensfang.

"A King must harden his heart, and act in the interests of his people. And if I show mercy now, it will be the end of dragons."

Hiccup had no idea what was being said. He only knew that he had to speak now. His voice sounded very small and weak, and indeed he barely could speak at all, with the burning heat tearing at his throat. But still he spoke, in Dragonese, trying to reach out to that alien otherness that the dragon Furious had become, trying to make some connection with him, and bring him back.

"I have not come here to die, Furious," shouted Hiccup hoarsely. "I have come here to give you my own promise. I promise you: Now that I am the new King, I will make the Wilderwest a Kingdom in which humans and dragons can live together peacefully—"

"Humans cannot change," roared the dragon Furious, and his eyeballs spat with electricity, and two thunderous lightning bolts shot from them to either side of the trembling Hiccup. "Do not think that you can use your treacherous forked-tongued words to change anything. Words change nothing. You see...When I look at you, I do not see a *new* King of the Wilderwest. I see the old King of the Wilderwest. I see...*Grimbeard the Ghastly*...

"I see Grimbeard the Ghastly sitting there before me, as if it were a hundred years ago, right here today!"

The little spark of hope that had lit in Hiccup when the dragon started talking died abruptly.

He isn't talking because he is wanting to bargain; he's going to play with me before he kills me, thought Hiccup. *Like a cat with a mouse...*

"Look at you," roared the dragon, in a screaming

taunt. "You little human *King*, you, all dressed up with the King's Things. The Crown...the shield...the second-best sword...the lobster necklace... the ticking-thing. You are Grimbeard the Ghastly to the life!"

The dragon Furious reached out a talon and jeeringly swung the ticking-thing so that it swayed back and forth from where it dangled on Hiccup's belt beneath the hovering Windwalker. *Tick-tock tick-tock tick-tock.*

"I am not Grimbeard the Ghastly!" Hiccup shouted up to the dragon. "I will never be like him! I am a Hiccup, and I will always be a Hiccup!"

"I have a GRUDGE against Grimbeard the Ghastly," growled the smoldering dragon Furious. "He killed my Master, and kept me captive in the darkness for a hundred years...Do you know how long a hundred years can seem when you have nowhere to go, nothing to do but to keep on thinking about the past, the present, and the future?

"If I had that Grimbeard here before me, oh how I would RIP him...

"I cannot rip Grimbeard but I *can* rip you...

"So FLY AWAY, little King, and let us see how far you get before I RIP you..."

The dragon opened up his great bloodstained jaws so wide that Hiccup could see his cavern of a throat, and the fire-holes preparing to shoot thunderbolts…

"Windwalker!" he screamed. "Fly! Windwalker, fly! Fly around his head to confuse him!"

Windwalker gave a snort of terror but nodded bravely. Windwalker had once been a very odd-looking dragon, an extraordinary bundle of fur that looked remarkably like a cross-eyed duckling mixed with an anxious wolf cub. But over the last couple of years, in his adolescence, Windwalker had gradually shed his hair and become sleeker, faster, and more aerodynamic.

His ankles had strengthened, his bending wings had become an advantage as he gained control and mastery over them, and he was now almost as fast as a Silver Phantom. Soon he would enter a chrysalis stage, and after that a truly extraordinary transformation would occur…But that's another story. For now, the Windwalker had turned into one of the swiftest, most maneuverable dragons in the Archipelago. Only a dragon like the Windwalker could even *think* of getting in so close to the dragon Furious, and elude his thunderbolts.

So as the thunderbolts were unleashed, the terrified Windwalker zigzagged back and forth, back

and forth, so quickly that the thunderbolts barely
singed his wings.

"Listen to me, Furious! Listen!" Hiccup shouted
down, crouched low on the Windwalker's back as the
Windwalker dodged and flickered and twisted around
the dragon Furious's head in an extraordinary display of
aerial artistry as the dragon Furious swatted at him.

"WORDS...CHANGE...NOTHING!" screamed
the dragon.

The dragon's eyes followed the Windwalker's
incredible loops and turns like a jaguar following a
bluebottle, and then he grew still, and the Windwalker
hovered behind his great head, to avoid the
thunderbolts...

"No, Windwalker!" squealed the Wodensfang.
"Furious has eyes in the back of his head!"

And so it was—oh, what a time to find this out!—
that adult Sea-Dragons do indeed have eyes in the back
of their heads that begin life as spots or moles, and grow
into eyes as the dragon grows, and then as the dragon
ages and gets smaller, the skin closes over them, and
buries them, and they dwindle into nothing again.

But the eyes in a Sea-Dragon the size of Furious are
very much there.

At the back of his head, behind his ears they

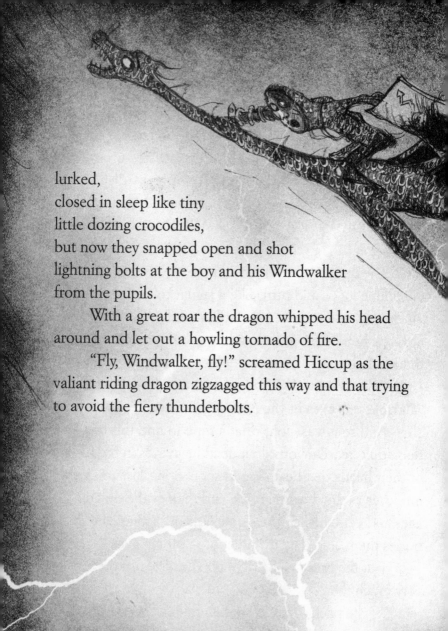

lurked,
closed in sleep like tiny
little dozing crocodiles,
but now they snapped open and shot
lightning bolts at the boy and his Windwalker
from the pupils.

With a great roar the dragon whipped his head around and let out a howling tornado of fire.

"Fly, Windwalker, fly!" screamed Hiccup as the valiant riding dragon zigzagged this way and that trying to avoid the fiery thunderbolts.

And the Sea-Dragon's talon nipped
the Windwalker's tail and flung him down,
so that the Windwalker spiraled down out
of the air and had to make an emergency
crash landing on the reef below, with such
out-of-control speed that Hiccup fell off
on the landing.

And then the dragon
Furious pinned him down
on the reef with two of his
talons, and Hiccup was
looking up, helpless, into
the implacable eye of
the dragon.

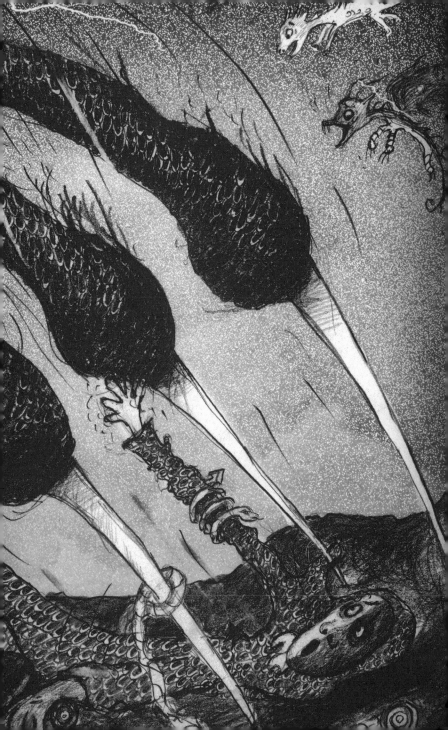

♪♪ ♪♪

I didn't mean
to come here.
And I didn't mean
to STAY

It's just where
the sea wind
blew me

ONE ACCIDENTAL
DAY! ♪♪

17. SOMETIMES WHAT YOU ARE LOOKING FOR IS RIGHT HERE AT HOME

"History repeats itself," said the dragon grimly. "And it will KEEP ON repeating itself, until somebody like me steps in and stops it."

The dragon had stopped playing, and now meant business.

He inhaled, about to send flames of fire down to kill Hiccup. The force of the dragon's inhalation was so strong that it was dragging Hiccup toward those open jaws...He could smell the rank fishy smell of the dragon's breath...

Hiccup shut his eyes and waited for the terrible pain of the flames.

The only thing that could save me now is the Dragon Jewel, thought Hiccup.

And at that *exact* moment, the alarm on Grimbeard the Ghastly's ticking-thing went off, probably in protest at the dragon dragging on it, in a peal of tiny clockwork bells, ringing to the sound of the Hooligan national anthem.

A typical Grimbeard the Ghastly touch.

You have to admit it—the guy did have STYLE.

Hiccup looked down, and two of the arrows on the ticking-thing, the one shaped like a lightning bolt and the one shaped like a question mark, were going around and around and around.

The dragon Furious started, and was distracted for one crucial second, trying to figure out where the sudden and unexpected noise was coming from.

And coincidentally—what are the impossible odds against this?—the distant voices of the Vikings on the clifftops were singing that very same Hooligan national anthem that the ticking-thing was playing. You could hear their tiny, faint voices carrying on the wind:

"I didn't mean to come here,
And I didn't mean to stay…
But I lost my heart to these rainy bogs…
And I'll ne-e-ever go awa-a-ay!"

The dragon Furious suddenly realized what was making the noise.

"It's Grimbeard's ticking-thing, sounding out the second of your death, with the Hooligan national anthem..." said the dragon bleakly.

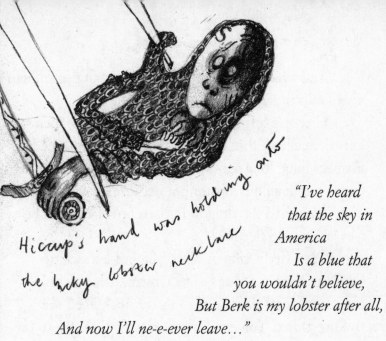

Hiccup's hand was holding onto the lucky lobster necklace

"I've heard
that the sky in
America
Is a blue that
you wouldn't believe,
But Berk is my lobster after all,
And now I'll ne-e-ever leave..."

The dragon inhaled again, ready to unleash his fire.

But a little bell had gone off in Hiccup's brain, like the alarm on a ticking-thing.

That Hooligan national anthem—what did it mean? The same thing that Hiccup had learned when he returned from the Quest to find the sixth Lost Thing, the arrow from America, and he saw the little Isle of Berk for the first time after a long absence.

Maybe there are lands with bluer skies and richer soils somewhere over the horizon...But sometimes what you are looking for is right here at home.

Love never dies…

And what was that nonsensical part in the anthem about a lobster?

Hiccup's left hand was holding on to the lucky lobster necklace that Fishlegs's mother gave to the baby Fishlegs long, long ago when she was forced to put him out to sea in an old lobster pot because he was a runt…

What had the dragon Furious just said when he was jeering at Hiccup?

"You little human *King*, you, all dressed up with the King's Things. The Crown…the shield… the second-best sword…the lobster necklace…the ticking-thing. You are Grimbeard the Ghastly to the life!"

Why did the dragon Furious mention the lobster necklace? It was a bit odd for him to say that because the lobster necklace wasn't one of Grimbeard the Ghastly's Lost Things. Was it?

WAS IT?
BUT WHAT IF IT WAS?

The dragon Furious had known Grimbeard the Ghastly well. He obviously remembered Grimbeard the Ghastly wearing a lobster necklace.

What if it had been *this* one?

And then a perfect *storm* of interlocking thoughts and questions came jostling into Hiccup's head, all

The past never really leaves us…

Sometimes second-best is BEST…

... When you fight for your friend, you are also fighting for yourself ...

pointing at how to unravel Grimbeard the Ghastly's riddle, all of the questions and the answers he had learned during the course of twelve long and exciting Quests...

Love never dies...When you fight for your friend, you are also fighting for yourself...The fang-free dragon...You have to keep on trying even though you are beaten before you start...Sometimes second-best is best...Accidents happen for a reason...

And *SOMETIMES WHAT YOU ARE LOOKING FOR IS RIGHT HERE AT HOME.*

What if what he was looking for had been with him all along?

Hiccup had never had to look for the things; they had just *found* their way to Hiccup, as if they were seeking him out. What if the lobster necklace had kept Fishlegs safe all those long, long years ago not because it was lucky, but because it was searching for Hiccup?

Accidents happen for a reason...

What if the dragon Guardians had not dropped Hiccup by accident after all, but because they knew he was carrying the last and most important of the Lost Things?

... Accidents happen for a reason

What is within is more important than what is without…

Those were the words written on the back of the map to find the Jewel. What if those words were in fact a clue, a riddle to the real Jewel's true whereabouts? The Dragon Jewel had been hidden for so long in the hilt of a sword, what if it were now hidden **INSIDE** something else?

The dragon Furious was inhaling again, ready to shoot those fatal thunderbolts…

A fang-free dragon… Why a fang-free dragon? How did that fit into the pattern?

"Toothless," said Hiccup, very calm, very stern,

Toothless took
the lobster claw in
his fang-free jaws
and bit it in
half

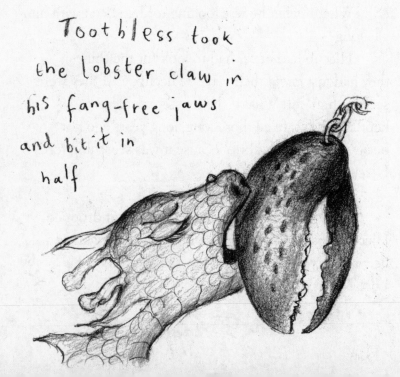

"I want you to pretend this lobster claw is a walnut. Crack it with your jaw without harming what is inside."

A fang-free dragon has a huge advantage in cracking a walnut without breaking the precious interior.

Toothless's hard little gums were the neatest, most efficient little nutcrackers in the whole of the Archipelago.

Toothless was so terrified he did not even argue. For once in his life, he obeyed without question.

He reached up his little shaking neck, took the lobster claw in his fang-free jaws, and bit it once, and into Hiccup's hand there fell what had been hidden there all the time, something small and light and bright and golden, a piece of precious amber with two little dragons caught forever in the gold: one dark and one light, and each with a tail in the other one's mouth…

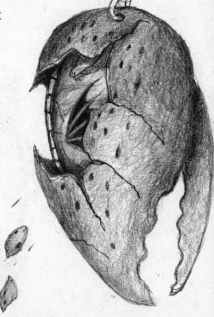

The alpha and the omega.

In my end is my beginning.

Past and present and future all together in an instant.

Toothless and Hiccup blinked at it in amazement.

Wodensfang let out a sigh of relief.

Above, the dragon Furious was on the brink of expelling his thunderbolts…

But he saw what Hiccup was holding in his hand, checked himself just in time, and loosed his grip. Hiccup leaped to his feet, holding the bright amber up in one shaking hand, and the dragon gave a snort of terror as a sudden shaft of sunlight sliced through the clouds and fire above and made the piece of amber wink up at the dragon Furious, so that he recognized what it was.

The Dragon Jewel.

The *real* one.

18. THE PAST NEVER LEAVES US...

Back on the cliffs of Tomorrow, the Vikings were singing their hearts out, willing their King and Hero to do well in this single combat, although they knew that the outcome of the battle would not be good.

They stood there, singing and peering through the fog and fire, hands shielding their eyes, trying to figure out what was going on.

Stoick was watching what was going on through his telescope-thingy,* so he narrated the news very loudly to everyone else.

"He's doing very well...He's flying brilliantly... Oh, well done, my boy, well done..." And then: "OH NO!" as the dragon Furious pulled Windwalker out of the sky..."OH NO OH NO OH NO! HE'S DOWN! THE DRAGON HAS GOTTEN HIM DOWN!"

Stoick handed the telescope-thingy to Valhallarama because he couldn't look anymore.

Her arm trembling very, very slightly, that iron woman Valhallarama put the telescope-thingy to her eye. "The dragon seems to be about to fire..." she said grimly. "He's throwing back his head...We should go OUT there! We must save him!"

---

*This first appears in Book 8: *How to Break a Dragon's Heart* and allowed him to see things from far away a bit more clearly.

"But that would be breaking the laws of single combat," gloated the witch. "And a *King* could not break such laws, or the world ends. It's a shame, a real shame…"

"SING THE HOOLIGAN NATIONAL ANTHEM!" ordered Gobber the Belch.

"HANG ON A SECOND!" cried Valhallarama. "Hiccup is holding something up. He's jumping to his feet. OH, BY THE BEARD OF FREYA THE MAGNIFICENT! THE DRAGON IS HOLDING HIS FIRE! THE DRAGON LOOKS AFRAID! WHAT IS GOING ON?"

The Druid Guardian snatched the telescope-thingy from Valhallarama to look for himself.

"Well, bless my soul," cried the Druid Guardian. "Hiccup has found the Dragon Jewel after all! He really IS a wonderful King!"

"What do you mean he's found the Dragon Jewel?" said Valhallarama, in a bewildered sort of way.

"HICCUP'S FOUND THE JEWEL!" Stoick roared. "HE'S FOUND THE REAL DRAGON JEWEL THIS TIME! WE ARE SAVED!"

And the Vikings broke off singing for a second and erupted in cheering, stamping applause.

"Impossible!" hissed the witch. "The real Dragon

Jewel can't just turn up suddenly on that reef over there for the little rat to find it at exactly the right moment!"

A sudden feeling came over the witch. Like Hiccup, she was good at riddles. She gasped, and nearly dropped to the ground.

"Unless...*Unless*...UNLESS HE HAD IT ALREADY!

"Alvin!" said the witch urgently. "I just had this horrible vision! Tell me again, Alvin—where did you find Grimbeard's coffin?"

"I've already told you this, Mother," said Alvin impatiently. "I heard a rumor that some girl and her dragon had discovered Grimbeard's grave, but were keeping it a secret out of respect for the dead. I disguised myself as a poor fisherman, romanced the girl, and persuaded her to tell me where the grave was. It was on that little island over there, the little isle of Hero's End. And after she had shown me, I sneaked back and dug it up. Very clever of me."

"And what was in Grimbeard's coffin?" hissed the witch. "The coffin that you opened long, long ago, the one that was booby-trapped and took off your hand?"

"I fail to see why this is important. We've been over this, Mother," answered Alvin. "There was no body in the coffin. The body had vanished. It was just the map to Grimbeard's treasure and the riddle."

"So there was nothing, nothing else?" asked the witch. *Nothing there at all?*"

"Nothing of importance," said Alvin, turning white now, as a slow, creeping realization like a little shiver came over him. "Certainly nothing worth losing my hand over…but there was…I suppose there *was* something… but it didn't matter…"

"What was it?" shrieked the witch, clawing at him as if she wanted to strangle him. "What was it? I told you to tell me EVERYTHING, Alvin…"

Alvin swallowed hard. "But it was nothing. It was just a smelly old pair of lobster claws hanging on a chain. A necklace fit for a slave. Typical Grimbeard the Ghastly, he always had a nasty sense of humor."

"WHAT DID YOU DO WITH IT?" screamed the witch.

Alvin was now a horrible sickly yellow. "Well, now," he said, "it was a long time ago…fourteen, fifteen years ago. I thought it wasn't important. Just an old lobster claw, one of Grimbeard's unpleasant little practical jokes. I gave it to this girl Termagant, the one that I was romancing at the time. I told her I'd lost the hand in a nasty fishing accident, and she nursed me back to health.

The necklace was fit for *her*, I thought. I wasn't going to give *her* anything NICE…"

"What happened to her? The girl, what happened to her?"

"Well…I abandoned her," said Alvin, as if that was obvious. "As soon as I was well again, and she had served her purpose. She wasn't worth ME."

"AAAAARRGHHH!" screamed the witch. "AAARGH! AARRGH! AAAAAARGH! Don't you see, you imbecile, the Jewel was hidden INSIDE the lobster claw? Of course it was! I know it was! You had it! You had it! And you gave it away!"

For, of course, what the witch was seeing in her mind's eye was the final piece of the jigsaw.

Fifteen years ago, Termagent placed her little runt baby in an old lobster pot, and set it out to sea in the old barbaric fashion, the way that the Tribes had dealt with their runts and their unwanted offspring for as long as the world could remember. Setting them out to sea, for the sea to deal with them.

And then, just before she pushed the little craft away, she reached up and took the necklace from around her neck, and placed it on her baby's lap. It was the only thing the poor girl had that the baby's father, Alvin, had given her.

Then she pushed the baby out to sea, like a little

Viking funeral. Not knowing, of course, that both the baby and the craft would survive the journey, cross the sea, and land on the beaches of the little Isle of Berk.

The baby, of course, was Fishlegs.

And it could be said that the lobster claw had saved his life. For inside the smelly claw was hidden the last Lost Thing, and as with all the Lost Things, it was almost as if it had been searching for Hiccup, who was the True Heir to Grimbeard the Ghastly.

That would be impossible, of course. How could that be?

Be that as it may, the hidden Jewel carried the lobster pot safely across the waves, safely through the storm, true as a star or a magnet, to the shores of Berk, where the baby Hiccup had just been born.

Perhaps Fishlegs's mother had instinctively known that?

Who knows? A mother's love for her child is so strong that sometimes she can know things without even *knowing* that she knows them.

All she knew was that the lobster claw might keep him safe, and she had been right.

Well, well, well.

Isn't Fate artistic?

I have said this before, perhaps, but...

Everything we do, you see, has its consequences and repercussions, every kind act, and every bad one, every friend we make, and every enemy.

Everything is connected.

Like the complicated interlocking wheels of a ticking-thing.

In that moment of suspended time, the truth broke upon Alvin, and he turned deathly white.

"I had it…I had the Jewel inside my hand and I threw it away…The most precious Thing I ever had… and if I hadn't thrown it away I could have been the King…" he groaned.

The Druid Guardian was regarding him with stern amusement, and he nodded his head. "For you know the price of everything, Alvin, and the value of nothing. *You* would have made a very bad King.

"*I* may have been blind," added the Druid Guardian, with deep satisfaction, "but the X-ray eyes of the dragon Guardians must have seen that Hiccup was carrying the Jewel with him, even when he did not yet know it himself."

Fishlegs was white as he listened to this, and realized what it might mean.

All around him, the Vikings were already celebrating, for Hiccup had found the Jewel…and

THAT MAN cannot be my father!

Fishlegs was over the moon too, of course, for Hiccup would be saved and they ALL would be saved, and it was all because of Fishlegs and the fact that he had given Hiccup his lucky lobster claw necklace.

But Fishlegs was feeling some rather more mixed emotions along with all the joy.

Oh for Thor's sake. Fifteen years looking for his father…fifteen years!

And his father turns out to be ALVIN THE TREACHEROUS?

"No," whispered Fishlegs, white to the lips. "It's not true…It can't be true…*That man* cannot be my father…"

He felt as if someone had just given him an enormous present at the same time as punching him rather violently in the stomach.

"HE HAS THE JEWEL! HE HAS THE JEWEL! HICCUP THE KING! HICCUP THE KING!" roared the crowd.

"Thumbnails and earwax and little twirly bits of Thor!" cursed the witch. She was looking really quite insane. "Oh, curse you, Destiny!"

The witch shook her bony fist up at the heavens.

"How *does* he do it? It is almost as if those Things were out there looking for him! As if he were some kind of horrible Hiccup-shaped magnet…"

What the witch hadn't learned, you see, old as she was, is that Hiccup had acquired these things as a result of his very own nature. His lifelong kindness to his good friend Fishlegs is what had led Fishlegs to give him the lobster claw necklace.

Whereas Alvin's habitual meanness toward others is what led him to give it away.

NO! It can't be true!

19. AND IT HAUNTS THE PRESENT IN MORE WAYS THAN WE THINK...

Hiccup held aloft the Dragon Jewel in one fist.

The dragon was blinded for a second by the ray of light hitting the Jewel—saw immediately what it was and, giving a snort of pure terror, he closed up his fire-holes in the nick of time, before those bolts of flame could be released.

The Dragon screamed, as if he had been hit by a gigantic spear, eyes turned black in horror.

And then…

"The Dragon Jewel," he hissed with a terrible sigh. "The *real* Dragon Jewel…"

"He's found it…" whispered the Wodensfang, his eyes alight with hope and desperate relief. "He's found it! Fate is on the side of the good after all…"

In that second that the Jewel was in his hand, Hiccup could feel its power.

The power to rule over the dragons, the power of life and death. The power to destroy them completely.

"I have the Jewel, Furious!" Hiccup shouted. "And I know its secret power!"

The dragon
paused. A moment caught out
of time.

The destiny of dragons,
caught up in a human hand.

"Then use it," hissed the
dragon Furious, panting, his eyes
black with pain. "Break it. End it.
Fate has landed on your side."

"We do not need to break it," said Hiccup.
"We can bargain; I can promise. I promise you that
now that I am King, dragons will be free. We can end
this war, we can make a peace, and dragons can be free
again to fly wherever they will..."

"But *you* will not live forever," sighed the dragon.

The boiling, steaming dragon was racked with a confusion of emotions: distress, fear, anger. His great body shivered, and his head twisted from side to side.

Hiccup looked the dragon Furious in the eye.

It was dangerous, but it was the only way to see what he was thinking.

There was a pause, and then within the stormy black depths, the pupils flickered and went pinprick bright with flame once more.

"End it! End it!" urged the dragon. "Whatever way, this must end now. I will not take your promise. We cannot go on like this. Dragons cannot be slaves again!"

"I cannot end it!" yelled Hiccup, tears streaming down his face. "It would break my heart!"

"You are a KING!" screamed the dragon Furious, angry once more, flames shooting out of those eyes again. "A KING must act in the interests of his people. You cannot hesitate. You have to make the kill; that is what we teach our dragon young from the very start...

"Look at me—that is *human* blood that you see here on my fangs, and those are *human* rags you see dripping from my claws. I am a MONSTER: Can you not see that? See that, and end it!"

"You are not a monster!" cried Hiccup. "You are no more a monster than Toothless here..."

"Well if *you* will not end it, then see what a monster *I* can be," roared the dragon, and he exhaled again. "Break it, or I kill you, and once I have the Jewel in my power, I will keep my promise and I will kill the whole human lot of you..."

This was the moment for striking.

The carnivore in the dragon Furious knew it. Only Hiccup now stood between him and victory for the dragons, an end to their misery of enslavement.

Prey, Hiccup is prey, only prey. Strike first, and think afterward...

The dragon Furious threw back his head, the fire-holes already filling with the deadly flames, his intake of breath so huge that Hiccup's body was dragged forward in the wind of it. One more second and it would be over...

Hiccup's arms were spread wide, the Jewel held aloft in his right hand. In that instant he knew, as he had always known, that he would not break the Jewel, he would not kill the dragons for all time, and he would not make the

He
could
not do it.

decision that a King ought to make.

Great hot tears rolled down his cheeks.

"I can't do it," whispered Hiccup. "I will not do this…I will not break the Jewel."

It was
not in Hiccup's
nature, and he could
not be anything other
than the boy he was.

Instead, he turned right around
and flung the Dragon Jewel as far as he
could, way, way out into the sea. And then he
turned to the dragon Furious.

"*You would not break the Jewel, either, if you were living in my skin*," shouted Hiccup passionately to the dragon. "*I know you would not do it. You are not a monster, and I trust you not to kill me. And I promise you in return that I will build a new world, a better world, a world worthy of both our species. Not our species as they are, but as they could be.*"

Hiccup shut his eyes and waited.

Hiccup **flung** the

Dragon Jewel as far as

he could, way out to sea.

The dragon could not believe it. The sheer unexpectedness of this action on the part of Hiccup made him halt once more. He started in shock, as if he'd been reminded of something, and after watching in confusion as the Jewel dropped into the ocean, he seemed to grow angrier than ever.

"What are you DOING?" roared the dragon.

The Vikings could not believe it either.

"I DON'T BELIEVE IT!" roared Very Vicious the Visithug, who was having his turn with the telescope-thingy. "THE KING HAS THROWN THE JEWEL AWAY!"

There was a cry of horror from the Vikings watching on the clifftops.

"NO! NOT POSSIBLE!"

And then a groan...

"WE ARE DOOMED..."

"SING, BOYS, SING!" roared Gobber the Belch, desperately, as if by the mere power of song they could reverse the doom that awaited them.

Half of the Vikings fell to their knees and began to sing. The other half prepared for the total war that they felt sure was now about to happen after Furious killed the King.

"I told you," hissed the witch. "I TOLD YOU!"

When you are doomed, there is still some small satisfaction in having been right all along.

"Fool," snarled the dragon Furious, recovering himself. "Fool...Your puny human arms cannot throw that Jewel far enough. You cannot lose it that way..."

The dragon's enormous eyes could see the Jewel as it dropped, like a speck of plankton, into the sea. He reached out and caught up the Jewel with his left paw as it fell through the ocean. The dragon held up the Jewel victoriously, so his dragon troops could see he had it.

"Our leader has the Dragon Jewel!" roared the dragon rebellion dragons in triumph. And then the dragon prepared to kill the boy. But in that second, when the dragon should have made the final deadly strike, something happened.

The dragon saw the boy in front of him, arms spread wide and defenseless in supplication. There is nothing more defenseless than a defenseless human.

No teeth, no talons, no thunderbolts, no fire. No Jewel, the wet hair sticking up around the Dragonmark on his forehead. The boy stood there calmly with his arms spread wide and his eyes shut, and around his head there flapped a tiny, selfish little dragon, Toothless, who was frantic with anxiety.

Finally, in a pathetic attempt to shield the boy,

Toothless settled over Hiccup's heart and spread wide his wings.

On the little dragon's chest there was a scar.

And in that moment in which the dragon Furious should have taken the kill, an old, old memory intervened, of another boy, another time, another scar.

For there had been three Hiccups: Hiccup the First, Hiccup the Second, and Hiccup the Third. And here there were three Sea-Dragons: one old, one young, and one in the prime and glory and power of middle life. Every one of the three had a scar upon his chest.

The dragon Furious had gotten his own scar from when he had once leaped, with the same terror and desperation as Toothless, to try and save his human brother, Hiccup Horrendous Haddock the Second. The Stormblade pierced his chest in that terrible, hopeless leap. It wounded but did not kill his younger dragon self, so much larger and grander than this ridiculous little creature. But for all the dragon's might, his muscles and his fire, he could not save Hiccup Horrendous Haddock the Second from dying.

The dragon Furious had thought he had forgotten.

He'd thought that one hundred years in chains, broken and in wingless solitude, had killed the love that had made him leap. But the past never really leaves us.

Love never dies, as the ruby heart's stone taught Hiccup, and even the Stormblade cannot kill love.

Once we love, we cannot forget, though the flesh hardens around the wound that once bled, though it be buried in one hundred years of chains and twisted around with the cruel, growing thorns of the choking forest. A door opened in the dragon's mind that he had been trying to keep closed for many long years so that he could carry out his rebellion. When it finally opened, it did so with the same sudden force with which Hiccup's memory had returned in the ruins of Grimbeard's Castle. And now that it had opened, even just a crack, it was impossible to shut once again.

The mind is a strange universe. In that precious second, that moment on Tomorrow in which the future of human and dragon hung in the balance, the long-distant past of yesterday came back to the dragon Furious as pin-sharp fresh as if it were right now, this minute...and he could not make the kill.

The dragon snorted, shook his head, tried to force himself to do it, to make those electric lightning bolts come out...but they would not come. The dragon bellowed with fury at himself, tried again once more...

"NOOOOO!" roared the dragon Furious. "I have to do it! I must fulfill my promise!"

But no, however hard he tried, thrashing his tail madly with anger, he could not make himself do it.

Far, far in the distance, Humungously Hotshot the Hero, and the Ten Fiancés, and Tantrum the Hero, and Valhallarama, and many, many more of the Vikings were on their knees, eyes closed, singing one of the old Viking songs, and you could just about hear it, very, very faintly, through the rain and the smoke and the fire:

"Once I loved truly, Thor, and my heart paid the price,
Let me love truly, Thor, let me love TWICE!"

The Wodensfang, trembling, opened his eyes. He, too, had been waiting for the terrible pain of the dragon's lightning bolts, the final scorching flames.

But they never came.

"My one true love vanished, and my heart broke that day," sang those beautiful Viking voices, very, very softly in the distance. *"But once you've loved truly, Thor, then you know the way!"*

20. ...IT CERTAINLY SCARES THE LIVING DAYLIGHTS OUT OF ME

Sweat was pouring down Hiccup's face. He was trembling, back braced, expecting to feel the fiery flames of the dragon...

...but they never came.

Hiccup opened his eyes.

The dragon was staring down at him with those tortured eyes, an extraordinary expression on his face, smoke snorting from his nostrils, shaking his steaming head from side to side as he struggled with conflicting emotions.

Hiccup's heart beat fast...Oh my goodness...His gamble might just work...Toothless's brave action had made the dragon pause, and Hiccup had a chance now, a chance to talk, and to change the dragon's mind.

"You have to give this new world a chance, Furious," cried Hiccup urgently, holding out his arms to the dragon in supplication, a trembling, shivering Toothless still shielding his Master's heart. "Look!" said Hiccup, pointing at his forehead. "This Dragonmark is a symbol of the brotherhood between humans and dragons. I will swear by this Mark that no dragon in this Wilderwest, where I am now the King, will ever be a slave again."

The dragon Furious trembled as he looked upon that Mark.

For now all the memories that he had been struggling to suppress for so many, many years came thundering back in a rush that nearly overwhelmed him. He remembered another time, another boy. Hiccup Horrendous Haddock the Second, who had once been the dragon Furious's blood brother.

He remembered playing in the Grimler Dragon cave, when the little, wild Hiccup the Second was still a baby and they could only speak to each other in Dragonese.

He remembered the days with Hiccup the Second upon his back, when the world seemed young and new and full of possibilities, flying high in the air together in such perfect harmony that you could hardly tell where the boy ended and the dragon began.

Throwing away that Jewel was just the sort of incredibly stupid thing that Hiccup the Second would have done.

The dragon Furious remembered when the defiant, teenage Hiccup the Second had put the Mark on his

the Dragonmark
(Mark of a HERO)

own forehead, to show his love for the dragon Furious, and how the boy's father, Grimbeard the Ghastly, had raged at him in a fury, for the Mark was banned and had become the Mark of a slave.

How his father had stormed! How Grimbeard had tried to wash it off, swearing to Thor as he rubbed away at it with his sleeve...But nothing would rub that Mark off, for the Dragonmark can never be removed.

The dragon Furious had thought that not one speck of love remained. Not a jot. Not a whisper. One hundred years in captivity had cured him of that love and turned his heart into a dark and hungry forest...

But it appeared that he had not been completely cured after all.

Human hearts can break and heal and beat again, and it appears that *dragon* hearts are the same.

Hiccup the Second was gone forever, separated from the dragon by an ocean of sky and time, and he could not come back to visit.

But still, somehow, a tiny part of him *was* here, in the raggedy, awkward shape of Hiccup Horrendous Haddock the Third.

And the dragon Furious loved him.

The dragon swayed back and forth, snorting and bellowing in pain and confusion. He had been stoking his anger for so long, feeding it, nourishing it. So this unexpected damming of his anger, this sudden uncertainty, was difficult for him to bear.

"We will miss our chance," said the dragon Furious. "This is the dragons' last chance..."

"No, no, that is not true!" cried Hiccup. "Dragons and humans can live together! I am the King now, and I will make this Wilderwest a better world, a world in which there is no slavery, and the two of us live freely. A world of equality and freedom..."

"It is too late," said the dragon, and now he seemed distressed and angry at himself, raking his own body with his long talons in his indecision. "Or it is too early. Whatever it is, it is the wrong time...Why can I not do this? I am failing as a King to my dragons if I do not kill you, boy..."

"Perhaps not," said Hiccup eagerly, for he could sense the great restless creature was open to persuasion now. "Perhaps being the best King you can be means giving this a chance again..."

"Ah, but we dragons are older than you are. We have seen all this before," said the dragon Furious, with a strange kind of longing in his voice. The Sea-Dragon brought up his gigantic, broken head.

"Maybe this is possible...Maybe...The boy

did find the Jewel, after all, and maybe that it is indeed a message from Fate…"

Maybe…

Maybe…

Maybe…

Hiccup waited, throat dry, heart beating. Had he said enough? Had he used the right words?

The dragon swayed from side to side, racked with indecision.

And then something dreadful happened.

Three boys named Hiccup.
Three dragons, each with a scar
above their heart.

333

21. THE WITCH INTERVENES WITH FATE

Just when it seemed as if things might be moving in the right direction, just when it seemed as if Hiccup might be able to persuade the dragon Furious to call off his rebellion…something dreadful happened.

It was, I suppose, an illustration of everything the dragon Furious was most worried about: that despite all that the good humans do, there are always the evil ones, hiding in the shadows.

The evil one in question was, of course, the witch.

She had seen Hiccup throw the Jewel. She had seen the dragon Furious hesitate. She had known that the horrible little rat would be *talking*, Thor rot him. She had watched it all, and she had the sense that everything she had lived for, everything she had worked for, everything she had *killed* for, was slipping through her bony fingers, and she could no longer bear it.

Twenty years trapped in a tree trunk, slowly growing white as a slug, quietly going mad in that darkness, gnawing on rats' bones, licking the bark for moisture, as she laid her plans like spiders' webs and looked back into the past, searching for signs and planning destinies and willing, willing, willing her son Alvin to be the King.

Now, at the last minute, was it all to be snatched away from her by one little rat-runt of a boy?

She realized that she needed to make her own intervention with Fate.

She bounded on all fours up to Madguts the Murderous, who had always been one of the most staunch of the Alvinsmen, trying not to wrinkle up her nose, for the repulsive diet* of Madguts the Murderous made him really rather smelly. "The little rat is giving us away! He's thrown away the Jewel!" hissed the witch.

"What are you talking about?" asked Gumboil, Madguts's henchman.

"The boy's actions prove he is not the real King," sneered the witch. "Giving away the Dragon Jewel when he has it in his hand! Dangerous foolishness. Trust me, I can look into the future. The dragon Furious has the Jewel, see, clasped in his ugly paw!"

"Oh…" Gumboil and Madguts could see the witch's point.

"You must lend Alvin your Stealth Dragon, and Alvin will kill the dragon Furious and retrieve the Jewel before it is too late," said the witch. "The dragon Furious will not have mercy. He is not capable of it, and the boy

---

*The Murderous Tribe lived on a diet of month-old rotten haddock stuffed with pickled onions and bad eggs, all washed down with enormous quantities of beer.

is a fool to risk all on the heart of a reptile. Dragons are monsters. They are not capable of the higher feelings like us human beings. Mercy is what distinguishes us from the beasts…"

Madguts the Murderous grunted in agreement, rubbing his filthy hands together, prettily decorated as they were with tattoos of human skulls (an artistic demonstration of the higher feelings of human beings, of course).

"But surely Alvin cannot intervene…" said Gumboil. "That would be breaking the rules…The world will end—"

"Pshaw!" spat the witch. "There is no time for scruples when the future of humanity is on the line! I repeat, the boy's actions make him a *traitor*, and Alvin, who is the real King, should be out there negotiating for us instead.

"Besides," the witch pointed out craftily, "if Alvin is riding the Stealth Dragon, the dragon Furious will not realize he is there until it is too late…"

"But that's cheating!" protested Gumboil. Even the Murderous Tribe still had a twisted sense of honor.

"The future of humanity is worth a little cheating," said the witch. "Besides, it is not really cheating, is it, when Alvin is the true King?"

Madguts the Murderous never lent anyone his Stealth Dragon, ever since an unfortunate incident a couple of years earlier when Bertha of the Bog-Burglars had stolen it for a bet.* But it did seem that this was a rather special occasion.

So he reluctantly grunted his approval.

Gumboil scurried toward the Stealth Dragon and ordered him to follow Alvin on this one special occasion.

"Mother, you have to stop interfering!" whispered Alvin furiously as the witch pushed him toward the Stealth Dragon, headbutting his reluctant ankles, dragging her teeth on his trousers. "I don't want to go! It's like a furnace out there! We can bide our time...wait for our moment to strike in the darkness—"

"You have run out of time for biding!" spat the witch. "Where is your sense of ambition? This is the moment for striking, Alvin. For seizing your destiny!"

They were alone now, beside the shadowy outline of the obedient Stealth Dragon patiently awaiting orders.

"This isn't my way of doing things, Mother!" howled Alvin. "You have to let me do things *my* way...I'm more of a skulker, a lurker, a poisoner in the shadows. I don't like to put myself in personal danger unless I know I can win."

---

*Please see Book 6: *A Hero's Guide to Deadly Dragons.*

"Cowardice!" hissed the witch. "Whining! I'm not interested in that wishy-washy personal stuff; just get on that dragon's back before I bite you! Don't worry, I will do your killing for you, but I need you there. Give me your second Fire-Suit and the Stormblade."

Sulkily, Alvin handed them over. Sulkily, he climbed onto the back of the Stealth Dragon.

You have to hand it to the witch: For an elderly woman, she certainly had courage.

She wrapped herself in the Fire-Suit, seized the Stormblade, vaulted onto the back of the Stealth

Dragon, kicked her bony heels at the dragon's flanks, and with a whoop from the witch, the Stealth Dragon took off. As he leaped upward, he turned from the browny hue of a brackish bog to the exact color of the flames and blackened clouds of the sky above.

"You have to let me do things my way, Mother..."

22. THAT'S WHY THEY CALL HIM ALVIN THE TREACHEROUS (THE CLUE IS IN THE NAME, REALLY.)

So while Hiccup and the dragon Furious were talking, while the dragon Furious was wondering if he should indeed call off the rebellion, they could not see the witch and Alvin coming toward them from across the Bay.

You cannot sense a Stealth Dragon approaching. That is what makes them such an effective military weapon. No sound. No sight. No smell.

The Stealth Dragon, when he swoops, can even slow down his heart to such a muffled beat that the most hearing-sensitive of little dragons cannot hear it approaching. Nobody quite knows how they can do that without dying, or how the beating of their wings is so quiet that it is undetectable.

Crouching down low on the Stealth Dragon's back, the witch and Alvin were invisible too, hidden by his camouflaged spine fins and his silent beating wings.

They had seen the dragon Furious take the Jewel in his hand, and it was the Witch's amiable intention to attack that hand, so that Alvin could steal the Jewel. In the meantime, she would kill Hiccup.

"Are we all quite clear on the plan?" snapped the witch. "First we fly to the dragon's hand, Stealth Dragon, so Alvin can steal the Jewel. And then I deal with the boy…"

The Murderous Tribe knows how to train dragons, and the Stealth Dragon obeyed without question. Alvin was more mutinous, muttering darkly under his breath.

The dragon Furious and Hiccup were so busy concentrating on each other that it was almost as if the world around them had ceased to exist.

The distant sounds of the chanting rebellion dragons, the songs and battle cries of the humans, had all faded into nothingness as their world narrowed into a conversation between a boy and a dragon.

On, on, the Stealth Dragon flew toward the reef, with the boy and the mighty dragon unconscious of their approach.

Despite himself, the shaking, wavering dragon Furious was allowing himself to believe, to hope, in the future.

But some instinct deep within him sensed approaching danger, and his ears pricked up, and he sniffed the air.

"What's wrong?" whispered Hiccup as the dragon

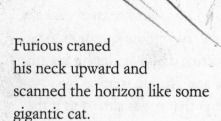

Furious craned
his neck upward and
scanned the horizon like some
gigantic cat.

Hiccup drew his sword. A cold,
cold feeling had come over him. He peered
around, shading his eyes as he tried to see
through the drifting smoke. There was
nothing to see but the fires that marked
the boundary of the Combat Ring, and
way, way in the distance, the restless
dragons and the restless Vikings,
hoping for peace, but ready for war.

The dragon Furious's beautiful
eyes were so acute that he could spot a
field mouse hidden in a bog from a distance
of ten miles. He could see stars and moving
comets that were invisible to the human eye. It was

342

even said that he could see through walls, and into time itself, although I do not know if that is possible.

But even a dragon Furious cannot see something that is invisible, and although he sensed there was danger, he could not see where it was coming from. A threatening rumble rose deep within his throat, the sound an animal makes before it strikes. His head swiveled around, searching, searching with his eyes, his nose, his ears...but finding nothing.

Cooee, thought the witch gloatingly to herself. *Cooooeee... You can't see us, you stupid great fire-spurting reptile. And you won't see us until it is too late.*

Even Alvin smiled, beginning to enjoy himself as they drew nearer, and it was clear that the dragon Furious could not sense them.

The dragon Furious's eyes scanned the entire Bay without finding anything. His nostrils wrinkling, he drank in the smell of burning trees, of wet Vikings, even the faint but distinct stink of the Murderous Tribe. But nothing else.

The dragon's hearing was so acute that he could hear the soft beating wings of the Neverbirds, even though they were flying at a very safe distance indeed, and the fast beating heart of Hiccup, trembling at his feet, and the even faster beating hearts of the little dragons and of Windwalker. But nothing else.

The dragon gave a great snort and shook out his wings as if to shake off his ugly anxieties. There was nothing to be afraid of. He turned his head back toward Hiccup to continue their conversation…

And then he gave a great yowl of startled surprise.

Alvin's hook had buried itself in the dragon's hand, and in the shock of the moment, just as if you or I had been stung by a wasp or a bee, the dragon Furious opened his great paw and shook it in pain.

The dragon Furious's hand opened, and out of his hand fell the Jewel.

DOWN
DOWN
DOWN...

…and Alvin kicked his heels into the Stealth Dragon's flanks and the Stealth Dragon dived after it.

Hiccup ran across the reef, barely noticing the sting of the rocks beneath his feet, slipping and sliding on patches of slimy seaweed. He saw it all, for the Stealth Dragon turned visible for a second in his excitement as he dived, and while the Jewel itself was too small for Hiccup to see, what he *could* see was the Stealth Dragon diving after something, and Alvin and the witch crouching on the Stealth Dragon's back.

Out on the clifftops, Luna saw it too, with her sharp dragon eyesight, and she beat her wings in anxiety.

Valhallarama, watching through the telescope, asked uncertainly, "What's going on?"

Alvin! thought Hiccup. *Alvin and the witch! Those traitors...those villains.*

Furious has dropped the Jewel! They have made him drop the Jewel!

And then there was another moment in which the Stealth Dragon's excitement briefly turned him visible again. The Jewel was too small to see, but Hiccup clearly recognized the moment that a dragon takes his prey. The Stealth Dragon's mouth opened and he caught something in it and soared upward, Alvin punching the air in triumph. It was a momentary vision, before the Stealth Dragon turned invisible again.

The dragon Furious saw it too, and gave a snort of fear and fury.

"NOOOOOOO!" cried Hiccup in despair, falling flat on his face in the seaweed. It was so cold beneath his knees, so cold on his cheek, as he groveled there, helplessly caught in the slime, and then he looked up at the uncaring heavens above, where you could still hear the echoes of Alvin's triumphant whooping.

"Noooo..." whispered the Wodensfang. How could Fate be so cruel?

Alvin had the Jewel. And he knew what he had to do with it.

At the very last moment, Alvin the Treacherous had snatched away the beginnings of hope and turned it into despair.

23. TOTAL WAR

"DRAGON REBELLION DRAGONS!" trumpeted the dragon Furious, all his indecision gone, and incandescent with rage, shooting thunderbolts and flames in random directions, hoping to hit his invisible assailants. "BETRAYAL! TREACHERY AND BETRAYAL! The humans have broken the rules of single combat! COME TO MY AID!"

All along the clifftops, with screams of fury, the great and terrible army of dragon rebellion dragons, like many clouds of locusts, launched themselves into the air and flew into the Bay, or swam up from the depths, their predatory fins slicing through the water, spouting fire from their blowholes as they made their way to the battle.

Dreamserpents, Flamehuffers, Firestarters, Riproarers, Grimlers and Monstrous Nightmares, Raptortongues and Triple-Header Rageblasts, Horrors and Dreaders and Breathquenchers joined the dreadful invasion that blasted into the Bay.

Rhinobacks lumbered into the air like gigantic armored rhinoceroses. Driller Dragons with their revolving horns, Razorwings shooting their dreadful barbed arrows, Tongue-twisters, Savagers, and

Brainpickers spreading their terrible wings and flying like nightmares toward the reef. From the snowy north came white Polarserpents with their horns like unicorns, Saber-Toothed Driver Dragons and Leviathorgans, launching their bone spears, venturing south for this occasion only.

Worst of all, there came the horrors from the greatest depths of the oceans: Sharkworms cutting through the water with their serrated fins, braving the cold waters despite the lack of the Summer Current.

Darkbreathers who live so long in the darkness that their hearts have slowed to a terrible coldness and they have a longing for the light. Thor's Thunderers sending out crackling bursts of electricity, churning up the waters so that great rolling waves spread across the Bay and threatened to swamp the reef.

The dreadful bulk of the multi-eyed Woden's Nightmares, nearly as huge as the dragon Furious himself, lighting up the sky with their eyebeams, and pouring out a strange, black substance across the waters, which they then set fire to, so that the whole of Wrecker's Bay turned into a sea of flame.

"The dragons are breaking the truce!" yelled Stoick the Vast. "Quick, everyone, get on dragonback to fight them! My son is out there, all alone!"

The Vikings rushed for their dragons.

They too made a dreadful and frightening army of surprising numbers, seated on dragonback and screaming defiance, and shooting their arrows, and yelling their chilling war cries as they rode into battle.

For many fierce dragons had joined the human side during the war: the intelligent dragons out of loyalty to their human masters, the less clever ones out of fear or obedience.

Gronckles, Marsh and Red Tigers, Bullroughers, Rocket Rippers, Devilish Dervishes, Deadly Nadders, Common or Gardens and Basic Browns, Gloomers, Two-Headed Gormatrons, the dreadful armored Eight-Legged Battlegores that could carry up to ten Vikings at a time, Bullguard Slavedragons, all carrying their human masters into battle, or flying by their side, shooting flames at the enemy.

Stoick on his Bullrougher, and Valhallarama on her Silver Phantom, Mogadon the Meathead, and all the other Dragonmarker Tribes of the Archipelago; the Alvinsmen, led in Alvin's absence by Madguts the Murderous, the Villains, Hysterics, the Bashem-Oiks, the Visithugs, Danger-Brutes, the Berserks, and the Uglithugs. Barbara the Barbarian on her Lightwing, her cat balancing on the dragon's head.

Then the humans from farther afield: the Wanderers, the Outcasts, the Nowhere Men, not to mention Humungously Hotshot the Hero and his wife Tantrum the Hero and the Ten Fiancés.

The humans had their own terrible weapons.

Axes, spears, arrows, swords—of course they had all of these.

But when Alvin and his Alvinsmen had been besieged every night by the dragon rebellion in Prison Darkheart, that great fortress in the Amber Slavelands, they had been forced to develop new and terrible weapons in order to defend themselves.

From the cliffs of Lava-Lout Island, great catapults shot rocks at the advancing dragon rebellion army, and strange heavy balls that exploded on impact and caused terrible injuries.

Even mighty Rageblasts, or Savagers, or Brainpickers, when hit by those cannonballs, fell shrieking from the sky.

Such is the destructiveness of the clever human mind when it turns to invention.

"I SAW THE FUTURE!" roared the dragon Furious. "IF WE DID NOT DESTROY THE HUMANS, IT WOULD BE TOO LATE! AND LOOK, IT *IS* TOO LATE!"

NO-O-

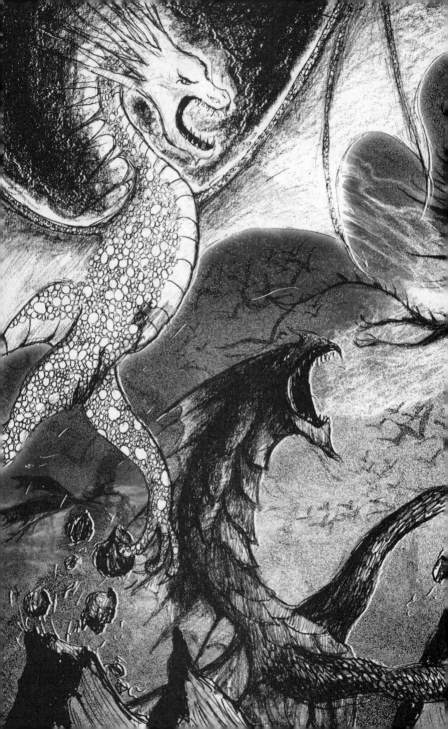

"No!" shouted Hiccup. "The final battle. The ultimate confrontation…I saw it in my dream, back when I was hidden in the underground hideout…This is everything I hoped would not happen."

He crawled forward, desperately trying to get to his feet, with Toothless holding on to him, holding him tight, just as he used to sleep with him a lifetime ago in their little bed on Berk, Hiccup feeling his lovely, wriggly warmth for what he hoped would not be the last time.

Oh, please, begged Hiccup. *Please let this not be the end of dragons…*

I do not want a world without Toothless…

I do not want a world where I am wingless, crawling in the mud like this, rather than touching the stars on the back of the Windwalker…

Up above, it was as if the heavens knew the significance of this moment. The thunderclouds had gathered, and it was hard to tell whether the lightning blasts shooting across the sky were thunderbolts from the storm, or the dragon Furious, or the Woden's Nightmare dragons, or the Thor's Thunderers.

"Giveitmegiveitmegiveitme!" giggled Alvin, forgetting his safety in his excitement, and wriggling along the Stealth Dragon's neck, gleefully stretching out his hand.

The Stealth Dragon, very proud of himself, turned his head, and gave the Dragon Jewel to Alvin.

"The Jewel..." sighed Alvin contentedly. "The real Dragon Jewel, in my hand at last!" Alvin smiled a slow and very nasty smile indeed. "And *now* I know its secret. All I need to do is break it, and the dragons are destroyed forever!"

"Oh, well done, my darling!" cooed the witch. "I told you we could do this."

And then...

"Uh-oh..." as she saw the advancing dragon army almost upon them. If one of those flames or bolts of electricity were to accidentally hit the Stealth Dragon, he might be shocked into visibility.

"Quick!" the Witch urged. "You need to break the Jewel!"

Alvin bashed the Jewel against the spiny fin of the Stealth Dragon's back. Nothing happened, for the fin wasn't really hard enough to break anything. He bashed it a little harder. Again nothing happened.

"Break! Break! Break! You stupid thing!" hissed Alvin, walloping it as hard as he could, but the Jewel remained obstinately unchipped.

"Break it Alvin, break it!" screeched the witch, biting Alvin on the shoulder. "Why are you hesitating?"

"It's harder to break than it looks, you old bat!" snapped Alvin furiously.

Alvin held the Jewel firmly in one hand, and tried to rip at it with the hook at the end of his other arm, but the Stealth Dragon swerved abruptly, jiggling his arm, so Alvin missed the Jewel entirely, and dug the hook into his own palm instead.

"Ow!" howled Alvin.

Trying to smash a Jewel while you are sitting on the back of a Stealth Dragon who is traveling at considerable speed and swiveling to evade random lightning bolts is a harder proposition than you might think.

If you've ever attempted to open an oyster with your bare hands while riding sidesaddle on a galloping horse that is being chased by wolves, you might have some idea of what I mean.

"Curses!" swore Alvin. "What I need is a *nutcracker*!" But of course he didn't have a nutcracker *on* him, so that wasn't very helpful.

He put the Jewel in his jaws and tried to clamp down on it, but only succeeded in breaking a tooth.

"Oh for Thor's sake," cursed Alvin. "This is ridiculous."

He was running out of time. He would have to

break this beastly Jewel somehow, and fast. It needed to be smashed between two hard objects, and all he could think of now was the ground, and his boot. That would do it. He'd smashed mussels like that all his life.

"Stealth Dragon! I want you to land on the rocky end of that reef, as far away from the Hiccup boy as possible!" ordered Alvin.

Obediently, the beautiful dragon landed elegantly on the reef. Alvin jumped off the Stealth Dragon's back while the witch stayed crouching in between his spine fins, clutching the Stormblade.

With trembling, excited fingers, Alvin placed the Dragon Jewel down on a rock.

He raised his boot.

Hiccup saw him.

Saw the outline of his wicked figure, framed against the flaming sea.

But he was too far away for Hiccup to catch and stop him, slipping and sliding on the seaweed, though he was running with all his might.

"Furious!" cried Hiccup despairingly.

Furious could have intervened.

But Hiccup's voice was so small and thin, and the human forces and the dragon forces had now joined in bloody, terrible battle in the air above the reef. The

Alvin brought down his boot in a swy

dragon
Furious,
way up above,
was being attacked
by the humans, and
although he was searching
desperately through the smoke and
the lightning bolts for the Stealth Dragon
and the Jewel, he could not hear the tiny sound
of Hiccup's voice calling up to him.

"TREACHERY AND BETRAYAL!"
snorted the dragon Furious. "TREACHERY AND
BETRAYAL!"

Alvin brought down his boot in a swift
stamping motion.

stamping motion...

24. DID I MENTION THAT THE PAST HAS A WAY OF CATCHING UP WITH US EVENTUALLY?

But before Alvin's boot could land, he was knocked violently sideways, as if he were being booted himself by the boot of Destiny.

Hiccup blinked, unable to believe what was happening.

But there it was, clearly, in front of his eyes. One second Alvin was bringing down his foot on the Jewel; the next he was soaring through the air, and landing on a rock some twenty feet away with an "*Oof!*" of infuriated surprise, and remaining pinned there by an invisible force.

Hiccup watched, open-mouthed, as the air above Alvin solidified into the Deadly Shadow pinning down Alvin with his two front feet, and Camicazi and Fishlegs sitting astride him—Camicazi making the Bog-Burglar victory salute.

Back on the clifftop, Camicazi's sharp Bog-Burglar eyes had seen the witch and Alvin sneaking away on the back of the Stealth Dragon, and so she and Fishlegs had followed them on the back of the Deadly Shadow.

One invisible dragon following another.

And the past had at last caught up with Alvin the Treacherous, as the past eventually has a way of catching up with all of us.

Fishlegs, on the back of the Deadly Shadow dragon, wanted some answers.

"The Jewel…maybe the Jewel is all right…I don't think Alvin's boot came down in time…" gasped Hiccup. "Oh, thank Thor and Woden and the great bushy plaits of Freya herself!" cried Hiccup, hugging Toothless with all his might—lovely, wriggly Toothless, still very much alive, and licking him all over his face with his little forked tongue.

Despite his best efforts, Hiccup wasn't making much progress across the slippery, slidy, seaweedy rocks. Above them raged the chaos, screams, and terror of the final battle, talon against shield, arrow against dragon skin.

"Toothless, quick, fetch the Jewel before somebody else gets it," Hiccup gasped.

Toothless squeaked in excitement, and dashed off to find the Jewel, lying horribly exposed on the reef.

Camicazi hopped off the Deadly Shadow's back

feeling emotional brought out the Berserk in Fishlegs

to look for the Jewel too. Fishlegs got off to question the cursing, squirming Alvin.

Fishlegs was feeling extremely emotional, and feeling emotional brought out the Berserk in him. An excitable rash was spreading across his face and confusing his feelings further.

"I have been looking for my family for fifteen years," said Fishlegs, looking down at Alvin, squirming in the iron clasp of the Deadly Shadow's talons. "Fifteen years of searching, fifteen years of wondering, and I have to say, whoever I dreamed my father would be, I never in a thousand years thought it might be *you*..."

"I deny everything!" spat Alvin the Treacherous. "LET ME GO! I have a Jewel to break!"

"I mean, I don't even *like* you," said Fishlegs. "How can I have a father I don't even like?"

"It's perfectly possible; I have a mother I've hated for years," raged Alvin. "And speaking of mothers, one thing she was right about: This is no time for the personal touchy-feely stuff. I'm on a mission here, so kindly get your ugly three-headed dinosaur to remove its claws from my neck; its bad breath is making me feel sick…"

"How sick would you feel if we removed your head?" cooed Arrogance.

Alvin understood a little Dragonese, and he turned pale at this.

"There must be *something* nice about you," said Fishlegs hopefully. "Do you like poetry?"

"I *hate* poetry," ground out Alvin. "I hate poets. I hate boys-with-faces-like-haddocks-that-somebody-trod-on, and if I were to have a son like you who was a runt, I would be the first one to bundle him in an old lobster pot and toss him out to sea. We have a saying in the Outcast Tribe: 'Cast out the weird, so your Tribe may be feared.' That's the only thing to do with runts."

Poor Fishlegs turned white, as if Alvin had hit him.

365

"Yes, we have a similar saying in the Hooligan Tribe: 'Only the strong can belong…'" he said miserably. "But what about my mother? Why did you abandon *her*?"

"Oh, these girls," snarled Alvin. "I have always been a good-looking man, and the Treacherous have a nice smooth way of talking. Is it my fault that some Viking vixen gets ideas above her station and thinks she can pin me down over some pathetic I'm-so-in-love-with-you nonsense? ME with my brilliant future?"

"You were married to her!" cried Fishlegs.

"I was crossing my fingers," said Alvin. "Then it doesn't count."

Now the Berserk rage really *had* gone to Fishlegs's head and he was trembling all over with temper, and a bright red itch had gotten into his eyes. His eyes streamed, and his nose ran with snot.

"RELEASE HIM, DEADLY SHADOW!" he shouted.

"Are you sure?" said Innocence, hugely disappointed.

"ALVIN THE TREACHEROUS, YOU FALSE-HEARTED YELLOW-BELLIED

MOLLUSK!" roared Fishlegs, very dignified for someone in a Berserk rage, and drawing his sword with a flourish. "I CHALLENGE YOU TO A DUEL FOR ABANDONING MY MOTHER AND LEAVING HER TO DIE OF A BROKEN HEART!"

The Deadly Shadow reluctantly released Alvin, who leaped to his feet, brushing off his

The king of the Wilderwest does not duel with RUNTS.

sleeves as if they'd been tainted by the Shadow's touch.

"*I* am the true King of the Wilderwest," sneered Alvin, "and I do not duel with *runts*. Tell you what though, runt. We'll try a little test to see if you really are a Treacherous."

Alvin threw wide his arms.

"Kill me," said Alvin softly. "One shot, and I will not hit you back, runt. See, I have not even bothered to draw my sword. Kill me…"

The Berserk rage was running through Fishlegs's veins, hot and pure as poison. But furious though he was, Fishlegs could not do it.

The temper left him, and he drooped sadly.

Alvin leaned forward and poked his iron mask in Fishlegs's face.

"You see," purred Alvin. "A *Treacherous* could

do that. *You* are not a Treacherous, you No-Named accident." Alvin turned his back on Fishlegs with a contemptuous swirl of his cloak, striding off to look for the Jewel.

Slowly Fishlegs lifted his downcast head.

And then he shouted after his father's departing

YOU are not a Treacherous, You No-Named accident.

I am Fishlegs No-Nam, the First of his Tribe!

back: "You are right! I am not a Treacherous! And YOU do not disown *me*, Alvin the Treacherous! I disown *YOU*! I cast you out as my father! I EXPEL you! I am putting you in a great big imaginary lobster pot RIGHT NOW and sending you out to sea!

"For *I* am Fishlegs No-Name, the First of his Tribe!" Fishlegs punched his fist up at the stormy heavens for emphasis. "And the motto of the No-Name Tribe is: 'Be of good cheer, ALL welcome here!'"

Fishlegs suddenly spotted a flaw in this motto, and added hurriedly, "...and everyone is welcome except for YOU, Alvin the Treacherous! *You* are OUTCAST from my Tribe!"

Camicazi still hadn't found the Jewel. She was running all over the rocks, desperately trying to find it, muttering to herself, for Bog-Burglars do not have a great deal of patience, "I mean, where is it? I'm not sure I would even recognize the beastly thing if I saw it..."

Toothless had joined her, and he had even less patience than Camicazi, so he was practically crying with annoyance. "T-t-toothless hates stupid Jewels that look exactly like all the other rocks on this stupid stupid r-r-reef..."

As he hurried off to join them, Alvin called back to Fishlegs over his shoulder: "A *Treacherous* would stab me

371

in the back right now. Whoever you are, you are no true son of mine!"

Motionless, Fishlegs watched Alvin go.

"Who am I kidding?" he whispered. "I've never been any good at the whole Viking grunting and thumping, stabbing and jabbing thing. I like playing the *lyre*, for Thor's sake. Even in a Berserk rage, I couldn't kill anybody."

"That's because you take after your mother," whispered Innocence, pressing her nose consolingly against Fishlegs's cheek.

"You're the spitting image of her," said Patience, "which is one reason we love you so much."

"She loved poetry," said Arrogance, simply. "Always singing, and laughing, and she'd have been so proud of you, Fishlegs, just like we are."

Fishlegs did not understand what they were saying, but he put his arms around the Shadow's heads and hid his face in Arrogance's neck.

"You are my family now," said Fishlegs.

"We are," "We are," "We are," hissed Innocence, Arrogance, and Patience all together. "We are yoursss forever..."

There was a horrible, screeching, screaming noise from above. A noise so screamingly, desperately awful that it felt as if the hairs on your head were being dragged out by the roots, a noise that sent terror to the very depths of your soul.

Alvin froze for one moment, and then gave a yell of pure fear as he saw what was racing down toward them.

The dragon Guardians of Tomorrow were coming for Alvin…

That was *their* terrible sound as they hurtled through the air, changing as they flew from air into fire and back again. One second they were howling tunnels of wind, the next they were flaming bullets; and so fast was their descent you could only see the vague outline of their thunderbolt progress.

They had been watching languidly from their airy perches in the upper atmosphere to check that the rules of single combat were observed correctly.

They saw Alvin and the witch sneak into the Combat Ring, they saw them strike the dragon Furious, and they saw Alvin steal the Jewel.

"He has desecrated the rules of single combat!" howled the dragon Guardians of Tomorrow, as they dived downward at unimaginable speeds. "Come, Fates, come my dragon Valkyries, come, my pretty kittens of Destiny! *We* know the fate for those who transgress the iron laws of the Archipelago, for we

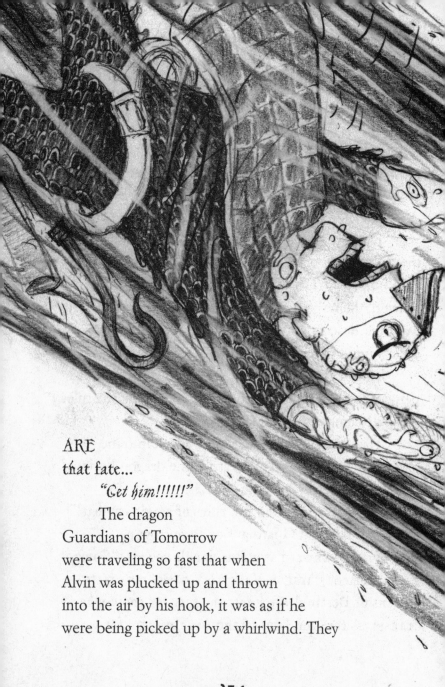

ARE
that fate...
   "Get him!!!!!!"
      The dragon
Guardians of Tomorrow
were traveling so fast that when
Alvin was plucked up and thrown
into the air by his hook, it was as if he
were being picked up by a whirlwind. They

hit the reef like an exploding bomb, bounced off
it, and caught Alvin, yelling with fear, and
took him up and up...

The dragon Guardians of
Tomorrow had taken Alvin
the Treacherous in their
invincible iron grip,
up and up and
up to drown
his frail

human flesh in the ice and fire of the upper atmosphere, so that he could never again return to earth, except as dust or purple rain.

Alvin the Treacherous had often said that a Treacherous was very hard to kill, and in his case, that saying could not have been truer.

Alvin had survived the booby trap of Grimbeard's coffin (that was when he lost his hand), being swallowed by a Monstrous Strangulator (that was when he lost his hair), falling into a Sharkworm feeding frenzy (that was when he lost his eye and his leg), being eaten by a Fire-Dragon that dived into a volcano (that was when he lost his nose), dropping into the inferno when the woods of Berserk went up in flames (that was when he found his mother and started gaining an unpleasant skin condition).

But surely even ALVIN could not survive this time.

Alvin blamed Hiccup for all of his misfortunes, so the very last words you could hear him say, as he was taken ever upward into the ice and fire of Airy Oblivion, were:

"This is all your fault, Hiccup Horrendous Haddock the Thi-i-i-i-ird!"

And then he was gone.

"He's gone…" said Camicazi, gazing upward,

open-mouthed. "I don't believe it…He's really gone… This time I really, really *do* think that's the end of him. Not even Alvin could get out of that one. Wow, it's quite a way to leave this world, I have to say. You can't get more spectacular than that…"

Fishlegs felt as though he'd been hit by the same whirlwind that had snatched up Alvin. All this was rather difficult to digest. He'd spent fifteen years (and twelve books) trying to find his father, and then when he finally *did* find him, he turned out to be the most evil, wicked person in the entire Archipelago.

This is one of the tricky things about Quests. Sometimes they lead you to a disappointment or, worse, an unpleasant surprise.

One of Alvin's spare hooks came clanging down onto the reef, and his eye patch must have dropped off as he was taken upward by the dragon Guardians. The eye patch now came fluttering down from above like a malevolent black butterfly, circling a few times in the wind before landing a couple of feet from where Fishlegs was standing. Fishlegs picked it up and stuffed it in his waistcoat pocket.

So that he could think about it later.

With an excited squeak, Toothless spotted the Dragon Jewel, glistening and sparkling in a rock pool.

"T-t-toothless has found it! Toothless is b-b-brilliant! Toothless is marvelous! Toothless is best Jewel-Finder in the whole entire universe!" gloated Toothless, pouncing down toward it.

But just before Toothless reached the Dragon Jewel, the dragon Furious, desperately fighting humans in the air above, saw through the smoke and the fire and the confusion of screaming, fighting dragons and humans, down to what was happening on the reef. His magnificent eyes, which could spot a fish moving at the bottom of the ocean from the distance of a mountaintop, saw the tiny wink of the amber, nestling in the rock pool.

The dragon Furious's hand came down upon the Dragon Jewel…

SLAM!

…just before Toothless could get to it, sending a great shower of water raining over the little dragon.

"Look what you did, you great b-b-big bully!" complained Toothless as the giant hand of the dragon Furious snatched the Dragon Jewel upward.

25. HOW CAN I TRUST YOU?

The dragon Furious caught up the Jewel.

Alvin was dead. The Dragon Jewel was safe, unbroken, and in the dragon Furious's hands.

But had Alvin and the witch ruined everything nonetheless? Had they taken away the dream of a new Kingdom of the Wilderwest, even before it had really begun?

All around the Bay, the humans and the dragons were fighting the final battle, just as Fate had foretold. The air rang with the terrible sound of metal on dragon fang, the smell of burning flames, the shriek of reptile and of humans.

Had everything that Hiccup had fought for, over twelve long Quests, had it all been snatched away from him at the very last minute?

"Stop this!" cried Hiccup, yelling helplessly up at the dragon Furious. "Stop it! Alvin is dead! YOU HAVE THE DRAGON JEWEL! There is no need for this anymore!"

But the dragon Furious threw up his head to the heavens and roared in fury and in pain.

He turned his brilliant eyes upon Hiccup.

"No need? NO NEED?"

The dragon was incandescent with rage, torn with conflicting emotions. He was so burned up with fury his skin actually caught on fire. He leaned down his head toward Hiccup and opened up his mouth and roared at him in a burning hot roar so violent that Hiccup was blown back in the rush of it.

"Why did I hesitate? Why did I trust you, even for a second? Why could I not make the kill? You see what humans are? You see how your promises are worthless when there are people like those humans, waiting in the wings to poison every single promise that you make?

"HOW CAN I TRUST YOU? HOW CAN I BARGAIN WHEN HUMANS CANNOT CHANGE?"

Hiccup was sheltering in the little nooks and crannies of the Wrecker's Reef, with the dragon tearing up the rocks around him in his frustration.

"LOOK WHAT WE HAVE DONE TO OUR WORLD!" shouted Hiccup, throwing out his arms at the blackened devastation all around. "LOOK AT OUR FRIENDS, OUR COMPANIONS, DYING AND BEING WOUNDED UP THERE IN THE BATTLE!" screamed Hiccup.

The dragon did not seem to be listening, still

crumbling up the reef as fast as Hiccup could run away from him, as if Hiccup were a mouse running through a warren of little mouse holes and the dragon were a vengeful cat.

The dragon caught Hiccup in his hand, at last, and brought him up to his giant head.

"You hesitated for good reason, Furious," shouted Hiccup, tearing uselessly at the dragon's fingers as the dragon bore him upward.

"Tell me that reason," spat the dragon fiercely. "See what has happened to me? See how I am repaid for my hesitation and the curse of my love?

"My dragons are fighting the last battle, and now it seems more important to me than ever that they *should* fight it, with all the rage that they can put into fang and tooth and claw. They should not hesitate, like I hesitated, to wait for the humans to strike them down. Tell me one good reason why I should call off this rebellion now!"

Tears were pouring down Hiccup's face. "Let me talk..." replied Hiccup. This was his last chance.

He knew it.

"Just call off your Red-Rage for one moment," he begged. "Halt the war, and let me talk—"

The dragon Furious gave a long, low hiss.

"Talking changes nothing, Hiccup. Words cannot alter human or dragon nature. Has the Alvin-man taught you nothing?"

"Yes, they can," said Hiccup. "Words change everything. Let me explain," pleaded Hiccup. "Give me a moment, just a moment to explain...I ask you this in memory of Hiccup the Second."

Every time Hiccup used that name, a shiver went through the dragon.

The dragon poured lightning bolts here, there, and everywhere, shot out his deadly flames in all directions, steamed out his anger as if he would burn up the world...but he could not bring himself to kill Hiccup.

He was defeated, and he knew it.

"I am betrayed by my former self," said the dragon at last.

"You have broken me. I can no longer kill you myself, for my heart will not let me, but that does not mean that I will tell my dragons to end their battle.

"I shall halt them, but I promise nothing. Even after you have spoken, I may tell them to carry on. For what have we to lose? We dragons are lost anyway, so we might as well take as many of you humans down with us as we can..."

Oh thank Thor, thank Thor...

383

"I understand, Furious," said Hiccup. "Give me one minute, and then you can do as you wish."

Furious set Hiccup back on the rocks, and then threw back his head and poured out fire in a terrifying upward fountain.

"**HALT!**" screamed the dragon Furious. "**HALT and listen to your leader!**"

All around Wrecker's Bay, Savagers, Brainpickers, Thor's Thunderers, the whole mighty army halted in reluctant obedience to their leader.

"Listen to me, your King!" cried the dragon Furious. "Hiccup the Third, King of the humans, has something to say."

The snarling, fighting mess of dragon rebellion dragons closed up their fire-holes reluctantly, retracted their fangs a moment, and hung in the air, an angry, mutinous rabble, expecting to carry on again any second.

"Why are we stopping?" asked Very Vicious the Visithug. "These dragons will kill us all if we let them."

The humans had halted too, and sheathed their swords for a moment, all the while looking around with wary eyes.

Hiccup tried to calm his frantically beating heart. He couldn't mess this up.

"Stormfly," whispered Hiccup, to Camicazi's

hovering Mood Dragon. "I am going to speak in Dragonese, but could you translate for the humans as I go along?" Stormfly the Mood Dragon spoke Norse as well as Dragonese.

Hiccup had a chance now, a chance to talk and to change the dragon's mind.

Hiccup cleared his throat.

"Look at what we have done to the world around us," said Hiccup.

The dragons and the humans looked around at the smoking, blackened landscape.

"This war, this devastation, this violence, is all for nothing," said Hiccup. "Even if you kill me now, even if you win the final battle against my friends and fellow Vikings, you will lose many of your companion dragons in the battle. And that will not be the end.

"To the south of us is the Roman Empire, with its heavily armed and ruthless army. You may very well lose to them, Furious. You have already left it to too late, for the Romans have fearsome weapons indeed. And even if you destroy the Romans, there will be more humans...more and more of them...

"And once you have killed so many, you will have to go on, and on, and on, wading through blood and more blood, for even if there is only one human being alive, they will fight you for the sake of their dead brothers and sisters."

Hiccup's palms were damp. He rubbed them on his Fire-Suit, only succeeding in smearing them with seaweed.

"This is what total war means, Furious," he went on. "You and your dragons are not monsters, whatever you may be pretending. You may grow weary of destruction.

"Think of it, Furious," said Hiccup. "No more burning. No more smell of flaming villages. No more aching wounds and weeping for loved ones.

"No more war.

"The dragon rebellion dragons could go back home and swim happily, freely in the innocent cold snows of the north. You could fly up, up, up in the cold, clear air, pure and happy as birds. You could go home."

"Ah, home..." sighed Furious.

Home.

Furious knew that, like himself, the dragon rebellion dragons had long ago slaked their anger and revenge, and that now they were working themselves up to be angry, and that was so very, very tiring.

Their skin stung with a thousand sword cuts, pinpricks all of them, for human spears were so pitifully small, but nonetheless, tiny as they were, the sea salt made them sting as if the dragons were being pinched all over by malevolent midges.

They longed for rest, to close their eyes without always having to keep alert for danger, just to sink into a deep, deep sleep.

They were weary of the reeking smell of the blackened landscape.

The dragon rebellion dragons were tired of war, all right.

And deep in his heart the dragon Furious knew the boy was right.

Even were the dragon Furious to continue, there was always the chance that he might lose, mighty as he and his dragons were.

He had not wanted to admit, even to himself, until that very moment, that all this blood, all this violence, all this misery, might end in failure.

"Total war is not the answer, Furious," said Hiccup quietly. "Blood just draws more blood.

"You have the Jewel safe in your hand."

Uncertain, the dragon Furious clasped the Jewel tighter to comfort himself.

"Look!" said Hiccup the Third, pointing at his forehead. "This Dragonmark is a symbol of the

brotherhood between humans and
dragons. I will swear by this Mark that no
dragon in this Wilderwest that I am now the
King of will ever be a slave again..."

The dragon started, for of course the Mark
reminded him again of Hiccup the Second.

"And that I will fight for the whole of my life to
build a new and better world," finished Hiccup.

There was a long, long pause, where the dragon
Furious snorted restlessly, sending out thunderbolts
up to the sky, lashing up the ocean waves in Wrecker's
Bay so that they were churned up into frothing foam,
throwing his head wildly from side to side.

I will build a world worthy of both our species, —not as they are, but as they COULD BE!

For the dragon was at war with himself, and he knew already that he had lost.

He looked into the past, present, and future. And then he sighed.

That door that had opened in his mind, back when Toothless had protected his Master, it would not be closed again.

"You have a dragon's tongue, boy-who-has-a-name-that-I-love," breathed the Dragon. "You have snared me with your words.

"I will give the human beings one more chance.

"One more throw of the dice.

"I will give you the chance to build this new world of yours, even though I fear it is doomed."

And as he said those words, the last of his anger seemed to fade away. The flames in his eyes died down to embers.

The dragon Furious smiled, a bitter, weary smile, but a smile nonetheless.

He had not smiled in a long, long time, so it took quite an effort for him to remember how to do it. But eventually the broken, scarred, and stiff skin of the dragon's mouth twisted itself upward into something that looked a little like a smile.

"I knew it!" squeaked the Wodensfang, delirious with excitement. "I knew it!"

"BROTHER DRAGONS!" roared the dragon Furious. "LISTEN TO ME! CALL OFF THE REBELLION! I HAVE THE JEWEL SAFE IN MY HAND AND I WILL BARGAIN WITH THE KING OF THE HUMANS!"

So out there on the reef on the Doomsday of Yule, Hiccup, King of the Wilderwest, and Furious, King of the dragons, pledged their word to each other.

"I promise," Hiccup said solemnly, bowing to the dragon, "by this Mark upon my forehead, that I will strive throughout my life to build a new world, a better world, a world worthy of both our species. Not our species as they *are*, but as they *could be*. I give you my word, from King unto King."

The dragon bowed his ancient battle-scarred head to Hiccup. He struggled to make his words as loud as possible, so that all should hear them.

"I promise I shall call off this rebellion and this Red-Rage. I shall work fang and claw to make my brother dragons and the humans live together in peace. I give you my word, from King unto King."

The dragon Furious reached out a talon toward Hiccup, saying gently to Toothless, "Move aside, little toothless Sea-Dragon. You are a Hero, for you have saved your brother human today, and he has nothing to fear from me anymore."

Toothless gave a cry of alarm as the dragon Furious's talon gently tore the Fire-Suit, and there, across the scar over Hiccup's heart, the dragon Furious drew a faint scratch, just enough to draw blood.

And he took the same talon up to his own chest, and drew a little blood there too, so the human blood and the dragon blood mingled there together on the end of the dragon Furious's talon.

"We are blood brothers now, Hiccup the Third," said the dragon Furious. "Just as I was once, with Hiccup the Second.

"And...

"A PROMISE IS A PROMISE, IF IT IS MADE IN BLOOD."

The dragon sighed a deep, deep sigh, and it wasn't quite clear if that sigh was despair, or relief, or fear.

"It is love that has betrayed me," he said to the Wodensfang. "I hope your boy is worth it."

"Love is always worth it," replied the Wodensfang.

"THE DRAGON REBELLION IS OVER!" roared the dragon Furious, in the loudest roar he could manage. **"GET READY FOR PEACE!"**

"THE DRAGON REBELLION IS OVER!" cried Hiccup, punching the air in triumph. Now that the solemn moment was over, he was so wild with joy he leaped up, hugging the cartwheeling, ecstatic Toothless and the ancient Wodensfang, jigging joyfully in the air.

Up went the cry across the Bay.

"THE DRAGON REBELLION IS OVER!"

"THE DRAGON REBELLION IS OVER!"

"THE DRAGON REBELLION IS OVER!"

"I don't believe it!" Stoick the Vast was so astonished that he nearly fell off his Bullrougher riding dragon, the Thunderer. "Hiccup's done it! HE'S DONE IT! THE DRAGON REBELLION IS OVER!"

"I told you you should have faith in our son," said Valhallarama, that great Warrior, and she grinned like a little girl as Stoick embraced her across the gap between their hovering dragons.

"HE'S DONE IT! HE'S DONE IT! DIDN'T I *SAY* HE WOULD DO IT?" screamed Camicazi, wild with excitement, and Fishlegs danced with joy beside her on the reef.

The relieved cries went up from human to dragon, from dragon to human, and the cliffs of Wrecker's Bay

The Dragon Rebellion Is

echoed back the jubilant cry, over and over and over, and up in the ice and fire of the upper atmosphere the dragon Guardians of Tomorrow repeated the words to themselves languorously, and down, down, ticking in the grasses, Ziggerastica and his nanodragons repeated them lovingly:

"THE DRAGON REBELLION IS OVER, OVER, OVER..."

26.
THE PLEDGE

Ah, joyful times
indeed!

Against all odds, and
impossible as it may seem,
Hiccup had not only managed
to get himself crowned the King,
he had also averted the final battle,
and ended the dragon rebellion
without further loss of life.

But I almost dare not write what
happened next.

The jubilant dragons and humans had
forgotten about the witch.

The witch, who was crouching like a white frog
in the shadows, still hidden between the spines of an
invisible Stealth Dragon.

The witch had seen her beloved Alvin have his
Kingdom taken from him, had seen him taken up to his
death by the dragon Guardians of Tomorrow.

Everything she had worked for her whole life was over.

And it was all the fault of that Hiccup boy.

So there she was, holding the Stormblade, and she had only one thought now, and that was to kill Hiccup.

As we have just seen, those who have loved, and been loved, can never forget that love.

But there are some who hate, who cannot forget that either, and the witch's hate went on like an unstoppable clockwork thing. She charged forward, nursing her hatred like it was something precious, Stormblade high above her head, whispering sweet hate-thoughts and revenge-curses to herself like a Valkyrie.

"Swoop close in, Stealth Dragon," whispered the witch. "Land right next to him. I need to be very close, so close that I could hug the boy. So close that I can leap off your back and sink this blade into his

The Witch's hate went on, like an unstoppable clockwork thing

chest, before the little rat even knows I am there.

"This is our time," crooned the witch. "Ah, you know it, don't you, Stormblade? You have drunk the blood of Hiccup the Second, and now you are thirsting for the blood of Hiccup the Third...

"History repeats itself..." whispered the witch lovingly. "History repeats itself...History keeps on repeating itself..."

The humans and the dragons were erupting with joy, down there on the reef. Human was embracing dragon, and dragon was embracing human, and the whole world was celebrating, dancing for joy.

The dragon Furious lifted up his great head and shot thunderbolt after thunderbolt into the air.

"PEACE!" roared the dragon.

"PEACE!" roared the humans.

He even LOOKED a little like he might remember how to be peaceful, that great angry dragon, and he was smiling once again, those stormy eyes becalmed.

But as the dragon Furious turned his head downward, he caught, out of the corner of his eye, a tiny glint of something shiny in the air.

What was that?

He jerked his head up again.

There it was again, a little flash, a little speck of sunlight glinting off something moving.

The dragon narrowed his eyes.

What in the name of Thor and his mighty dragon Worldshaker could it possibly be?

There it was again, a bright spark, or a wink.

Great forked-tongued giants! *It was the sun shining on the tip of a sword! A sword levitating through the air!*

It was indeed, for the witch was so eager to make the kill that she drew the Stormblade a little early and held it high above her head, so that the tip of it was visible above the body of the diving Stealth Dragon.

If you had looked down on that scene, it might have seemed as if the Stormblade itself was flying through the atmosphere, on its own, as if it were magnetically being drawn toward Hiccup's heart...

And history might, indeed, have repeated itself, had the dragon Furious not seen that tiny pinprick of a sword slicing through the clouds.

The dragon Furious gave a great scream.

He acted without thinking.

In that split second, it was as if it was a hundred years ago, when Furious looked down and saw Grimbeard the Ghastly bringing down the Stormblade against an unarmed Hiccup the Second...

Back then, Furious had desperately dived, flying with all of his wing strength…

He had tried to place his body in between his beloved Master and the sword…

But he had leaped too late.

So now, one hundred years later, the dragon sprang forward, placing his whole body between the sword and Hiccup, shielding him. He spread wide his wings and stood up to his greatest extent, so that there was suddenly an entire dragon-mountain between Hiccup and the Stormblade.

The Stealth Dragon was traveling so fast he crashed straight into the gigantic Sea-Dragon's chest. Holding the Stormblade above her head with both hands and throwing her entire body weight behind it, the witch plunged the sword into the dragon Furious's chest.

The plunge made her lose her balance; she lost her footing on the Stealth dragon's back, and with an "ooh!" of surprise, the dragon dropped away from beneath her, and the witch was left swinging from the sword hilt of the Stormblade, at a dizzyingly high distance from the ground.

The dragon Furious started in surprise and shock, just as *you* might if someone had stuck a pin into you. He looked down to see the tiny little figure of the witch swinging from that pin, equally surprised to find herself attacking Furious rather than Hiccup.

The dragon reached down and plucked the witch off him, and flicked her away with his fingers from that astonishing height…

UP, UP, UP through the air soared the witch, her little limbs working back and forth like the legs of a white cockroach…and DOWN, DOWN, DOWN she fell, in a most satisfying arc for those of us who like people being given their just rewards, right *bang-splat-plumb* into the slimy depths of the blowhole of Woden's throat.

The blowhole, so deep that it was rumored to go down to the center of the earth itself, swallowed up the witch, and then with a great satisfied belch, it shot a triumphant trumpeting

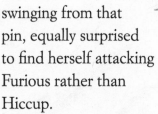

spout of
water way,
way into the air, as
if the reef itself were alive,
and were digesting its lunch.

"Oh thank Thor!"
whispered Hiccup. "The witch is
dead…"

After all these cruelties, all these
years, the witch, who was the boiled-
down essence of evil, eager for empires
and hungry for power, the witch, at last,
was dead.

It was difficult to feel any sadness for the death of
so very wicked a person.

"Are you all right, little blood brother?" asked
the dragon Furious.

"I'm fine…" replied Hiccup shakily. "I'm just
fine…Are you all right too?"

It was just a tiny scratch on his chest. The dragon
Furious would be fine.

Of course he would be fine.

The Stormblade was merely the size of a pin, or
a needle, in relation to the dragon's gigantic bulk. The
dragon had drawn out the Stormblade as if it were the

DOWN, DOWN, DOWN she fell . . .

annoying
sting of a wasp,
and flicked it away with
the same careless anger as
he had snuffed and flicked
the witch.

Surely, surely, he would
be fine.

"He's fine..." breathed the
Wodensfang, with relief. "He's
fine..."

"THE WITCH IS DEAD!
ALVIN IS DEAD, AND I HAVE
MADE THE HUMAN KING
HICCUP THE THIRD, MY BLOOD
BROTHER, A PROMISE! AND I
WILL *KEEP* THAT PROMISE," said
the dragon Furious.

The blowhole of
Woden's throat swallows
the witch

The witch was dead!!

a great trumpeting spout of water

He turned to Hiccup, and Hiccup could see the dragon's chest, where the tiny wound from the Stormblade showed an infinitesimal scratch.

"FOR A PROMISE IS A PROMISE, IF IT IS MADE IN BLOOD."

But then the great dragon stiffened and grew strangely still.

The great dragon in front of them, so splendid in the might and height of his glory, trembled and choked.

"No," said Hiccup. "No...no...no...I don't understand, Wodensfang. What is happening?"

"I don't know," whispered the Wodensfang. "But I feel a sudden dread..."

The dragon Furious had shrugged off a thousand pesky human sword cuts. The prick of a needle could not have any effect on a Sea-Dragon the size of a mountain.

Unless...

Unless the Stormblade was poisoned.

Unless it was poisoned, not with the slow-working poison of the Venomous Vorpent, for which Hiccup had found the antidote, but with the most potent and devastating drug that a wicked witch could lay her hands on.

However many good human beings there are,

trying to do good things, what do you do about the evil ones who are waiting in the wings, and who, in one second of destructive wickedness, undo all the work that the good human beings have been working on patiently for lifetimes?

No. NO.

"Wodensfang, quick! There must be something we can do," said Hiccup.

"There is nothing you can do," whispered the dragon Furious. "The witch has poisoned me..."

Hiccup gaped as the great dragon swayed before him.

"This is all my fault..." wept Hiccup.

"It is not your fault. You acted in good faith. But you see," said the dragon Furious affectionately to Hiccup, "this is what I have been trying to tell you, little blood brother...

"You cannot build this new world of yours within a generation, or even ten generations," said the dragon Furious longingly. "It will take a long, long time for humans to become better than they are now..."

He had laid his head down on the reef now, and was panting short, hard breaths. Steam came off his immense body and rose up into the air in great clouds.

The storm had passed, and all was quiet, except for

a gentle breath of rain that came down on them all like a blessing.

So many dragons and humans had died already in this battle. But there was something so dreadful about the sheer VASTNESS of this splendid creature whose life was now draining away, that brought home the destruction, the insanity, and the waste of this war.

There was a particular horror about a creature so mighty, so splendid, who moments earlier had been shooting out thunderbolts in the violent splendor of the prime of his life, being brought down so low and dying in front of their very eyes.

It made even the most bloodthirsty of the human Vikings think: *This must never happen again.*

Hiccup stretched up to the dragon's head, and held on to it with his tiny, insignificant hands, hands that could barely reach up to the dragon's great chin.

Once, a great whale had become stranded by the tide on the Long Beach on Berk. The entire village had tried to move the whale back into the sea, but they could not do it, for the poor creature was too large. Hiccup felt the same feeling of helpless rage that he was too small to do anything about this catastrophe, too tiny to prevent the dying of this enormous, terrifying, beautiful creature.

For the first time, Hiccup realized, deep in his

bones, that the dragon Furious might be right: that all Hiccup's efforts to re-create the world might be in vain, that Hiccup might need a plan to save the dragons, in the end.

And holding the dragon's dying head, the plan came to him, in the same brilliant flash as when he had found the Jewel inside the lobster necklace.

A *Jewel* of a plan.

Hiccup held the dragon's dying head.

"Do not worry, Furious," said Hiccup passionately. "You must not die worrying that because this has happened to you, the dragons will not be saved in the end. I will work my hardest to make sure that the second Kingdom of the Wilderwest is better than the first.

"But if it does happen that I get to the end of my lifetime, and it seems that humans have not improved sufficiently, then I have a plan that will save the dragons."

"Is it a c-c-clever one?" whispered Toothless.

"Clever-*ish*," said Hiccup.

"You have a plan, do you?" said the dragon Furious softly, and now his eye looking on Hiccup was definitely affectionate as well as ironic. "A plan that will save the dragons? Now, that would have to be a very clever plan *indeed*. We both know that saving the dragons may be impossible."

The dragon Furious smiled once more.

Hiccup swallowed hard.

"My plan will come into action only as a last resort," said Hiccup, his voice shaking, "if we feel it is the *only* way the dragons can be saved.

"At the moment of my death, whoever is King of the dragons at that time must lead the dragons back to the coldnesses of the north, far from men's eyes. Out in the deepest oceans, there are still parts of the world where men do not tread with their dirty feet...

"Dragons have told me that there are trenches in the darkness of the seas that are so deep, that even in a thousand years human beings will not be able to follow you there," said Hiccup. "And you dragons are of the chameleon family. You know how to hide."

The dragon Furious looked at Hiccup with a kind of thoughtful wonder.

A tiny spark of genuine hope had lit in the embers of his eyes. "We *do* know how to hide," said the dragon Furious. "We are supremely good at hiding."

"And you would get even better at it," promised Hiccup. "Even now, the nanodragons hide so brilliantly in the grasses and the heathers that unless you know they are there, and put your face right up to them, you can't see them at all.

"You would hide so effectively, so completely, that it would be as if you'd never existed. And as you begin to vanish, I promise you that I will make sure our bards and storytellers will spread the rumor that you were only ever mythical creatures, like chimeras or sphynxes. Humans of the future must never know that they share the earth with you, for then they would seek to dominate or destroy you.

"You would enter a Sleep Coma and wait for the human race to either improve its nature or to disappear. You were here long before the humans, and perhaps you will be here long after."

The dragon smiled again. He even laughed, a frail, explosive laugh.

"It is a crazy plan," said the dragon Furious, his eyes alight with genuine amusement and excitement at the thought of it. "A plan dreamed up by a lunatic or a fool. Just the sort of plan that Hiccup the Second used to come up with. He was always getting me into trouble with plans like that..."

"It *is* a crazy plan," admitted Hiccup. "And maybe I am a fool, but I *will* save the dragons, Furious;

I promise you this. Whatever happens, I will save them. I *will*, I *will*, I *will*."

He turned to the humans now, sitting silent in the surrounding skies on their dragons, awed by the dreadful sight of the great dragon Furious lying with his body slumped in the water, on the reef.

"Look! One of us humans did this!" shouted Hiccup, this time in Norse, punching the air passionately. "The dragons only fight us because they think we will destroy them. This is our fault! This must never happen again! Never! Save the dragons!"

Vikings are an emotional people. Only moments before, they had been fighting the dragons with everything they had. But the sight of this dying dragon, so close, and at the end of his life, suddenly so weak, so vulnerable, stirred them all. This was no monster, but a cornered animal, and as they all knew, a cornered animal would fight desperately, bloodily, and beyond all reason.

"Save the dragons!"

"Save the dragons!"

"Save the dragons!" cried the humans.

"Save the dragons," whispered the dragon Furious.

The dragon's eyes, though very, very dim, had now lit with sudden, real, genuine hope. He gazed at the horizon with a faraway look.

"You know," he said to Hiccup, with a kind of wonder in his eye, "looking into the future, I really believe that this crazy plan of yours might work."

And then he turned to Luna, hovering sadly among the dragons above Wrecker's Bay in all her glowing white glory.

"It may be that I am dying," said the dragon Furious carelessly, and as if that was not very important, "and will not be able to fulfill my pledge to you, Hiccup. In which case, I give my Kingdom to Luna, and she shall repeat the pledge after me, and keep the promise that I now give."

And so Luna repeated the pledge.

"As a sign of my faith in King Hiccup the Third, I am giving him this Dragon Jewel," said the dragon Furious.

The dragon Furious opened up his palm, and there within it was that speck of dust, the Dragon Jewel. The dragon rebellion dragons backed away with scared murmurs, such was the power and dread of this Jewel.

"Take it, Hiccup," urged the dragon Furious, letting the Jewel drop into Hiccup's hand. "There may be those among my dragon army, less forgiving than I, who will wish to carry on the Red-Rage. You will need it for protection."

415

Hiccup's eyes were full of tears. "You are giving this to me still? You trust me even though this has happened?"

"I trust you, little blood brother," said the dragon Furious.

The effort of his last speech seemed to have been too much for the dragon Furious, for he was seized with a paroxysm of coughing, and he lay down again on the reef, trembling and jerking and snorting.

"Nooo!" yelled Hiccup, and he started forward toward the giant head. "No! Do not die! You do not have to die!"

But the dragon *was* dying, nonetheless. The lamps of his eyes were fading fast. His voice trembled, the Dragonese hissing weakly out of the edges of his once-beautiful mouth, the smoke dying to a trickle. He closed his eyes.

Tears streamed down Hiccup's face. He laid his cold cheek against the burning heat of the dying dragon's skin, and that seemed to wake up the dragon again.

"Do not be sad," said the dragon Furious, opening his eyes once more.

"Listen to how happy everyone is. We have peace at last...and so do I.

"Do not mourn me, Hiccup, or any of you. This

is not a time for grief, but a time for celebration. You see, I have been dead for many years. I had not realized until this moment how much I had become like Grimbeard the Ghastly.

"I have been Grimbeard in dragon form. The less hope I had, the more I destroyed. I have killed and killed and killed again, and the more I killed, the more dead I became.

"Like Grimbeard, I have done some terrible, terrible things...

"But here, right when I am about to die, Hiccup, you have given me back my life.

No! Do not die!

"Although my rebellion failed, and I failed, perhaps there is, after all, a sort of nobility in my failure...Perhaps you were right, Wodensfang, and history really is a succession of noble failures."

"It is true," said Wodensfang, "that in this failure you have justified everything that I have lived for, everything I have fought for, my entire life."

The little old dragon's face was lit up with ecstatic joy.

"Dragons are just as capable of nobility as humans. We, too, can be merciful. We, too, can turn the other cheek...We, too, can love, just as humans do. You put Hiccup's life before your own, Furious, and you die a Hero."

"Ah, *love*," said the dragon Furious, and he smiled once again. "Love is a bad, bad business, as Grimbeard himself would say. Love has brought me to where I am now."

The dragon did not seem sad about this. He even heaved what might have been a dry laugh. "But for one hundred years in my forest prison, I went over and over in my head that moment where I leaped too late, and failed to save Hiccup the Second from the Stormblade. Over and over again I said to myself: If only I had seen earlier...If only I had leaped more quickly...

"If only...if only...

"But now I *have* leaped in time," said the dragon with deep satisfaction. "I made the leap...I saved the boy Hiccup...One hundred years too late, but still, it seems, in time. And look how I am rewarded!" said the dragon, smiling now for the fifth time, with the most untroubled, clear look in his yellow eyes that Hiccup had yet seen. The fires in his eyes had died completely, and now they glowed with a warmth and light that shone in that dark Bay with the brightness of mini suns.

"The boy Hiccup has a plan that will save the dragons!" cried the dragon Furious to his followers. "The dragons *will* be saved, and that is all that I ever wanted.

"So do not weep tears for me, dragons or Vikings. This little scratch is nothing.

"And you were right, Wodensfang," the dragon added. "The boy *was* worth it."

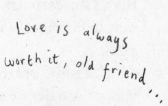

"As I said, love is always worth it, old friend," said Wodensfang. "Love is always worth it."

"I am born again," said the dragon Furious.

419

He did, indeed, look about a hundred years younger than he had a couple of minutes earlier.

The lamps of the dragon's eyes glowed with a fierce light once more, and he was seized with a sudden energy.

He forced himself to lift his head, to move toward the edge of the reef, and he spoke with a return of his old determination.

"I will not die *here* in Wrecker's Bay. I shall not be trapped *here*, on land, for the seagulls and the Vultureclaws to pick my bones, and for my skeleton to be a sad reminder of a dragon who dared to be a rebel, and fought perhaps too fiercely for what he believed in.

"A hundred years ago, when Grimbeard the Ghastly was about to die, *he* did not stay buried in Hero's End, where his grave is. No, he set out to the west in his ship *The Endless Journey*, never to be seen again.

"That is where *I* am going..." said the dragon Furious, and despite everything, he reared up to gaze at the horizon, a great, magnificent dragon-mountain, the Stormblade's cut a mere insignificant pinprick in his chest.

"*Home...*" sighed the dragon Furious, looking beyond Tomorrow, beyond Hero's End, out at the endless waves stretching away forever.

"The Open Ocean...miles and miles of glorious empty wilderness...Now, that is where a dragon can really spread out his wings and *swim*, as carefree and as wild as a dragon ought to be...

"And maybe I will not die after all," said the dragon Furious recklessly, his eyes burning more fiercely still, with brighter and brighter hope, or was it fever? "Maybe the cold, clear seas of home will cure me, and I shall have victory over death. A new beginning. It has happened before—the impossible has become the possible—so why should it not happen to *me*?

"Whatever happens," said the dragon, "*I go first...I shall be the first to hide.*"

There was a sigh among the listening humans and dragons.

He turned to Luna, shining softly silver, grave as a statue. "You are the new ruler of dragons now, Luna, and I hope that you shall be a better monarch than I have been. Remember your pledge."

And then he turned to Hiccup.

"Promise me again, O boy-who-has-a-name-that-I-love. Promise me one last time..."

"I promise that I will save the dragons," said King Hiccup Horrendous Haddock the Third.

With a last, desperate effort the dragon Furious

launched himself off the reef, drenching those Vikings and dragons who had landed on the rocks in the resulting tidal wave.

His first few strokes through the water were painfully slow. But was it Hiccup's imagination, or did he seem to be growing stronger, the farther he swam away?

They watched him go into the sunset in the final hours of daylight on the last day of Doomsday: the entire massed Tribes of the Archipelago, the countless armies of the dragon rebellion, the numberless little nanodragons, Luna and the dragon Guardians of Tomorrow, standing still and silent, saluting the great dragon as he left for the west.

They watched the dragon Furious swim past Tomorrow, through Hero's Gap, past Hero's End, and out, and on, and farther and farther into the future. And it really did seem that he was growing stronger and stronger, as the great dragon swam away, and got smaller and smaller in their eyesight, until when he reached the horizon, far, far away, he was almost the size of the Wodensfang himself.

And then, just as he dipped over the horizon and the last blink of sunlight vanished and the moon rose up, he had the strength to leap out of the sea, in one last, joyous, very-alive leap.

27. THE GHOSTS HAVE BEEN SET FREE...

The dragons and the humans watched the dragon Furious as he went, and cheered him as he disappeared from their sight.

He had said not to weep for him, but they all had tears in their eyes.

It was difficult to know whether they were tears of sadness or of joy, for the dragon was so joyous when he left them, and what he had achieved, as he said himself, was so impossible.

PEACE.

Peace in the Archipelago, after so many years of war. Who would have thought it possible at the dawning of this day?

And then slowly the dragons and the humans fell silent and looked at one another, panting, weary, ragged, crying for the dragon, and yet jubilant.

They looked at one another as if to say: "What do we do next?"

It was getting dark.

Luna gave a great roar of command.

The massed armies of the dragon rebellion spread out their wings and, almost of one accord, dispersed to their homes all over the Archipelago and beyond. The Sharkworms, Leviathorgans, and Thunderers to the Open Ocean; Firestarters and Nightmares to the caves, although a fair few of them stayed the night in Wrecker's Bay with Luna before making the long journey home.

At a cry from Ziggerastica, the little nanodragons rose into the air like a buzzing cloud of locusts, spread out in such numbers that for one moment the sky turned pitch black, as if night were long here already, before they disappeared, humming, to hide once again in the grasses, the bogs, and the marshes of the Archipelago.

Meanwhile the dragons who had supported the humans in the final battle looked to their human companions, to see what they should do.

And the humans, in their turn, looked to Hiccup.

All of them, great burly Visithugs, Wanderers, former Slaves, all of the Tribes of the Archipelago, standing out there on the reef, ragged, war-torn, tattooed Warriors, turned to Hiccup, looking at him expectantly.

Oh my goodness, thought Hiccup, with a start, for the second time that day, *I'm the King. They are all expecting me to know what to do...I'm NEVER going to get used to this.*

It was not as cold as it was that morning, but it was beginning to get very dark.

The humans were exhausted with the emotion of the day, and the sheer weight of the task ahead of them seemed almost insuperable.

They should go home, but where was home for the Vikings now? Almost every house in every village had been destroyed by the war. Whole mountains had been demolished, forests burned to the ground, and were smoking still. The entire Archipelago had been turned into a lunar landscape of craters and charred embers where once the trees had swayed, alive with chattering Squirrelserpents and Dreamserpents.

They had to rebuild their entire world, and that was quite a task.

"Fellow citizens of the Wilderwest," said Hiccup. "We have a peace to build, and a new city on Tomorrow, a great city worthy of this new Kingdom of the Wilderwest.

"It will take time, but we will do it. Any dragon who wishes to live alongside us, as a citizen of the Wilderwest, as valued as any human, is very welcome, but those who want to return to the wild are absolutely free to do so," said Hiccup, for many of these dragons had such strong attachments to their masters that they had no wish to leave, and indeed, it would be unkind to separate them from their human companions.

"In the future we will honor this day, the Doomsday of Yule, with a great celebration of Furious, his dragon companions, and our own human friends who died in this war, and who sacrificed their lives for this peace and so that there should never be slavery of human or dragon again.

"We shall call it the Celebration of the Black Star."

Hiccup held up Snotlout's Black Star, the highest award for courage the Hooligan Tribe can give.

"So, before we all return to our homes on the various different islands of the Archipelago, and start our new lives, we will camp out tonight on the island of Tomorrow, in the ruins of Grimbeard's Castle, and we will forget that we are weary, and that there is such an impossible task ahead of us.

"Tonight we CELEBRATE.

"We celebrate the end of the dragon and human war, and the beginning of the new Kingdom, and the lives of the Heroes who fought to make that happen."

"Oh goodeee!" Stoick rubbed his hands together. "A feast! A feast! Tomorrow was packed with deer. I think we could catch ourselves a huge feast of venison. I love a venison stew!"

So the Tribes of the Archipelago set off on

dragonback, back to Tomorrow in a great happy line, weary but excitedly chattering about the battle.

They rode on dragonback toward Tomorrow along the path of the moon, flying wing tip to wing tip, dragons and humans together.

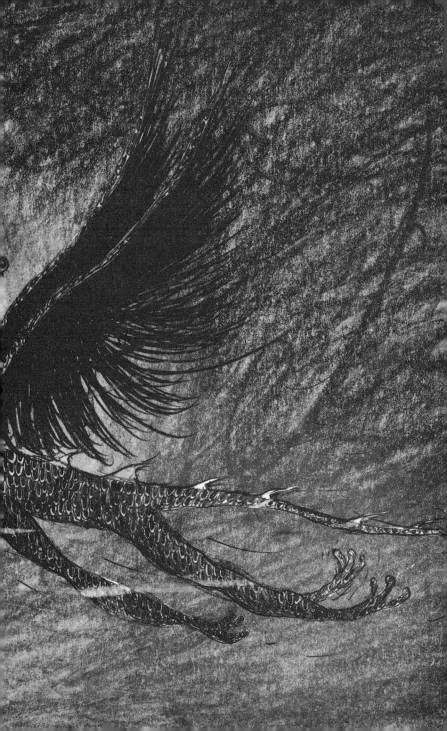

Stoick the Vast and Bertha of the Bog-Burglars led a huge party of Vikings in an evening fishing trip on dragonback across the sea of Wrecker's Bay. Within an hour, it was like old times once again, as Stoick swept down on the fish on the back of his Bullrougher, whooping loudly with excitement.

Hunting at night on dragonback was one of the favorite sports of the Vikings—the eyes of their dragons lit up at night, so that it was possible to hunt your prey even as darkness fell.

The hunting party returned with vast quantities of fish, and Bertha and Stoick argued loudly about who had caught the most.

There was a full moon that night and the clouds and the smoke had dispersed. The Druid Guardian came up to Hiccup, sitting a little uncomfortably on his Stone Throne.

"The dragon Guardians of Tomorrow would like to request their freedom, now that the curse on Tomorrow has been lifted, and peace has returned to the Archipelago," said the Druid Guardian with a bow.

THE CURSE HAS BEEN LIFTED!

It was the first time those words had been said aloud, and Hiccup's heart leaped with delight at the words as he heard them.

"*Of course* they should be set free!" said Hiccup, and the Druid Guardian held up his hand, and it was as if three thousand fireworks were going off all at once as the dragon Guardians rocketed away from the claustrophobic confines of planet Earth, breaking free from the clogging demands of gravity itself, up and up and up, reveling in the fires they generated as they entered the upper atmosphere.

What a glorious sight they made, as they soared on the edge of space for the first time in a century, rocketing and diving, and leaping in joyous squiggles, dancing in the glory of their newfound freedom.*

You would only ever see such a thing once in a lifetime, the entire massed Tribes of the Archipelago and their dragons feasting in the ruins of Grimbeard's Castle, eating and laughing and dancing around bonfires.

One hundred years ago, the curse had come upon Tomorrow when Grimbeard the Ghastly enslaved half his population, killed his very own son, and buried the dragon Furious in a forest prison.

Ghosts from that time had haunted the Archipelago throughout Hiccup's childhood.

Now, the curse had been crushed, and the ghosts set free, like the dragon Guardians of Tomorrow.

---

*Shooting stars, as we all know, are not really stars that are moving. How would that be possible? The idea is preposterous. Stars cannot move any more than stones. They are dragon Guardians, burning at the edges as they fly.

It was a wonderful sight to see former slaves and former masters eating together. How could Vikings—such a proud, wild, free people—ever have agreed to such a thing as slavery? It was almost as if for a hundred years the peoples of the Archipelago had been put under some terrible enchantment, and were only just waking from it.

There they all sat, mourning the past, enjoying the present, and planning hopefully for the future.

Come close before we leave them, take my hand, and hover above them, as if we were a couple of nanodragons, and you can hear them still.

"Ah, Snotlout, I am so proud of him," sighed Baggybum the Beerbelly, tears rolling down his face. "What a boy. What a fine, fine boy…"

"He was the greatest student I ever had," replied Gobber the Belch. "To get a Black Star for courage when he was only fifteen years old! It's unheard of…"

"The dragon Furious…I wish you could have seen him when he was young, in Hiccup the Second's time…" the Wodensfang was telling any of the dragons who would listen.

"Now that my *old* hut has burned down," said Stoick the Vast to Mogadon the Meathead, gulping down his supper with such relish that a lot of it was ending up in his beard, "I intend to build the largest Chiefly hut on Berk that this Archipelago has ever seen." And he drew his plans for this great building with a stick in the ash in front of them.

"T-t-toothless fought the dragon Furious all on his own using his SPECIAL POWERS," Toothless boasted to Stormfly. "The dragon Furious was terrified when Toothless suddenly t-t-turned invisible in a big puff of black smoke and poured out his poisonous darts and let rip his lasers and exploded his rockets and..."

Toothless and the rest of the Ten Companions of the Dragonmark were gathered around King Hiccup on his Stone, Old Wrinkly smoking his pipe close beside them.

"You can have your lobster necklace back, if you like, Fishlegs. I don't need the luck anymore, now that Alvin is gone," said Hiccup.

"Can you think of anything nice about Alvin at all?" asked Fishlegs rather wistfully.

"He was INVENTIVE," said Hiccup kindly.

"That's true," said Fishlegs in excitement. "He *was* inventive, wasn't he? That might be good for my poetry.

And he was a distant cousin of yours, Hiccup, so that means *we* are related, which is good…

"Also, Alvin did get worse, didn't he, over the years?" said Fishlegs. "He didn't start out quite so bad as he ended up. Maybe we could have saved him if we had gotten there in time."

"That's true," said Hiccup. "He wasn't so bad when he was just Alvin the Poor-but-Honest-Farmer. But I have to admit, Fishlegs," said Hiccup gently, "that even back then, it was already too late for Alvin. I remember the first swordfight I ever had with him. He said: 'The treasure has got me and I like being got,' and that wasn't a good sign if you think about it…"*

"It's typical," said Fishlegs. "Fifteen years looking for your father and he turns out to be the meanest man in the entire Archipelago. There is absolutely NO WAY I am calling myself Fishlegs the Treacherous."

"Maybe you could turn that name around. Like when the Slavemark became the Dragonmark," suggested Camicazi.

"*Nothing* can turn that name around," said Fishlegs. "Nobody's going to say: 'Have you met Fishlegs the Treacherous? He's such a nice guy,' are they?

_____

*You can read about this in Book 2: *How to Be a Pirate*.

"I'm starting my own Tribe," said Fishlegs firmly. "It's called the No-Name Tribe. Shadow has already joined. And we have some great new mottos, don't we, Shadow? 'Be of good cheer, ALL welcome here' and 'We are all kind, none left behind.' "

"But that's just what *I* want to do with this new Kingdom of the Wilderwest!" said Hiccup enthusiastically. " 'None Left Behind!' No more slavery. People like the the Quiet Lifes and the Peaceables and the Wanderers all having their say in the Thing...

"And you and Camicazi shall be the first Warriors of my Wilderwest. And when I have my first Warrior ceremony, I shall give you an extra name to add to your own: Fishlegs the Faithful, Chief of the No-Names."

Hiccup put his hand on Fishlegs's shoulder, as if he were naming him already.

"And Camicazi the Courageous, Heir to the Bog-Burglars...First Warriors of the Wilderwest..."

As Hiccup put his hand on Camicazi's shoulder, Camicazi turned red as a beetroot.

"And T-t-toothless is *not* going to hide," said Toothless to Hiccup. "T-t-toothless and Hiccup will never leave each other."

"Never," agreed Hiccup. "I will never give you up, and you will never give me up. I hope that whole

438

hiding thing will never have to happen, Toothless.
And it would only be right at the end of my life, if
at all. This is a whole new beginning. The witch is
dead, Alvin is dead...Peace has begun, and a whole new
world is starting."

At that very moment, like a bird of peace,
Horrorcow came flapping up from the direction of Berk.
Horrorcow was Fishlegs's vegetarian hunting dragon.

You are my First Warriors
of the Wilderwest.

"Horrorcow!" said Fishlegs, hugging her in delight. "Where **HAVE** you been?"

Hiccup grinned and translated for Horrorcow. "She says she doesn't like wars and she's been hiding underground on Berk until it was all over.

"You see!" said Hiccup triumphantly. "It's a sign! War is over, and Horrorcow is our bird of peace. Our *dragon* of peace, if you like.

"**EVERYTHING** will change from this moment on!"

"Ah, will it?" wheezed Old Wrinkly, puffing on his pipe in an interested fashion.

"Anyway," said Fishlegs, "I've finished my Quest to find out who my parents are, and even though it didn't turn out exactly the way I wanted, I can now concentrate on new horizons. **LOVE**, to be exact."

Fishlegs writing a poem to Barbara the Barbarian

Fishlegs was writing a poem to Barbara the Barbarian.

"I thought you were in love with Tantrum O'UGerly?" snorted Camicazi. "I thought you said after Tantrum married Humungously Hotshot the Hero, you would never love again…"

"Yes, well, that was before I saw Barbara the Barbarian," said Fishlegs, sharpening a piece of charcoal on the edge of Hiccup's Stone. "Can you think of anything that rhymes with muscles?"

"How about brussels?" suggested Hiccup. "As in 'brussels sprouts'?"

"This is a love poem," said Fishlegs crossly. "I can't start whiffling on about not-very-nice vegetables in the middle of a love poem!"

His expression suddenly changed.

"Oh my goodness! Barbara's looking in our direction!" he squeaked.

"She's moving! She's coming our way! Be cool, everybody! Be cool!"

"Hi, guys," said Barbara the Barbarian. Her black cat, Fearless, meowed threateningly as she walked past, followed by her six bodyguards and her frowning father,

BE COOL, EVERYBODY!!

Ballistic, the hairiest, scariest Chieftain in the northern Archipelago.

Fishlegs turned red as a sunset, and then pale as a piece of chalk, and then white with bright pink spots, as even this very brief encounter with Barbara's cat had given him an instant allergic reaction.

He gurgled something that was intended to be suavely charming, but in fact sounded something like "Urrgghghhh…"

Then he tried to itch his face, forgot he was holding the charcoal, accidentally shoved it up his nose, and fainted on the spot.

Barbara the Barbarian looked over her shoulder at him in a puzzled sort of way, saying to her nearest bodyguard, "Who *is* that weird boy? What does he have up his nose, and why does he keep falling asleep?"

"Wow, Fishlegs, you're a real sweet-talker," said Camicazi. "Fainting and itching and shoving charcoal up your nose—*that* is the way to impress a Viking Warrior princess."

"Do you think she might love me back?" said Fishlegs, getting to his feet, removing the charcoal, and scratching himself violently.

"Hmmm," said Camicazi, pretending to think. "SHE is a six-foot Amazonian daughter of a Chief, permanently attached to a murderous feline, and well known for her bare-knuckle fighting skills... While YOU are an unknown bard-in-training at least three years younger than she is, who faints dead away whenever he talks to her, and who is, to top it all off, completely allergic to CATS. You're made for each other! This is Fate! It's written in the stars!"

"Do you really think so?" asked Fishlegs anxiously.

"NO!" laughed Camicazi. "Face it, Fishlegs…You have NO HOPE."

"Yes, that's what I thought," said Fishlegs, resettling his glasses sadly on his nose. "Never mind, being unlucky in love is good for my poetry."

"Fishlegs," said Hiccup, suddenly uneasy, "remember what happened when you fell in love with Tantrum O'UGerly? Her homicidal maniac of a father sent me on that mission to the forest of Berserk, where I accidentally released the dragon Furious."

"You can't blame this whole dragon rebellion on *me*!" objected Fishlegs.

"I'm just saying," said Hiccup patiently, "don't you think you should try and fall in love with somebody who *doesn't* have six bodyguards and a father who is a homicidal maniac this time? I have this nasty feeling that this is going to get us into trouble all over again…"

"You can't choose who you fall in love with," said Fishlegs, opening wide his arms enthusiastically. "Love just happens!"

A little crowd of girls came up to the Stone— Camicazi's old team of Bog-Burglar Escape Artists: Sporta, Typhoon, Harrietahorse, and Beefburger—all giggling and blushing and punching each other.

"We were just wondering if the King

The King is BUSY, doing important Royal Business. With ME!!

wanted to dance with us?" asked Harrietahorse, giggling in what Camicazi felt was a very irritating fashion.

"The King is BUSY," said Camicazi firmly, drawing her sword for emphasis. "He's doing important Royal Business. With ME. Go on there, SHOO!"

And the girls scrambled away, for no one wanted to get on the wrong end of Camicazi's sword.

Camicazi nodded her head darkly. "It's a bad business, this 'love' business—a bad, bad business…"

"So things are going to change, are they?" said Old Wrinkly, his eyes bright with amusement. "Peace will break out? Civilization will appear, just like that?

446

You don't think that maybe, a little like *love*, *life* just happens?"

Sitting on his Stone, King Hiccup looked out at his subjects, feeling suddenly a little uneasy.

Everything had begun as merrily as anything, but even on a night as glorious as this one, you couldn't put all of the Tribes of the Archipelago all together in one ruined Castle without the odd argument breaking out.

A little way away, Bertha of the Bog-Burglars was boasting about how she could fly from the mainland to the Castle on Tomorrow in less than ten minutes on the back of her new Bullrougher, and Valhallarama said she could do it in *nine* on the Phantom, and Bertha said: "Would you like to make a small bet on that, Valhallarama?"

And Mogadon the Meathead was kneeling in front of Stoick the Vast's plans for his new Chiefly hut, looking for easy points of access, for he was already making his own plans for future burglary and raiding expeditions

It's a bad business, this "love" business, a bad, bad business...

that he would be
making to the little Isle of
Berk…

And Tantrum was in a sulk
with Humungously Hotshot the Hero,
because Valhallarama was there, and Valhallarama had
been Humungous's first, lost love.

"But of *course* I love you more, Tantrum my
darling!" said Humungously Hotshot the Hero gallantly,
down on his knees before her. "*She* may have been my
first love, but *you* are my last. How can I prove my love
to you? I will get you anything! Anything you want! I will
tear down the sky for you. I will bring you the moon…"

Tantrum tossed her hair petulantly. "Okay then,"
said Tantrum. "You can steal me that Hogfly. I've always
wanted a Hogfly." And she pointed at the Hogfly being
petted on Very Vicious the Visithug's lap.

Humungously Hotshot swallowed. "Does it have to
be THAT particular Hogfly, Tantrum, my sweetest?"

And up in the Castle's ruined turrets, a dragon
fight was breaking out, entirely caused by Toothless
and Stormfly, who had worked out a brilliant new

448

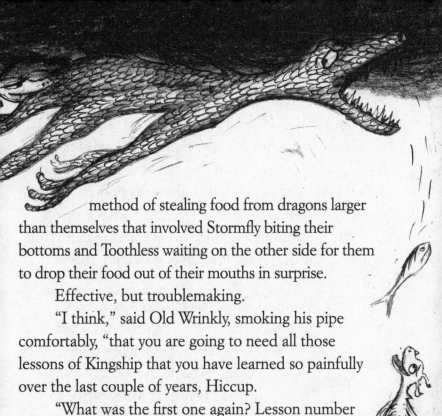

method of stealing food from dragons larger than themselves that involved Stormfly biting their bottoms and Toothless waiting on the other side for them to drop their food out of their mouths in surprise.

Effective, but troublemaking.

"I think," said Old Wrinkly, smoking his pipe comfortably, "that you are going to need all those lessons of Kingship that you have learned so painfully over the last couple of years, Hiccup.

"What was the first one again? Lesson number one: The search for the fang-free dragon—that dragons can be trained without fear and intimidation…

"Back then you were just trying to train one small disobedient dragon. *Now* you will be trying to train an entire disobedient nation."

Oh thank you, Old Wrinkly, very helpful.

"Okay," said Hiccup slowly, looking out over his quarreling, fighting, stormy new citizens of the Wilderwest. "We can't expect them all to change OVERNIGHT, can we? Civilization will take time… They are Vikings, after all.

"And now that I come to think of it," said Hiccup thoughtfully, "perhaps until they get used to this peace business it *is* quite a good idea that most of these Vikings will be going home to their different islands tomorrow.

"In the meantime, *I* know what will stop them from arguing…Barbara," said Hiccup now, "could I borrow your foghorn?"

King Hiccup stood up on his Stone, and blew the foghorn as hard as he could. The thrilling sound of the foghorn, when blown at full blast, was so magnetically loud that it hit the ears like an electric shock. It sent the hairs on the back of the neck electrically upward, and the old eardrums jangling. Even in the midst of their fighting, the dragons and the humans paused, as if turned to stone by the noise.

"Citizens of the Wilderwest!" yelled Hiccup the Third. "I remind you

We can't expect them all to change OVERNIGHT can we?

that this is a *CELEBRATION*—the Celebration of the
Black Star—not a time for fighting!"

The various combatants, dragon and human,
moved apart guiltily.

"I suggest we SING!" said King Hiccup the Third.
"Sing our hearts out, every old Archipelago song that we
know! Beginning with the Hooligan national anthem!"

The Vikings thought that this was an excellent idea,
and fighting turned to singing in the magic of an instant.

> *"I didn't mean to come here,*
> *And I didn't mean to sta-a-ay…*
> *But I lost my heart to these rainy bogs…*
> *And I'll ne-e-ever go awa-a-ay!"*

All of the Vikings joined in, their melodic voices rising up
with such beauty that it brought tears to the eyes.

The dragons sang their own wild song, putting up
their heads to the sky and howling joyously.

> *"I've heard that the sky in America*
> *Is a blue that you wouldn't believe,*
> *But Berk is my lobster after all,*
> *And now I'll ne-e-ever leave…"*

Civilization will
take time…

"What does 'Berk is my lobster' mean, exactly?" Hiccup asked the Wodensfang. "It was the line that told me the Jewel was inside the lobster necklace. But I've always wondered what it *meant*; it sounds like nonsense..."

Wodensfang sighed romantically.

"Lobsters, you see, are a symbol of love," said the old dragon, "because they mate for life..."

"The lobster necklace must have been the one that Grimbeard gave to his wife Chin-hilda when they got married, then," said Hiccup thoughtfully in Norse, "and she gave it back to him when she left him in a fury.

Grimbeard probably wore it because he regretted his lost love."

"Lobster necklaces are a symbol of love, are they?" said Fishlegs, looking interested.

"Fishlegs, if you start sending Barbara the Barbarian lobster necklaces I am going to get very cross with you," said Hiccup, waving his arms around in an agitated way. "*DON'T SEND HER ANYTHING! HER FATHER ISN'T GOING TO LIKE IT! THAT'S WHY HE'S GIVEN HER SIX BODYGUARDS! REMEMBER WHAT HAPPENED LAST TIME!*"

> "*I was on my way to America,
> But I took a left turn at the Pole,
> And I lost my shoe in a rainy bog,
> Where my heart got stuck in the ho-o-o-ole!*"

Fishlegs sang this particularly loudly, because despite finding out during the course of his Quest that he was part Berserk,

part Murderous, part Treacherous, and mostly No-Name…
he was still a Hooligan by adoption, if not by birth.

And then they all sang an old Viking Archipelago
song called *Not The Settling Kind*, that says so much
about the yearning wild spirit of Vikings (and indeed,
dragons), and sounds particularly good when sung in a
ruined castle under a starlit sky.

It goes like this:

> *"I have never cared for castles*
> *or a crown that grips too tight,*
> *Let the night sky be my starry roof*
> *and the moon my only light,*
> *My heart was born a Hero,*
> *my stormbound sword won't rest,*
> *I left the harbor long ago*

on a never-ending Quest,
I am off to the horizon,
where the wild wind blows the foam,
Come get lost with me, love,
and the sea shall be our home!"

All of the Viking voices were perfectly in unison, apart from Humungously Hotshot the Hero and Tantrum, who had never been able to sing. Tantrum had forgotten all about the Hogfly for the moment, and was happily embracing her Hero, singing with him, both wildly out of tune with everyone else, but happily in tune with each other.

Not the Settling Kind was Tantrum and Hotshot's favorite song, and as they reached the big notes together at excruciating volume, it was a happy reminder that, argue though they may, love was *always* worth it.

"Do you want your foghorn back, Barbara?" King Hiccup the Third asked Barbara the Barbarian as she sang at the top of her voice with all of her six bodyguards and the cat joining in.

Barbara broke off a moment, and looked thoughtfully at

Humungously Hotshot and Tantrum, wildly out of time . . .

the massed Tribes of the Archipelago, singing their hearts out.

"No, you keep it," she said at last. "I think you're going to need it."

Ah yes, how true that was.

It is one thing to decide you are going to create a new and more civilized world, and quite another to put that idea into action.

Things *would* change, in time, for Hiccup would never let them go back to that Old World of slavery and intimidation.

But there were some things that would never change.

Young bards would still fall hopelessly in love with princesses out of their league. Chiefs would quarrel, and dragons would fight, and storms would blow, and trouble would follow trouble, just as it had in the old world.

But all of this was in the future.

Right here, right now, the witch and Alvin were dead, and the dragon rebellion was over.

Right here, right now, Hiccup and his Ten Companions of the Dragonmark were all together. Hiccup, Toothless, Fishlegs, Camicazi, Windwalker, Deadly Shadow, Stormfly, and Wodensfang, not to mention

Horrorcow, all crowded around the King's Stone. Stoick, Valhallarama, Bertha of the Bog-Burglars, Humungously Hotshot and Tantrum the Heroes and the Ten Fiancés, the massed Tribes of the Archipelago and the Wanderers, Bearcub and his older sister Eggingarde, all the former slaves and their former masters—they were all there.

(Even Norbert the Nutjob was there, unbeknownst to anybody, complete with a Dragonmark and disguised as a Wanderer, but that is another story.)

None Left Behind…

The Vikings had changed tunes, perhaps realizing that they wanted to end this night on a high note, and they began to sing one of the most rousing, happiest Viking songs of all.

Because they had remembered who they were this day.

They were *Vikings*. A wild, wandering people, like the dragons, who fought for freedom, and equality in the eyes of Thor, and the wild places of the world.

"UP WITH YOUR SWORD AND STRIKE
AT THE GALE!
RIDE THE ROUGH SEAS FOR THOSE
WAVES ARE YOUR HOME!
WINTERS MAY FREEZE BUT OUR

HEARTS DO NOT FAIL!
HEROES...HEARTS...FOREVER!"

They were all there, singing their hearts out, all together, and out in Wrecker's Bay, Luna and her wild dragons joined in the Vikings' song, shooting great joyful fireballs into the air as the fins of Sharkworms broke in the Bay like dolphins. And down, ticking in the grasses, the nanodragons were singing too, rubbing their hind legs together as they sang joyfully, in tiny squeaking voices:

"YOU MAY BE SMALL BUT YOUR HEART CAN BE LARGE
WORK ALL TOGETHER AND MOUNTAINS MAY MOVE
DON'T JUDGE A GRUB BY THE SIZE OF HIS WINGS
FOR YOU CAN'T ALWAYS SEE...A HERO!"

It is dark, so the humans and the dragons cannot see the blackened world about them. But that is fine, for they can already see, in their minds' eye, the whole world green once again with the shoots of spring. The humans are building those castles in their minds already: finer houses, newer villages, better harbors. The dragons hear the wild north calling them with the promise of a free Open Ocean and impossibly blue skies, where death has

458

no dominion and they can fly forever, like the dragon Guardians shooting and rocketing above them in endless black space.

"YOU ARE NEVER ALONE IF THE SEA
IS YOUR FRIEND...
RIDING THE WAVES OF IMPOSSIBLE
QUESTS...
IF IT DOESN'T END WELL,
THEN IT ISN'T THE END...
A HERO...FIGHTS...FOREVER!"

There they are, all of them together, singing their hearts out on the top of that ruined Castle on Tomorrow. War is over; their bellies are full of fish and deer, and they are full of hope and joy, and excitement about their future. They sing long, long into the night, bursting with happiness, the quiet moon shining down on them, under a brilliant canopy of stars.

"THE HERO CARES NOT FOR A WILD
WINTER'S STORM,
FOR IT CARRIES HIM SWIFT ON THE
BACK OF THE WAVE,
ALL MAY BE LOST AND OUR HEARTS

MAY BE WORN,
BUT A HERO...FIGHTS...FOREVER!"

And if *this* moment doesn't last forever...then it really
ought to.

So that is where we will leave them, Hiccup and his
friends: forever young, forever hopeful, singing their
hearts out on the island of Tomorrow.
BECAUSE...
If it doesn't end well, then it isn't

THE END

This is the love letter Fishlegs
wrote to Barbara the
Barbarian

Dear Barbara the Barbarian,

~~I really love your splendid muscles~~
~~I bet you eat up all your brussels (sprouts.)~~

Roses are red,
Violets are blue,
Muscles are lovely
And so are you.

Yours sincerely,

?

EPILOGUE BY HICCUP HORRENDOUS HADDOCK THE THIRD, THE LAST OF THE GREAT VIKING HEROES

So that is the story of how I became the King of the Wilderwest and ended the dragon rebellion.

Now that I am an old, old man, it feels so strange to look back at my younger Hiccup self, whom we just left among the ruins of Grimbeard's Castle, looking into the future, so confident, so hopeful, so sure in what he was going to do.

And now I look back and I wonder, just as the dragon Furious wondered long ago as he lay dying on the reef:

Was my life a failure, or was it a success?

I *did* build my new Kingdom of the Wilderwest. I rebuilt Grimbeard's Castle, and the flags fly from twenty towers, even stronger and more solid than they were before. There is now a bustling city on Tomorrow, a harbor crowded with life and ships. Looking at it now, you would never believe that when I was young this was a desolate ghost of a town, where the wind howled through the empty streets and the ruins had fallen into the bog.

And more importantly, just as I pledged to myself when I came back from discovering America, the land-that-does-not-exist, I built a Barbaric Archipelago in which might was no longer right, where it is not only the strong who belong. I built a world where weaker Tribes such as the Peaceables, and the Wanderers, the Nowhere Men, and the Quiet Lifes all have their vote and a say at the Thing.

None Left Behind…

The world of my childhood was a wondrous world indeed, full of excitement and adventure, but it was also a world in which small children lived in daily fear of death by wolves, by dragons roaming wild, by starvation, and by war.

That is no longer true.

We barbarians are proud barbarians still, but along the way we have grown up. We have put down our swords and picked up our pens instead, and have almost become, dare I say it…civilized.

So, in that, my life has been a success, and I have done good work as a King and as a Hero.

But as I grew older, and older, and realized that I

would not live forever, I began to wonder whether I had really changed the world sufficiently for it to be safe for dragons in the future when I am gone. And I know that human nature has not changed enough yet.

So, in that, I failed.

But as the Wodensfang and the dragon Furious said, perhaps it is a *noble* failure, and history is a succession of these noble failures.

I never spoke to Luna directly about this. But I did not need to. She knew it, maybe always knew it, and slowly, slowly, almost imperceptibly, over the course of my lifetime, the dragons began to hide.

They did not leave immediately. It did not happen like that. It was a very gradual retreat. At first, a few of the wilder species retreated to the north, to the oceans, to the deep seas. But still more stayed in the Archipelago. Our riding dragons and hunting dragons did not want to leave our side, so they stayed with us, out of their own free choice.

Thank Thor, I myself have still lived a life that has been full of dragons.

All my life I have flown on the back of Windwalker, high, so high. All my life Toothless has been there, sitting on my shoulder, answering me back, stealing the food from my plate when I'm not looking.

A Sea-Dragon like Toothless, of course, lives for many thousands of years; throughout my life, he barely grew up at all. While I, of course, grew up, got married, became a powerful King, and had children of my own, Toothless remained the same.

But we taught our own children to ride horses and train hawks as well as dragons—just in case.

When I was a young man, the world still seemed full of dragons, very much awake, very much as fierce and as dangerous as they had ever been, out in the wilderness of the Open Ocean. One of them, the Doomfang, saved my life a dozen times or more out there. And many more nearly took my life away from me as well...

But maybe the dragons felt a little uncomfortable with the new, civilized world that I was building. Dragons have always been wild creatures for wild times. Or maybe they sensed what Furious sensed, that my struggles to change the world could never be successful in one generation alone.

As I have said, they began to hide.

They retreated north to be with their fellow dragons. They migrated into the deep-sea trenches I was telling you about, and put themselves into Sleep Comas. Many of them developed the chameleon skills of a Stealth Dragon, and disguised themselves so effectively in the grasses and the rocks and the seas, that you would not even notice they were there, particularly if you did not know you were looking for them.

Sometimes, I used to lie very still on my stomach in the bracken, and stare very hard, and if I stayed there for a long time, then slowly, slowly, I could begin to see again the dim outline of a Tiddly-Nip Tick-Botherer, or a Drowsy-Tipped Dragonmouse, materializing in front of me for one second as it scurried camouflaged through the grasses—and then it was gone.

That was how I knew they were still there.

It has only been in the last couple of decades of my life that the dragons have begun to hide in earnest.

Gradually, in the last few years, even Toothless and Windwalker began to spend time away from me. They were restless for the fellowship of the other dragons in the pin-sharp cold waters, the innocent cruel snows of the north. They began to leave me for short stretches of time, and then slightly longer, and longer again. They always returned, however. Toothless would never leave me forever.

And that was when I began to fulfill my promise to the dragon Furious.

I instructed Fishlegs and his fellow bards to create

stories suggesting that the dragons were only ever fictional creatures. People do not believe that yet, of course, for they have seen dragons with their very own eyes. But as the dragons disappear into hiding, and the people who have seen dragons with their own eyes grow old and die, well…

…the stories will live on.

Stories always do live on, and the stories that Fishlegs tells are that dragons do not exist and have never existed.

This belief will keep the dragons safe.

So, you see, I *did* save the dragons.

It was not in the way that I hoped, perhaps, but I kept my promise to the dragon Furious, and I saved the dragons nonetheless.

My plan, crazy though it was, is working.

And in fact, it is working so effectively that sometimes even I, in my childish old age, cannot remember—did they exist or did they not?

Although it was all my own idea to make a fantasy out of their reality, I myself can get confused, so completely have they vanished. Could such magnificent creatures *really* have flown the skies, and swam the seas of my childhood?

I am feeling a little weak now—weak, but also

excited. I sense an ending coming, or should I call it a new beginning?

When Toothless flies to me next, it shall be for the last time.

I am waiting for him now, just to see him one last time, just to remind myself that, yes, he really does exist. The window is a black, empty square, but the Dragon Jewel is a warm, golden promise, heavy in my hand, that he *will* fly through that open window, he *will* shake out his wings and demand some food, some choice snack (I, of course, know all his favorites), and settle down in his old familiar place lying on my chest, blowing perfect violet-colored smoke rings right above my heart.

Here it is, the Dragon Jewel, and there they are, the two little dragons suspended in the amber: one dark, one light, each with a tail in the other one's mouth, like the alpha and the omega.

Here I am, watching, waiting.

(When I die, I shall be buried at sea, in a proper Viking funeral, just like the one we tried to give Toothless long ago when I was a child, when he wasn't really dead. The sword and the Jewel, I have asked to be buried with me, for the sea is a safe place for things to be buried. Things can be lost there, only to be found again when the time is right.)

Once, when I was a child, I dreamed that Grimbeard the Ghastly, on the deck of his ship *The Endless Journey*, threw the sword Endeavor up into the air.

Up and up it spun, through the inky blackness, across the cavernous span of a hundred years, until, entirely of its own accord, my own left hand sprang out of space and stars and never-ending time and caught it.

Now that I am so very old, I am dreaming once again.

And in my dream *I* am the one throwing the sword.

It is spinning now, in the black starlit waters of my dream, right above *your* head, dear reader.

A sword that may look second-best, and secondhand, but carries the memories of a thousand lost fights, a history lesson in itself.

Reach out, and catch it by the hilt.

Swear by its name, Endeavor, to do your utmost to make this world a better place than when you arrived in it.

For look! There will be dragons all around you, as camouflaged as a Stealth Dragon. Maybe they are hovering over your head, just out of your line of sight, looking after you without your realizing, just as the nanodragons were for me. Put your head down in the heather and lie very still, just as I did long ago. If you lie there long enough can you too see the faint outline of a nanodragon moving?

Toothless will be out there, lying hidden and asleep in some water-fed cave by the cliffs, just as small and disobedient as ever, waiting to be found by a brave and kind human child of the future.

And maybe there are fiercer dragons too, sleeping down there in the unreachable depths of the ocean, in those trenches so deep that even humans of the future will not be able to explore them—and they may awake again.

If those fierce dragons *do* awake, if they do open their bright cat eyes, and shake out their terrible wings, the Dragon Jewel will still be lost in the infinite vastness of the ocean.

So you will just have to make sure that the dragons will awake in a better world than the one that I have lived in. I have made it a little better, but it needs to be much better still.

Or else there will be fangs and fire and everything that is awe-ful.

And then we will need a Hero, and that Hero might as well be…

...YOU.

In my beginning is my end...

There were dragons when I was a boy.

Books are like dragons…If we do not believe in them,
and read them, they will cease to exist.
How, then, will we learn the language and understand
the stories of the dear dead ghosts of the past?

SAVE THE DRAGONS.
SPEAK DRAGONESE.
READ A BOOK.

ACKNOWLEDGMENTS, THANKS, AND GOOD-BYES

A wise person once said that a writing Hero needs three things: innocence, arrogance, and patience. So maybe Fishlegs has found the right dragon. But no Hero can write alone. These are the peoples of my own Archipelago, who have loved and supported me—some for fifteen years, and even further back.

The early Hachette Tribe:

Marlene Johnson, Kate Burns, Les Phipps,
Alison Still, Venetia Gosling, Claudia Symons,
Harry Barker, Margaret Conroy, Mary Byrne,
David Mackintosh, and Erin Stein

And the Warriors of today— many of them with numerous years' service:

Fritha Lindqvist, Rebecca Logan, Andrew Sharp, Nirmal Sandhu,
Susan Barry, Helen Marriage, Sally Felton,
Daniel Fricker, Hilary Murray Hill, Emily Smith,
Jason McKenzie, Charmian Allwright, Camilla Leask,
Jo Hardacre, Megan Tingley, and Andrew Smith

Special big thanks to Jenny Stephenson
and Naomi Greenwood

And most important of all, my longtime editor
Big Chief Anne McNeil, Mighty Sword and
Defender of all things Dragon

The DreamWorks Tribe:

High Chief Jeffrey Katzenberg, Chris Kuser, Bill Damaschke, Chris Sanders (who codirected the first movie), Pierre-Olivier Vincent, Nico Marlet, Simon Otto, Will Davies, John Powell, Jay Baruchel, America Ferrera, Gerard Butler, and the whole animation and acting team

And most especially, Bonnie Arnold, Producer-Hero, and His Most Bardic Brilliance, Dean DeBlois

Swords-for-Hire and Bardiguard Protection:

Staunch Defenders and Protectors, my agents Caroline Walsh and Nicky Lund, and my lawyer David Colden

With special thanks to Traveling Troubadour and Acting Genius:

David Tennant, a one-man Archipelago all on his own

The Cheerers-on:

Amanda Craig, Nicolette Jones, Julia Eccleshare, Nick Tucker, Peter Florence, Martin Chilton, Emily Drabble, Michelle Pauli and the team at Guardian Children's Online, Lorna Bradbury, James Lovegrove, and the teams at BBC Breakfast, Newsround, and Blue Peter

The Fiery Tribes of Knowledge, Wisdom, and FUN:

Booksellers, librarians, and teachers everywhere

The Friends-and-Family Tribe:

My parents, the Great Chieftains Michael Blakenham and Marcia Blakenham O Hear Their Names and Tremble Ugh Ugh, without whom the whole adventure would never have started,

Judit Kumar, Lauren Child, and the dear dead Heroes Alan Hare, Jill Hare, and Nancy Blakenham

The Hares who live in the land-that-does-not-exist:
Caspar, Melissa, Thomasina, and Inigo

The Five Fearless Faccinis:
Emiley, Ben Francesco, Delfina, and Bay

And last but not least,
The Cowell Companions of the Dragonmark:

My True Viking Heroes,
MAISIE, CLEMMIE, and XANNY

And most of all to Simon, who (of course) wrote all the best parts…

BECAUSE:

Love Never Dies,
What Is Within Is More Important
Than What Is Without,
The Best Is Not Always the Most Obvious,
and Once You've Loved Truly,
Thor, Then You Know the Way

A Hero is Forever.

This is Cressida, age 9, writing on the island.

Cressida Cowell grew up in London and on a small, uninhabited island off the west coast of Scotland, where she spent her time writing stories, fishing for things to eat, and exploring the island looking for dragons. She was convinced that there were dragons living on the island and has been fascinated by them ever since.

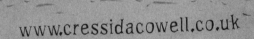

www.cressidacowell.co.uk